PARADIGM

PARADIGM

YVONNE HEIDT

SAPPHIRE BOOKS

SALINAS, CALIFORNIA

Editor - Tara Young
Book Design - LJ Reynolds
Cover Design - Fineline Cover Design

Sapphire Books Publishing, LLC
P.O. Box 8142
Salinas, CA 93912
www.sapphirebooks.com

Printed in the United States of America
First Edition – October 2018

This and other Sapphire Books titles can be found at
www.sapphirebooks.com

Dedication

For my Daughter,
Kerri-Ann Lynn
Wouldn't we have had a blast?

Acknowledgments

As always, my undying gratitude and love goes to Sandy for – well, everything.

Without Chris, the entire staff at Sapphire books, and their long suffering, enduring patience with me, this book would not be in your hands right now. Thank you seems like such a small thing to say for all you've done.

For my editor, Tara Young. Thank you for making the journey as painless as possible. You were a joy to work with.

Apologies to Lori Reynolds for drawing the short straw! You absolutely deserve the ice cream, chocolate, and cherry on top.

I also would not have made it through this process at all if not for the encouragement from my friend, JD Glass. Thank you for being there when I needed to laugh, cry, scream, or on occasion, all three at the same time.

I'm blessed to have beta readers who are also friends. Cris Perez-Soria, thank you for the time you took to help and to let me know that yes, the story had you leaving the lights on at night!

A huge shout-out and hugs to Susan Thompson, who went way above and beyond. Your input was invaluable and very much appreciated. She's an excellent cook too! Hugs and flowers to Shelia Mason Howell for always being a one-stop shopping paranormal expert when I have questions I can't answer myself.

I'd also like to take the time to thank Jove Belle and Andi Marquette for letting me ramble and play over at Women and Words every 4th Monday.

Life gets busy and the miles separate us, but no one gets me more than Maralee Lackman. For that she deserves a medal. Or two.

Kisses and hugs to my sister, Suzie Baldwin, my unpaid publicist.

And last, but never least, thanks and love to each and every member of my tribe. You know who you are.

par·a·digm
ˈperə,dīm/
ˈpair,ah,dime/

noun
A model, pattern, template, standard, prototype or archetype.
A set of established beliefs.

Bad things happen in the dark.
Leave the lights on...

Prologue

From her desk, Jazz Miller watched the wall monitor designated for camera three, located in the former hospital's basement. The areas selected for the tours were pitch-black, but her view of them had night vision and the latest audio capabilities.

She heard Maeve, their guide working that night, whisper loudly, "What was that?"

Jazz hit a button on the control panel in front of her. She counted off in her head—one, two, three—before a door slammed and reverberated like a gunshot. As a unit, the amateur wannabe ghost hunters flinched and shouted.

One of the women began to cry. Jazz hated when that happened, but her job required her to run with it. And Jesus, she needed this job or she and Dad would be out on the street. The responsibility of paying the rent, groceries, utilities, and a variety of other bills fell on her shoulders most of the time.

His drinking had become worse, and he was in a stupor for the better part of each day.

Jazz could only be grateful Dad wasn't a mean drunk. When her mother ran off, he broke. Her wonderful strong hero snapped under the heartbreak and betrayal. Jazz wasn't immune from her own baggage, but Dad was forced into an early retirement, and what he received each month was never enough to carry their household.

Hence, her working in this freaky-ass place.

She realized she'd missed her last cue when Maeve's voice rose in volume. The group walked down a predestined hall, and Jazz activated the machine that caused a cold wind to rush around the group. In reality, forced air pumped through the doorframes.

"Oh, my God!" a woman screamed. "Something pulled my hair."

She checked the camera and recalled several tours involving hair pulling, especially women with long blond hair and blue eyes, and it made her glad her own was short and brown. Her eyes were, as well, but Stacy, her girlfriend, described them as tawny. Jazz had always thought it was a sissy description but didn't have the nerve to say it. She was drawn out of her thoughts by another shout, from a man exclaiming he was freezing and something must be trying to manifest.

She sincerely hoped not.

Over the speaker, Jazz heard wailing and footsteps thunder away from the area. For the stragglers remaining, a loud groan emanated from a closet in a room Maeve randomly on purpose made sure they walked into.

And that's a wrap. She absently spun her office chair and waited for the buzzer to sound the all clear. It signaled the tourists were finished for the night.

Jazz had a hard time comprehending that people paid to be terrified during these tours. She knew it wasn't real, yet the screams played an endless loop in her mind. Nightmares and wet pants didn't appeal to her sense of adventure. What the hell did they get out of it other than a T-shirt that claimed they'd survived a night in the most haunted sanitarium in America?

What if someone had a heart attack during

the tour? She wondered if the current owners had insurance for that shit. Then again, her minimum-wage contribution to the job wasn't privy to that information. God, she had to get out of this place.

It had been their last group of the night, and Jazz's eyes burned with fatigue while she gathered up her stuff and waited for Eric, her ride home.

The place gave her the serious creeps, and she never stayed late if she could help it.

If they asked her, and they didn't, the owners didn't need to fake anything anyway.

In her opinion, it was haunted enough.

She'd seen the shows, in addition to legitimate scientific studies they'd filmed at this location, along with their EVPs and photographic evidence.

They had all convinced her she wouldn't and shouldn't walk these halls alone.

She despised that the offices and gear for the staged encounters were hidden in the basement. As if it weren't scary enough, her equipment constantly screwed up. Again, they hadn't asked her, but she could have told them, as many genuine psychics had, angry spirits could and did drain energy from electronics. Why were they always surprised?

In her opinion, the whole setup was a beacon, and it created a vortex for the real scary shit. The more fear created, it seemed as if more shit happened.

What's taking him so long? Jazz put on her coat and scarf, sat down again, and waited while she fiddled with her gloves. The graveyard shift sucked. She was always tired and felt her life revolved around the attempt to catch up on her sleep. She missed going out with her friends whose schedules were directly opposite of hers. Jazz rubbed, then closed her eyes while she waited for her ride home.

She startled when she realized she'd dozed off and frantically checked her watch.

Holy shit! Three hours had passed. Where was Eric? Jazz shot up from the chair, grabbed her phone, horrified to find she hadn't turned it back on after the shift ended. Management recently banned them during working hours, and after the last employee got fired, she hadn't dared to push it. Jazz fumbled it, and her eyes widened when she'd seen she missed the text that he went home sick six hours ago.

No, no, no, no.

Full of nerves, she checked the minutes available to her, and anxiety continued to rise rapidly in her chest as call after call to other co-workers went unanswered. Like her, most employees got the hell out of this place as fast as they could. She couldn't call her best friend, Billy, as he didn't have a cell yet. The only reason she owned one was to be able to check on her father. In any case, the effort would have been lost anyway as she'd run out of time on hers.

Jazz's nerves kicked into a higher gear as she considered she just might be stuck in the basement in one of the most haunted sanitariums in America.

Alone.

She stood at the door and reached for the knob several times, while trying to talk herself into opening it.

Jazz heard a loud squeak behind her, looked over her shoulder, and caught the sound of a metal desk screeching across the floor. That made up her mind, and she bolted out of the room. It wasn't any particular trick they had on tap in the control room.

Though her hands were shaking, she reopened

her phone, and the dim screen only allowed her to see a foot in front of her as she peered down the hall and made her way to the exit. Jazz felt it was better than nothing at all.

She hurried her pace when the noise of a creaky wheelchair came from somewhere behind her. It had to be a joke, she thought. It was set up to fuck with her. Even as she thought it, she concluded no one she knew would be so cruel. She tried to rationalize the computer was malfunctioning but knew she'd turned it off after her shift. Against her will, memories of evidence she'd seen from the studies intruded, freezing her blood.

There was no sign of anyone else remaining in the building. Of course, after three hours, not one employee she knew would dare to be alone in the wretched, horrible place. Maybe one of the fringe groups of ghost hunters had illegally broken in. That had happened before.

She never thought she'd be praying for an intruder.

But better human than…*other,* she decided.

Jazz tried to steady her heart rate, but something in her knew, just knew it wasn't trespassers. They usually came along with equipment and flashlights, and she heard no giggling, talking, or the horrible sound of their spirit boxes that claimed the dead were talking to them.

Jesus, those freaked her out.

She made it to the exit, and her pulse banged when she found it locked. Even worse than realizing she'd have to go upstairs and through another hall was the feeling she wasn't alone.

She turned from the basement's exit and backtracked toward the stairwell. Worried about what might be in front of her, Jazz was afraid to look back. She swung the heavy metal door and ran up two treads at a time, grateful for her long stride. Jazz reached the first floor, and the sound of the cellar door slamming below caused her to stumble against the wall.

She quickly righted herself, ignored the sharp pain in her elbow, ran around the corner, and sped up.

She saw shadows in every corner and in each open doorway, and it was hard to keep convincing herself her eyes were playing tricks on her. Logic refused to take hold when she heard scuttling coming from someplace behind her. Her mind refused to attempt to explain the noise.

Jazz was not at all ashamed of being terrified.

She wanted to cry with relief when she saw the neon green exit sign and the glow in the small reinforced window lit by the parking lot streetlight. She escalated into a full sprint, hit the door's metal bars at full speed, and was knocked back several feet onto her ass. The phone flew out of her hand.

This can't be happening.

Terror battled her denial as she crawled to where it landed, but as soon as she reached for the phone, the screen turned black. She trembled when an evil demonic laugh was followed by a dragging sound from one of the rooms on her left.

Don't turn around. Don't look.

Jazz got up and pounded on the doors until her knuckles split. She noticed the blood seconds before she felt sharp claws skitter down her neck to the base of her spine.

And she began screaming.

Chapter One

Thirteen years later

Gypsy Tanner was having a hard time staying detached as she soothed the hysterical guest in the interview chair across from her. She motioned cut for the cameras. "Do you need a moment?" she asked while handing her a small envelope of tissues.

"I'm so sorry," the woman said.

Gypsy offered a small smile. "It's fine, Mrs. Edgar."

"Alayna, please. Since I'm sharing such a personal experience with you, we might as well be on a first-name basis."

"Okay then." Gypsy rose from the chair as their director, Smiley, called for an early lunch.

The spotlights were turned off, and there was a rustle of movement as most of the crew headed to craft services. Gypsy turned to her personal assistant. "Could you please get me a cup of coffee, Tangie?"

"Sure."

Across the studio, the production manager, Roger, threw his hands up, clearly frustrated they hadn't been able to get through the umpteenth attempt to film Alayna's back-story.

Gypsy understood his exasperation but knew it was better to take a break than to keep pushing at her. It was going to be a long day, and she knew she was going to hear from Roger, an expensive one, as well.

Gypsy kept her arm around Alayna as she gently guided her to makeup.

Again.

Her sister, Rhiannon, who had been watching off set, patted one of the stools and began opening her magic jars. "We'll get you fixed up, honey, don't you worry." She wrapped a towel around Alayna's shoulders.

"Thank you, I'm sorry."

Rhiannon smiled at her. "Don't be," she said. "It's no problem. Would you like a touchup, too?"

Gypsy checked the mirror over the long counter with a critical eye. "Maybe just the gloss."

"Is Gypsy your given name?" Alayna asked. "Or did you change it to match your coloring and appearance?"

"It's my real one." Gypsy lifted her long mass of hair. "Up or down?"

"Down," Rhiannon said, then directed her conversation to Alayna. "We used to have a cat with those freaky green eyes."

"Oh." Alayna shifted in her chair. "I think they're exotic. I can hardly believe you're sisters."

"I was a year behind her, but they used to call us Vice and Versa." Rhiannon moved to Gypsy's hair and arranged her curls. "Here, you do only need the gloss." She handed her the tube. "I'll bring her back over when I'm done."

"Thank you." Gypsy patted Alayna on the shoulder, relieved to see some of the anxiety had drained from her expression. Or maybe, it was her sister's golden touch. She'd take either one. "Take your time, we have an hour for lunch."

Her heels clicked on the cement floor as she walked back to the set where Tangie waited with her fresh coffee.

Gypsy smiled. Her personal assistant was a true godsend, and she adored her. Her short hair, purple this week, stood up in artful spikes, which brought her height to about five-one. The diamond in her nose glittered, and her big blue eyes blinked behind her black large-rimmed glasses.

Snap. Tangie popped her gum as Gypsy stepped next to her. "I thought we broke you of that annoying habit."

She snapped it again and then smiled wickedly. "Yeah, well, at least I don't do it during taping anymore."

"There is that," Gypsy said and took the offered go-cup. "Go ahead and take your lunch, Tang. I'm going to avoid Roger and go over notes in my dressing room."

"Do you want me to get you something while I'm there?"

"I brought my own today."

After eating her salad, Gypsy spent a quiet hour reading before she headed back to set where the crew was straggling in. Smiley motioned her over. "Since the Edgars aren't back yet, we'll get yours done instead."

"Sure," she said. Gypsy spotted Tangie joking with the gaffer and gave her a come here signal.

They walked around the green screen they used for formal interviews and into an old abandoned and dilapidated room. The set designers had done an excellent job making it appear as if it had been empty for decades. Fake cobwebs, dust, and falling plaster were artfully arranged, and antique silver candlesticks graced the vintage hand-carved mantel.

It gave every appearance of a haunted mansion.

Gypsy adjusted the seams on her skirt and straightened her jacket. She hit her mark at the boarded window and waited.

Smiley took his position and grinned at her. "Let's keep Roger off our backs and do this quickly."

"Quiet on the set, and action."

The first camera assistant leaned in front of her with the storyboard. "Gypsy's intro. Edgar family. Oak Street. Take one. Mark it."

After the sharp snap, Gypsy smiled. "We believe our loved ones go on to a better place." She paused, and then grinned. "Well, I do anyway." Always at home in front of a camera, matching her expressions to her narrative for the greatest effect was second nature.

"But what if your late relatives didn't care for you when they were alive?" She layered on a troubled expression before she continued. "What if they came back to haunt you and make your life miserable? This is what the Edgar family says happened to them. Tonight, we'll see our professional investigative team at work and hear from the family about their experiences."

"Cut!" Smiley looked around from his stool behind a monitor. "It's not your fault, Gyp. Harry, go around and cut the light behind the window, please."

She waited patiently while they restarted.

"Take two."

"We'd all like to believe that our loved ones live on in a better place and watch over us with love."

Pause, smile.

"I know I do." Turn slightly, show concern. "But the Edgar family would have to disagree." Angle to the side, look into the second camera. "This is *their* story. I'm Gypsy Tanner." Pause, then look back to the first lens. "And welcome to *Paradigm*."

"Cut. Fantastic," Smiley yelled. "And how about a bumper?"

"Anything for you, Smiley." Gypsy grinned. Bumpers were short and sweet, meant to promote the show during commercials.

"And go," he said.

"Welcome to *Paradigm*." Gypsy started again. "And stay tuned. You won't want to miss seeing our professional crew investigate the Edgars' home, and later, we'll hear from the family personally as they share their experiences with us."

Snap.

Gypsy rolled her eyes at Tangie. "Stop with the gum."

"It was like a period at the end of the sentence. You know?"

Before she could argue with her, Roger came around the wall of the set. "Great job," he said.

Grateful he hadn't launched into a tirade about costs, Gypsy nodded. She returned to her interview chair and took a few to meditate briefly and recharge. The noise of the set didn't bother her in the least; she was used to it and wouldn't trade any of the hardworking crew on her show.

They all pulled together to find genuine stories because she believed most viewers wouldn't be fooled and would know if the fear and apprehension the guests brought with them were real.

It came across in the interviews.

Gypsy mused on instances in the past where guests had been less than truthful. She'd had an advantage since childhood, she called it her bullshit detector. Though sometimes tempting, she didn't call them liars to their face, but in the end, she refused to let their stories air.

The canceled episodes cost thousands of dollars.

Roger had had a fit, but veto power was built into her contract.

She refused to be bullied, believed her integrity was valuable and ultimately unshakable. As long as the network wanted her to continue to be attached to this show, Gypsy wouldn't let her reputation be tarnished. She'd worked too hard for it.

She insisted they vet the guests. In this day and age, everyone was plugged in and had cameras and recorders. If someone was being terrorized by something, it shouldn't be all that hard to provide some kind of proof, take pictures of scratches and other strange phenomena. Hell, they even had EVP—electronic voice phenomena—apps anyone could download onto their phones. She, along with the investigative crew, also went over any evidence they collected. She liked to be completely informed.

In the beginning of their television show's three-year run, Roger had been overheard muttering comments about former models being spoiled and making his life miserable, but he didn't say much to her face.

What Roger thought or said behind her back was none of her concern, really.

And in the end, she'd appeased him by pulling together and producing a best-of episode that received huge ratings and kept the advertisers happy. Then he whined about not receiving credit. She couldn't win for losing with him.

If the hauntings occurred before the electronic age, Gypsy had made sure she did pre-interviews with the guests to discern if they were actual victims of the paranormal or attention seekers who would do anything for their fifteen minutes. This was where her little secret psychic advantage didn't hurt.

It was a small unknown advantage. *Paradigm* had won awards by mixing her interviews with the families, investigations by her competent crew, perusal of gathered evidence that Gypsy believed to be authentic, and her absolute commitment to make sure of it. The show also included guest spots with various acclaimed paranormal experts. Last but not least, though never her favorite, they had panels of skeptics. Most of the time, Gypsy thought of their explanations as unbelievable as they claimed *Paradigm*'s evidence to be. Some of their condescending attitudes straight up pissed her off.

Gypsy wasn't dumb. Her success as a former model had everything to do with getting the job in the first place. She'd been hired because of her instant recognition to the public.

But she liked to believe her looks were only a small part of her success. They got her in the door. Gypsy had plenty of intelligence to go with them. If people forgot that or assumed different, it was their bad. She swept away the ignorance with a flip of her hair and could verbally destroy her critics with a smile.

When she finished with her touchup with Rhiannon, she headed back to the interview set. On the way, she passed Alayna's husband.

"I don't think she'll break down again. Don't worry," Ted Edgar said. "I slipped her a little something."

Gypsy hesitated for a moment. There was already an issue that his wife might not make it through their next attempt. Now if she was impaired, there was a possibility things could get worse, and production would stall again.

Before she could reply, Ted quickly added,

"Only a half, she'll be fine. She has a prescription." His knowing look said he'd been through and done it all before, as if he were sharing a secret with her.

Her instincts told her he wasn't being mean. She'd seen them together between takes, and his love for her was obvious. He was more worried about his wife's emotions than about the interview.

And wasn't that refreshing?

❧❧❧❧

Jazz threw her keys on the entry table.

There wasn't a dark spot *in* this house, and that was a very welcome relief.

Compared to the crappy apartments she'd lived in, the restored Craftsman was a bright palace. She'd been thrilled when her best friend, Billy, whom she'd known since she was twelve, invited her to live with him in sunny Los Angeles.

"Hey, Billy, are you home?"

She riffled through the mail they dutifully put in the basket each day. Most of it was for their other roommate Candace, who'd moved in a couple of weeks before Jazz.

Candace went to casting calls all day, looking for that big break, and if she wasn't reading for a director, her other job as an escort kept her busy.

Jazz never judged, and Candace never brought her work home. Jazz had almost become used to the constant bombardment of her different scents of perfume and hair products in their Jack and Jill bathroom.

Because of their different schedules, they hardly saw each other, though Candace seemed nice enough when they did.

At least she kept her things tidy. Billy would have had her head if she didn't.

"Are you here?" she called out again. Jazz heard Cleo yapping in her crate. Billy must have planned to be gone for a few hours.

Probably out gallivanting, she thought with affection.

Jazz walked over and picked Cleo up, and the dog covered her face in kisses. Jazz laughed. She was the damnedest, ugliest, cutest, dog she'd ever seen. No one had ever determined her breed, but Jazz thought she kind of resembled a guinea pig on steroids. She grinned when she noticed Billy had painted her toenails pink this week.

Jazz carried Cleo to the back door and walked outside with her to the side yard, away from the pool, to let her do her business.

It was hot outside, and sunlight hit the pool, creating sunbursts in the water. As much as Jazz wanted to fall into the blue, her clothes were covered in sawdust and drywall paste.

She'd have to change first. Jesus, she was dog tired, and her muscles ached.

After waiting five weeks to get her transfer in order, the union had sent her to Universal Studios that morning. And now she was going to have to get used to the routine again of being up and out of the house far before the sun rose.

On the bright side, she got off work early in the afternoon, with time left to enjoy it.

She reminded herself to call her father later. It was strange not having him to take care of, as she'd done most of her life. She'd been worried about leaving him alone, though he hadn't had a drink in years.

His sobriety had been surprisingly difficult for her. She'd had to cut the strings of codependency that had roots going far back into her childhood. His latest lady friend, Bea, had all but moved in, Jazz was fond of her, and really, Dad didn't need her anymore.

He encouraged her to move and have fun. "Meet new and exciting people," he'd said. "You'll *love* it!"

Exciting indeed, Dad.

The only people Jazz had really interacted with since she arrived were Billy and his revolving choice of company.

She wasn't being fair. Billy had been her best friend for—what? Almost two decades now? And she'd loved him since the day they met.

That long? Good lord. They were a long way from being known as the fag and dyke from those taunts from ignorant assholes.

Cleo ran over to her, and Jazz picked her up in time to see their buxom neighbor over the fence. Jazz ducked quickly. She was nice eye candy, but she'd passed the point of intrusion with Jazz a month ago.

Too many times to be coincidental, when Jazz was outside, Dalia, if that was her real name, popped up over the fence and tried to engage her in conversation. That wasn't the problem. No, the issue was Dalia felt the need to be topless when she did so, and it made Jazz uncomfortable. Dalia didn't listen to Jazz's subtle hints or take notice when Jazz had become more abrupt. Then again, she could have been ignoring Jazz's signs on purpose.

It had been a long time since Jazz had gone there with anyone. Dalia would not be the one she'd break her fast with.

She took the dog back into the house. Cleo

promptly grabbed her threadbare tiny stuffed pig, then took it to her fancy designer pillow by the hearth, color coordinated, of course. She'd be fine there while Jazz took a shower.

In her new bedroom, Jazz silently blessed Billy. The room was full of comfortable, homey touches she'd never had before—fresh flowers, tasteful knickknacks, and stylish furniture. Even if she'd had the inclination to decorate her father's house or her previous apartment, she could have never matched Billy's impeccable taste.

She mentally shuddered while remembering the house she'd grown up in had been stuck in stasis going back to when her mother left them, full of pink, mauve, and mint green.

Jazz sat on the big bed to appreciate Billy's touches. She felt cared for, and it had been a long time since she had.

The thought formed a small ball in her throat just as a light tapping caught her attention. She turned to the window, and the sound grew progressively louder.

Hair rose on the back of her neck, and a familiar fear chilled her skin.

Jazz didn't want to believe it had followed her. She clenched her fists and shut her eyes tightly. When the taps became insistent knocks, she covered her ears and rocked.

PTSD anyone?

Whether it was post-traumatic stress or not, the sound kicked her nerves into high gear.

"It's not real," she yelled, hoping it would dissipate the illusion.

"Who you screaming at, Jazz?" The noise stopped.

She jumped and swallowed her yelp. "You scared me. Don't sneak up on me."

"You're the one shouting and talking to yourself."

"Huh." Jazz shook her head while she studied her friend.

Billy had always been pretty, pretty enough to be a leading man in, well Hollywood, but Billy had no inclination and he made no apologies for who he was. Instead, he put his considerable talent to styling, both hair and wardrobes, and was quite successful at it.

In high school, he'd been on the skinny side, worn his hair in a blond mane. He'd shortened it since and now had it styled so his dark hair was overlaid with white spikes.

After she arrived, he'd done her hair similarly, and with both of them having dark eyes, she felt they vaguely resembled fraternal twins. It still felt strange when she passed a mirror.

"I thought you would be close behind me," she said.

"Been that and a little more, Jazzy. Are you okay? You look a little pale."

"Fine." Her tone belied her nerves. *Just dandy.* How had she lost thirty minutes of time?

"Maybe you should lie down."

"I need to take a shower."

"Okay," he said. "You do that. Then I think you should lie down. I'll get something together for dinner."

Jazz nodded, but the second he left, she plopped back onto the bed and was asleep within seconds.

❧❧❧

"Alayna, are you ready?"

She appeared to be relaxed, but if Alayna wasn't plugged in, so to speak, to her memories, Gypsy would postpone it again or skip it altogether and use only her husband's introduction. They hadn't taped their son's interview yet, so she had no idea how he was going to come across on camera.

She needn't have worried. Alayna's hysterics were gone, but her story projection was genuine and believable. If she hadn't seen her earlier, Gypsy wouldn't have even noticed the slightly glazed look.

"From the top. Edgar interview. Take sixteen."

Gypsy gave Alayna props. To her credit, she'd hardly twitched when the clapper on the slate was snapped down. Her eyes went distant as she talked of the past.

"It all started long before we moved back into the house. My husband and I were newlyweds and barely out of high school. We had to live with his parents. It was the recession, you see, and jobs were almost impossible to come by. And to top it off, I was pregnant.

"His mother didn't care for me, you know? And really, to be honest, that's an understatement. She hated me on sight. In her eyes, no one was good enough for her son. She said I ruined his life by trapping him." Alayna leaned forward. "As if I got pregnant all by myself.

"She made my life unbearable. Oh, never when Ted was around or even my father-in-law. She was careful to reserve her viciousness for when we were alone."

"That's terrible," Gypsy said and meant it. She was truly interested in the story's progression now that Alayna was able to actually tell it without falling apart. She silently applauded Ted for his foresightedness.

"I could tell you a thousand stories of what she did to me, the verbal abuse, the petty arguments she started, the times she lied to my husband about things I did—or didn't do—but it all comes down to there was absolutely no love lost between the two of us.

"It took me years to find my voice, but I when found it, I used it. Let me tell you."

Gypsy internally cheered when Alayna pulled herself straight in the chair, as if showing her backbone.

"Well, I finally stood up to her—the bully—and she told me rather cruelly I was not welcome in her house from that moment on, and get this, she thought her son would choose to stay with *her*. She also said it made no difference to her if her grandson stayed or not."

Alayna hadn't paused for Gypsy's reaction to her comments, but she was fine with that as her guest needed to tell her story.

"Can you imagine? Obviously, Ted did not choose her, and we've been married twenty-two years."

Gypsy smiled. "Congratulations."

"She never forgave me, and I never walked through her door again while she was alive."

"That must have been hard on you," Gypsy said.

Alayna waved her hand to brush it off. "Not on me, I couldn't care less if I saw her face again, but surely it was on my husband and son. I never asked him to choose one of us over the other. Because it was his mother, after all, but she refused to consider forgiving me, as if I needed forgiving, and my husband clearly told her, if his wife wasn't welcome, neither was he."

Gypsy was tickled with her sarcasm. "It's tragic his mother put him in that position."

"Right?" Alayna rolled her eyes and continued. "As hard as that was, compared to what we've gone through, that part was the easiest. Ted's father passed away first, probably to get away from her, and she died two years ago. As an only child, Ted—I mean we—inherited the house. It was a beautiful home, but I got rid of anything and everything that reminded me of her." Alayna's eyes lit up, and she grinned wickedly.

It must have felt wonderful and freeing for her. "It sounds to me you had a little justice," Gypsy said, knowing a well-placed comment would move the story along. "And just the right set of circumstances to create the perfect storm." Instantly, she was sorry to see the little gleam dull in an instant but analytically, knew the close-up would also register the reaction.

Alayna's distress grew in the space between them, and even as she sympathized, Gypsy hoped it wouldn't interrupt the flow. "How long was it before you noticed things were off in the home?"

"Shortly after we moved in. We hadn't lived there in years, the house had aged, so little things that began happening, we rationalized. The knocking we attributed to bad pipes, the cold spots we excused as a bad furnace. When it got to be more yet, I still thought it was my imagination because I was back in a house where I'd been hated so much. No matter how many possessions of hers I gave away, it seemed her hateful vibes were still flying around."

"Did you talk to your husband about it?"

This was the moment the editors would cut to Ted's solo interview with a few scenes of the investigation and from there break to the B-roll re-enactments that would be spliced in intermittently along with snippets of their joint interview and their son's.

They'd yet to share the evidence they'd caught nearly a month ago with the Edgars. Things were never filmed consecutively, and Gypsy thought it an art form to make it seem so.

Out of the corner of her eye, she caught Smiley's thumbs-up signal.

She would keep Alayna talking. They weren't done yet, but they'd finally got Alayna's entire intro on tape without interruption.

❧❧❧❧

Jazz screamed into her pillow and had another moment of true terror when she felt a body land on top of her. She pushed herself up violently and heard a squeal and loud thud as something hit the floor.

"Ow, what did you do that for?"

Billy.

"Holy shit. What's *wrong* with you?"

He peeked over the side of the bed. "I think you broke my arm."

"I did not, you big baby."

"I came in to wake you for dinner, and you wouldn't budge."

"So you threw yourself on my back?"

He grinned. "It worked." Billy stood and appraised her. "You're filthy and you stink."

"Love you, too, buddy. I agree with you. Let me shower really quick, and I'll be out."

"Ciao," he said and left the room.

Billy, she thought, was the only person she knew who successfully managed to flounce out of a room and look good doing it.

Her heart rate was almost back to normal after she stripped and went into the bathroom. For a second there…

Nope.

Since moving here, she finally remembered

what it was like to have slept an entire night without interruption.

She let the warm water hit her full in the face and tried to wash the memories away. Who was she kidding? She would never forget the horror. But right now, right this minute, she could tuck it in the back of her mind again.

After a quick check out the window, she decided she still had time for that dip after dinner and put on her swim bra under her sleeveless tank and pulled on her shorts before padding in her bare feet down the spotless hardwood floors.

She rounded the corner and found Billy talking with someone she'd never met before. A slim man with beautiful caramel skin sat across from him, sporting spiked dark hair and striking green eyes.

"Yum-my," he said as she approached. "You're right."

Billy laughed. "She's as gay as you are."

"So? She's built better than my last boyfriend."

"Flex your muscles, babe, make him jealous."

Jazz grinned and showed off her arms in a body builder pose. "Hi."

"This is Jorge, our friendly neighborhood florist."

"Oh, did we get flowers?" Jazz asked.

Jorge blew her a kiss. "Ain't I a daisy?" He pinched Billy. "I'm not the florist, you ass." He tilted his head. "We work in the same business. It's nice to finally meet you. You haven't had the pleasure, but this is not my first ride on Billy's merry-go-round."

Billy blew him a kiss. "Right, darling?"

"Hmm." Jazz walked to the island to see what Billy had made. "So what are we having for dinner?"

"Takeout." Billy pointed to the bar.

"Just water, thanks," Jazz said.

"You can get that yourself then. We're eating outside." He picked up his own drink and walked out the French doors with Cleo at his heels.

"I brought Chinese," Jorge said from behind her.

"Great, I'm starving."

Billy had set the table. He never ate out of cardboard. Takeout dinners were always plated on his matching dinnerware, complete with crystal glasses. Jazz wouldn't have minded eating out of the cartons, but when in Rome and all that, she thought. She plopped down in one of the chairs and stretched her legs out. "This is awesome. Thanks, guys."

Billy passed a serving dish of pot stickers. "How was your first day of work?" He turned to Jorge. "Jazz got a call to work at the Universal lot today."

"Exhausting," she said. "And very weird to see a New York City street end abruptly, then to appear on a street in *Tombstone,* and after the next turn find myself in Middle America."

Jorge fanned himself. "Kurt Russell."

Jazz laughed while she helped herself to more food. She listened as they discussed their own experiences at Universal. Maybe everyone here had a story about it. Once again, she was reminded she was far, far from home.

Billy took a sip of his drink and turned to Jorge. "She hasn't had sex in over a year."

Jazz choked on her sweet and sour. "Gawd, Billy." She shook her head. "I can't believe you just said that."

He feigned innocence. "What?"

"My, my, my," Jorge said. "We're going to have to do something about that."

"Please tell me you're not offering."

"Honey," Jorge said and waved his fork. "You're yummy and all, but not even in the dark." He gestured toward her breasts.

Jazz laughed. "As if I'd want to." She mimicked him and pointed between his legs.

"I know this girl—" Jorge said.

Billy jumped in. "Absolutely not. Don't even think about it."

"But—"

"I know who you're thinking about," Billy said. "And double dog not."

"What are you—twelve?" Jorge waved his arm. "She's a nice woman."

Billy turned back to Jazz. "Her face met an iron skillet," he whispered dramatically. "Twice."

"You are so bad," she said.

Jorge covered his mouth and giggled.

It was kind of funny, she thought, to have the two of them bickering over her. "Thanks, but no thanks, boys. I can find my own girls."

"And I'm sure she'll be the pick of the litter." Billy stood to clear the table.

"Hey," she said. "Give me that last crab thingy." He tossed it at her.

"Go on," he said. "Dive in, I know you want to."

"I do," Jazz said with her mouth full and rose to help.

Jorge picked up his empty glass. "No, don't touch, we've got it."

And there's another reason to love living here, she thought. Billy took care of her. She was used to the shoe being on the other foot. It was strange but entirely welcome.

She felt lighter than she could remember, and

she could so get used to this.

Jazz balanced herself, her toes on the edge, and let herself fall back into the pool. The cool water refreshed her, and she turned weightlessly a few times before surfacing.

When she opened her eyes, she saw a dark shadow dart from the shallow to the deep end underneath her. Out of breath, she pulled herself up and out of the pool. Jazz sat at the edge and searched the water.

It had probably been a cloud passing under the sun, but the moment had ruined her desire to swim, and she felt goose bumps rise in the wake of a cold chill.

She wrapped up in her towel and started to the house.

Billy stepped out of the French doors. "We're going out for a drink. Do you want to join us?"

Jazz shook her head. As much as she didn't want to think of the shadow, the feeling stayed with her. "No, you guys go ahead. I'm tired and have to get up super early."

"Bor-ing. Girl you better go and get yourself some nookie soon," Jorge said. "Ouch, don't elbow me."

"We're going," Billy said. "Don't wait up."

"Oh, I won't."

After Jazz waved them off at the door, she left a light on for Billy and headed back to her room. She paused when she spotted the open drawers in her dresser. She was certain she'd closed them.

Hadn't she?

Chapter Two

Gypsy walked into the studio and straight to Tangie, who held out her first cup of coffee for the day. "Thanks." She took a sip and sighed. "Breakfast of champions."

"You know it," Tangie said. "Roger and Smiley are going over the dailies."

"Okay. What are you doing now?"

"Fan mail, searching our Twitter account for some questions you might want to use during the Q and A show."

"Oh, awesome. Let me know how that's going. I'm going in. Wish me luck."

Tangie shook her head. "As if you need it."

She laughed and shooed her off.

When Gypsy went into Roger's office, they were already watching the second interview they'd done the day before, and she caught the end of it.

She looked at the scene with a critical eye toward her own reactions. Sometimes, she felt as if she might be too detached after hearing the same stories, and it was not at all how she wanted to come across. It certainly didn't mean that she didn't empathize with the victims because she did. She didn't *want* to become jaded to a guest's emotions.

She turned her attention toward the monitor. Ted's interview had been quick and to the point. Smiley dubbed it perfectly in only three takes, and she'd gone home shortly after.

"Ted, what your family has experienced is terrifying, especially for your wife. I have to ask, why didn't you move?"

His gaze shifted to the floor before he looked back up at her. "After we inherited the house a year ago, we foolishly took out a loan against the equity. For the first time, we had money to take a long honeymoon, pay off the credit card bills, help my son, Junior, with his student loans. And they were all excellent reasons at the time. My wife wanted to remodel, and I didn't blame her. We took that long vacation, and I hired a contractor to remodel while we were gone."

"From what she's told me, I don't either. I heard she cleaned it out."

He smiled. "And had a grand time with it."

"You didn't mind?"

"Heck no. My mother was evil to her when she was alive."

"How was your relationship with her?"

"My mother? Growing up with her was difficult, to say the least. It's hard to live with a narcissist. She wasn't vicious to me, at least not in public. Had to keep up the appearances, you know. She reserved her cruelty for when we were at home where it was private. Anyway, back to why we couldn't move. The markets, both stock and real estate, crashed, I was outsourced at my job, and just like that, we were upside down. We didn't have the money to leave. Alayna was the only one working, and we were living paycheck to paycheck."

"So you had to stay," Gypsy said and noted the camera would catch how helpless he felt, his dejected expression before he got ticked off. Most of the men she interviewed in this position felt the same way.

"Yes, and damn it, it was a big part of my childhood. I grew up there and had wonderful memories of my father. I didn't want to give up the house my father built. He worked hard to maintain it, and he loved it. When I was young, he took me to the river to help pick out the stones for the hearth in the family room. Every board and nail hammered into it has a piece of his spirit."

"That's a charming thought," Gypsy said. "And how awful is it that your mother is trying to tear it away from you?"

"It's breaking my heart to see my wife go through this."

"Has she ever hurt you or Junior?"

"Yes." His tone was clipped and short.

"So," Gypsy said. "You don't think it's the house that's being haunted. It's personal."

"Very much so," he said. "I think she'd follow us even if we abandoned the house."

The scene finished. Roger, who had his back to her, must not have known Gypsy entered because he began muttering. "She handles them with kid gloves. I don't know why she lets them ramble on like that."

"Because," Gypsy said, amused when he startled. "They need to tell the story at their own pace, and I think the interviews are better because the Edgars are not being influenced by the fearful energy in their house. Also, without patience, Alayna would have never gotten through it. When it all comes down to it, she felt safer here."

"I agree," Smiley said. "We've a lot of footage to choose from. Here," he said and clicked a button. "We're going to add this bumper to close the episode."

Gypsy saw herself standing by the fireplace.

"Thank you for watching. We want our viewers to know the stories are real. The video and audio are real. Their fear is genuine. In this field, there is a plethora of ghost hunters and accusations of fake evidence. Here on *Paradigm*, we welcome your skepticism. If you have a legitimate argument, we invite you to come speak on our show."

The number the studio set up for these calls flashed at the bottom of the screen. Thank God, she wouldn't have to wade through the crazies to get to professional, so-called skeptics who would eventually sit across from her.

Poor Tangie.

Of course, they could use skeptics from past shows, but as many times as Gypsy cut them down, they'd have to be gluttons for punishment. *Paradigm* viewers *loved* it when Gypsy contradicted their opinions with incredulity. *Their* conclusions were so far out of left field and so far-fetched that in her opinion, they made them look rather stupid. They'd rather be ignorant than believe in anything not seen. More often than not, they came off as pompous asses.

In addition, the self-professed ghost experts themselves? The Boys Club? She thought them rather arrogant. She hated when other shows debunked legitimate evidence in their attempt to appear more professional; their conclusions were almost as ridiculous as the skeptics' take.

Gypsy, as well as her fans, loved it when she unsheathed her velvet claws and ripped them up.

If she'd had any skepticism when she started this job, it had all dissipated when faced with real paranormal experiences and presented with irrefutable proof.

She didn't believe herself to be overtly psychic, nor did she claim to be, but she had an innate bullshit detector, excellent insight, and instincts. So she could consider herself somewhat gifted.

"What do you think of using that clip?"

She turned her attention to Smiley. "Whatever you think is best." Gypsy looked back to Roger. "We could have a panel of guests against the skeptics."

"We'd have to budget it." Roger looked as if he'd sucked on something sour.

Great, she thought. Her work here was done. She finger-waved to Smiley and backed out of the office.

Thanks to her ever-efficient assistant, the travel arrangements to San Francisco were made, and—*yay*—her budget allowed Tangie to come with her. She took care of things before Gypsy even knew there were things to take care of.

And bonus, since Tang was straight, Gypsy never had to worry about getting hit on and being uncomfortable afterward. That was a blessing in and of itself.

Gypsy headed over to makeup to gossip with her sister between takes. Maybe she could convince her to join her at the mall later that afternoon.

As she passed the haunted sound stage, a loud thud was followed by what Gypsy thought was some rather creative cursing. She chuckled as she walked down the hall.

❧ ❧ ❧ ❧

Jesus, that hurt.

On the other side of that wall, Jazz swore again and stuck her thumb in her mouth.

Should have been paying more attention to that last nail.

She was a little afraid to look at it. It had been a long time, but the last time she'd hit a finger with her hammer, she'd needed stitches.

Totally not what she needed when she'd just started this job. And she certainly wasn't going to file an incident report on her own stupidity. She carried Band-Aids in her lunchbox for just that reason.

Her supervisor told the small crew their job was done for the week and to take off at lunchtime after they picked up their checks. Jazz sincerely hoped that she would get another ticket to continue working at the studio. She thought it was cool, but she wouldn't know until she called into the union office.

Her thumb wasn't as bad as she thought as she swept up her area. Now she was off the clock and unfortunately, had no ready excuse not to join Billy on one of his mall trips. Damn, the man could shop a blue streak. It was far, far down the list of things she wanted to do, but she did love his company, and he'd been so kind to her.

She jumped into the little blue truck he'd lent her and turned on the GPS to go home. She didn't know if she'd ever get used to this traffic or learn her way around. The insistent sound of horns blaring when nobody was moving anyway, as if hitting them while being bumper to bumper was going to fix and move the metal snake the cars had created.

Four long hours later, she sympathized with the toddler who was throwing a fit outside the Neiman Marcus entrance. She was holding on to seven of his colorful bags. "Can we go now?" Jazz asked Billy.

"Stop whining. Looking fabulous takes work."

He gave her the once-over. "You could use some."

"What's wrong with the way I look?"

"Do you really want me to tell you?"

"No." She laughed. "You probably have a list."

"I do. Yes, we can go, right after I stop in here."

Jazz looked for a space on the benches currently occupied mostly by men waiting for their wives and plopped down.

When Billy came out again with two more bags, she shook her head. "Now?"

"As soon as we stop by the little boys' room."

She groaned. That could take a while, too.

As she was waiting for him to come out, Jazz leaned against the wall next to the clear escalators.

Sparkles.

It was the sparkles that caught her eyes as they flashed along the moving stairs. They came from a pair of strappy rhinestone-studded high heels attached to slender ankles catching the light as they descended lower, and long, long legs were revealed.

Jazz couldn't look away from the white-beaded fringe on the long lacy vest as it caught more of the light and dazzled her further.

Dark purple nails rested gracefully on the rubber rail, several silver bracelets lined her wrist while under the duster a violet dress clung like a second skin to a body straight out of Victoria's Secret. Jazz blinked twice to make sure she wasn't imagining her. But no, the woman was still coming down, and with her face turned away, all Jazz could see was a mass of dark brown curls, which brushed the middle of her back.

It felt as if she'd waited for an hour for the entire woman to appear. In reality, she realized it was less than five seconds. She couldn't see her face yet, but then again, it was the fringe swirling around her thighs that begged for attention.

Look at me, look at me.

And she did for a brief second before she turned and walked the other way. She'd been drop dead gorgeous, and even as Jazz's blood heated, her feet were dead and frozen to the floor. If anyone had told her she'd be a victim of it at any point in her life before this day, she would have laughed it off. She may have even felt a twinge of sadness, but in the end, she'd still believe love at first sight was created here in Hollywood and at the very least, a fairytale.

Hell, two minutes ago, she didn't believe, but now found herself frantically searching the crowd for the woman who'd caused her heart to flip.

"Close your mouth, darling, you'll catch flies." Billy studied her. "What?"

Jazz stuttered while she pointed in the direction the woman had taken through the breezeway.

Concerned, he put a hand on her back. "Are you okay? Did something happen?"

"No, no, I'm fine. I just saw the girl I want to marry."

He spun quickly. "Where? You know I need to approve."

"She's gone forever."

"That's too dramatic, darling. What does she look like?"

Jazz sighed. "Perfect. And I'll never find her again."

"You're such a pessimist. You'd do better to believe in puppy dogs, rainbows, and that all good things come to you."

For a second, Jazz felt the sadness of her past. "I haven't had much cause to, buddy."

A shadow passed over Billy's face. "Oh, honey, I'm so sorry." He tried to lighten the mood, handed over his bags, and patted her. "I'm sure you'll see her again. If the Universe means for you to be together, she'll pop into your life at the exact right time."

Jazz didn't know if there would ever be a right time. Her life to that point when she'd moved here hadn't been a walk in the park. In fact, it was a downright nightmare. She possessed more baggage than anyone she knew. With her luck, her dream woman would turn out to be straight and married anyway. Either that or run away screaming.

The want she'd felt would likely never be answered. The moment passed, and she noticed the weight in her hands. "How come I'm carrying all of these?"

"Manicure, darling." He blew on his fingernails.

"You had your nails done today?" She checked her phone. "Jesus, Billy, we've been here for over three hours."

"And you've been such a doll about it. Come on, let's go home." Billy took off toward the exit with his fast mall walk on and zipped to get around the crowd, and Jazz, carrying his purchases, struggled to keep up.

After they fought the traffic home—and damn, did it ever slow down? —Jazz dumped his bags on the couch. "You exhaust me," she said. "I'm going to go change."

Billy wasn't paying attention to her as he was too busy emptying his bags, oohing over his treasures.

Jazz went into her room and looked around to see if anything had been moved or was out of place. She'd nearly accepted the logical explanations made over the last few days about the slight instances she'd felt threatened, but vigilance was second nature for her. Jazz's shoulders relaxed when she realized nothing was amiss, and she changed into shorts and tank top, then double-checked she'd tightly closed the drawers in her dresser. After she took a mental picture of her room, she went back out to the main part of the house and into the kitchen to get some water.

She heard conversation coming from the television but ignored it. It was rare for her to watch anything. "Do you want a sandwich?"

"Sure, if you're making it," Billy called back to her. "And fruit."

After she put together two plates, she joined him in the family room just as credits were rolling on the show he'd been watching.

"You should tell them your story."

"Who?"

"*Paradigm*," he said.

"And what exactly is it about?"

"Interviews with people who are being haunted and house investigations."

"A paranormal show? I lived it. And you know I don't have fuck-all to do with that crap." Even the thought of it caused a nauseating tap at the base of her spine.

"Language. You're such a brute."

Jazz chuckled. "Someone has to be."

"Seriously, don't you want to find answers?"

"Nothing has bothered me since I've moved here, and I don't want to open myself for any of that energy again. It would feel as if I'm daring it."

A door slammed in the back of the house, and Jazz felt the blood drain from her face. "See?"

Billy looked at her and quickly blurted, "It must

be Candace."

"Are you sure?"

He shook his head.

Jazz and Billy walked to the entry, although neither was in a hurry to go check. They held hands and their breath.

Not again.

Billy's hand tightened around hers, cutting off the circulation to her fingers, and he gasped when the knob turned and the door creaked open.

Candace appeared carrying a laundry basket in front of her. "What are you looking at?"

Shaken, Jazz laughed nervously. "Apparently, you."

Billy shook his head, and she heard his relieved sigh. "Go get ready, girls, we're going out."

"Not me." Candace said. "I'm tired of going out. I'm looking forward to relaxing and getting small chores done."

"Are you sure?"

"Going out usually means I'm working. No, thanks." Candace turned away, then walked toward the utility room.

"Billy, I don't want—"

He interrupted Jazz. "Yes, you're going. Go change again."

She knew it was childish, but Jazz mentally stomped her foot as she knew there would be no arguing with him. Besides, it might be fun.

Maybe.

❧ ❧ ❧ ❧

Gypsy headed straight back to Rhiannon after

her trip to the mall. She was running late for her joint interview with the Edgars, and she only had a few minutes to get touched up.

She hated being late and was annoyed with herself, but her delight in the siren red shoes she'd purchased negated some of that.

"You don't have time to change." Rhiannon brought out her brushes while she hip-nudged Gypsy onto a stool.

Gypsy glanced down at her fringed duster. "This is fine."

"You're right, it is. Let me punch up the color in your eyes, you don't need much else. What's in the bag?"

She grinned into the mirror. "My fabulous new shoes."

"Oh, let me see."

"I'm out of here. Go ahead, take them out, drool, and then put them back. I don't have time to put them in my dressing room."

Rhia nodded. "I'll take them over there for you."

Gypsy arched her brow.

"What?" Rhiannon feigned innocence.

"Don't wear them home," Gypsy said on her way out the door. Rhiannon's laughter followed her down the hall.

The Edgars were already in their chairs. "Sorry," she said while they attached her microphone. "I was held up."

"You're not late yet," Smiley told her. "It's fine."

She faced the couple. "Ready?" She sat back, crossed her legs, and waited for the mark. "Welcome back." Gypsy looked straight into the camera. "We're with Ted and Alayna Edgar. Their story continues on

Paradigm." She looked over at them. "Thank you for joining us."

Ted nodded. "We appreciate this opportunity."

"It's a shame Junior couldn't be here today, but we'll be talking with him soon."

Again, Ted nodded.

Alayna's mouth turned slightly at the corners. It wasn't really a smile, and Gypsy was a little worried she'd break down again, but with Ted holding her hand, she might be okay.

Please let her get through this.

"I know that we've talked separately, but I've always found interviews with the family as a unit to be helpful in understanding the circumstances, synergy, and the details that may have been missed."

"Different dynamics and points of view for the same experiences?"

Gypsy nodded at Ted. "Exactly right." She glanced down at her notebook, though she didn't need to. "When we talked earlier, Alayna, you said you were the first to experience activity in the home."

"Yes. But now that I think back, there was always this feeling, you know? That someone was looking over my shoulder. I believed, of course, it was because Eunice hated me. I thought clearing her things out would make that go away. Considering all that's happened, it was incredibly naive of me."

"If you've never experienced it, the idea of a haunting would never be your first conclusion," Gypsy said.

"Therein lay the fault of being skeptical," Ted said. "Because we didn't believe, the events escalated until they became a kind of paranormal terrorism."

Alayna nodded. "And it made Eunice stronger."

She shuddered visibly.

"As we've said," Ted began, "there were times we heard knocking in the walls. Of course that had to be the pipes, right? The extreme cold and changes of temperatures had to be a faulty furnace. For me, those were easy things to reason away. In the beginning, only my wife was having experiences while I wasn't there. It took me longer to admit what was happening was unexplainable and after all consideration, must be something paranormal."

"But it started first with Alayna." Gypsy redirected the conversation back to her.

Alayna took a deep audible breath. "Along with that creepy feeling, I started misplacing things. My keys, glasses, my phone, and things like that. Sometimes, I wouldn't find them for hours or in some place so ridiculous, I know I would never have left them."

"I once found my remote in the freezer." She'd never had, but Gypsy knew her comment was relatable.

Alayna visibly relaxed, leaned forward, and lowered her voice. "I found my keys in the medicine cabinet."

"Good one," Gypsy said. It was the first genuine smile she'd seen from Alayna since the interview started, and she was glad to see it.

"That went on for a few months. Then one day, I was alone and passed through the dining room, into the kitchen, and a vase flew out of the china cabinet at me. At the time, I was more upset it was a family heirloom."

"I think I told her it was an earthquake or some kind of tremor," Ted said and shook his head. "Now I realize how silly that sounds."

"Is that when you, Alayna, got the first inkling it

might be your mother-in-law, Eunice?"

"No, not yet." She patted Ted's arm as if comforting him for his poor excuse. "I was still in full denial myself and making excuses of my own, asking myself if I was crazy or if my imagination was running wild."

"Which was another one of my bright justifications," Ted said.

Gypsy appreciated his honesty and willingness to admit he'd been wrong. She liked him better for it and in her opinion, also went a long way as far as validation toward their story for her.

"It's okay, honey," Alayna said. "At that time, I was willing to believe I needed medication." She looked back at Gypsy. "I started to see shadows. First, I just had glimpses in my peripheral vision, then more substantially and more often. When I saw one standing at the edge of my bed, I began thinking it might be Eunice."

"How about you, Ted?"

"It took me a bit longer. I mean, really, who wants to believe their own mother would haunt them?"

"It's not like getting a warm fuzzy from a loved one, is it?" Gypsy glanced down at the pad again. "Let's talk about the poltergeist activity that escalated from that point."

"I know it sounds cliché," Ted said, "but it was in the kitchen. Alayna was grocery shopping, and I was cooking dinner. I turned from the stove, and a drawer opened. I closed it, went back to the counter, and *heard* it open again."

"That's when I came in," Alayna picked up the story. "I came in the back door, and had I not ducked, the cupboard next to my head would have bashed me in the forehead before my pretty teapot flew out." Her cheeks colored. "I'd just bought that."

Ted shifted in his seat. "That's when I went from skeptic to believer. I couldn't deny or rationalize what I'd just witnessed."

"When your paradigm shifted?" Gypsy smiled. "Alayna, was there ever a time you thought this could be random and not Eunice?"

"No." She shook her head. "After we'd eliminated the obvious, we knew it had to be. And if I'd had any doubt, I was completely convinced the day I saw her name written in the steam after I'd showered."

Gypsy jotted a note. "It could be said that it was there before she died."

"No," Ted said. "We'd had the master bath completely remodeled from the studs up. Everything was brand new."

"Did you get a picture?" Gypsy asked, though she knew they did. She'd seen it and knew the final cut would edit the shot in during their conversation. "It must have terrified you."

"And Eunice would have known that," Alayna said. "From that day forward, it only got worse. She made my life hell when she was alive, and now she gets to keep doing it? How fair is that?"

"Some spirits stay just as mean after they pass," Gypsy said. "And don't seem to want to move on."

"One night," Alayna continued, "she yanked the covers off."

"That's when I took this photo." Ted handed it to Gypsy. "It scared me so badly I dropped the camera, so it's a little blurry. You can clearly see a face on that one." He pointed to the second picture. "And *that's* my mother."

When the showed aired, the viewers would be able to see the shots side by side. "The resemblance is uncanny, and I'm convinced, but we'll let the audience make up their own minds." Gypsy knew the panel of skeptics would tear the evidence to shreds. She was used to that, but she also knew the experts would prove there had been no tampering involved. She believed the Edgars were telling the truth; their sincerity was undeniable.

Gypsy understood the show focused on the paranormal aspects for entertainment value, but something about this case tugged at her heart about this couple clearly in crisis.

❧❧❧❧

It was a short ride, and Jazz noted the crowd lining up around the block. Billy went straight to the front and winked at her while the bouncer made eyes at him.

Straight in the door, she hated waiting.

"See there?" Billy asked and beelined to the bar. "That little redhead is giving you a come-hither look."

"Why?" Jazz asked. "There are plenty of attractive people here."

Billy looked her up and down. "Sun-streaked blond hair, muscles to die for, washboard stomach under a skimpy tank, long legs, and…Do I need to go on?"

She felt herself blush. "No. But thanks for the style." She pointed to her bangs.

"Love how they hang in your dark mysterious eyes," Billy said. "Even the gay boys are looking at you."

"Stop it."

Embarrassed, she looked around. One of the major things she noticed about Los Angeles, the greater percentage of everyone here was good-looking in one way or another. Her gaze lingered on the dance floor. God, they were young. Had she ever been so loose? Maybe at one time she might have been, but her youth had been destroyed in the aftermath of *that* night.

She peeled the veil off her eyes, and appearances began to crack around the seams. Some of the partyers had an almost desperate look and air about them, but not the compact redhead who was weaving around the crowd with a predatory gaze.

Because Billy had so recently pointed out that she'd been celibate for months, Jazz considered whether or not she'd break that streak tonight. In the meantime, there was no reason she couldn't appreciate the hot body poured into a little black dress and killer fuck-me shoes.

When the woman was a few feet away, Billy chuckled and excused himself. "I see Jorge at the bar. See ya!"

"Hey!" she shouted at his back. "Don't you dare leave me here—I don't know how to get home!"

He threw a saucy look over his shoulder and disappeared in the crowd. Though irked by his abandonment, she knew he wouldn't actually ditch her.

She didn't move from her spot, and within seconds, the woman reached her and with a breathless sigh introduced herself as Brittani with an "i."

Up close and personal, Jazz could see the meticulously applied makeup melting in the heat of the club. Obvious hair extensions and a decade-plus more on her than the distance had showed. Not that age bothered Jazz, more it was the frantic need to hang on to youth.

Someone bumped Brittani from behind, and she slipped in her high heels. Instead of the expected soft press of her breasts hitting her in the chest, Jazz received a double jab punch.

Hollywood. The land of illusion.

Maybe she was a silicone snob. God, was there such a thing? Jazz had always loved women of all shapes, sizes, and color. Each had her own feminine allure, but it was the confident women she was most attracted to.

She straightened Brittani up to her feet and gently excused herself. The music was giving her a headache, and the smells of alcohol, perfume, aftershave, and sweating bodies were making her a little ill.

Damn, maybe she was too old for this. It certainly wasn't because she'd had too much alcohol because she hadn't ordered a drink yet.

"Wait!" Brittani called out. "Don't you want some company?"

"Not tonight, love, but thanks."

Brittani smiled sadly and walked back into the crowd.

It was a little depressing, but all Jazz wanted to do at that moment was go home.

She found Billy and told him she was going to leave. His disappointment was obvious, but he didn't argue. He called her a cab instead.

Jazz wasn't going to lie to herself. When the taxi pulled into the driveway and the house was completely dark, she was a little spooked. Candace must have decided to go out after all.

She ordered herself to pull up her big girl panties

while she walked up to the door and let herself in. The first thing she did was turn on the hall light and was then greeted by Cleo. Candace hadn't put her in the crate. Good thing she came home first or Billy would have had a fit. Cleo had severe separation anxiety, and only her nest and stuffed dog helped.

Jazz checked for doggie accidents, and finding none, looked for a note. How did one deal with a roommate who went on dates for a living? When should she be alarmed? She'd have to ask her because she didn't know if there was etiquette for this situation. Better yet, she thought, she would ask Candace in the future if she would let her know anyway. How could they send in the cavalry, if they didn't know where she was?

She would probably tell her she could take care of herself and had been doing so long before she moved in, but still, Jazz's protective nature wouldn't shut off like a switch.

She felt a little uneasy, though it might have been because she hadn't spent much time here alone when it was dark.

The overhead light in the hall buzzed then flickered, and Jazz laughed nervously.

It could be anything.

Then again, she could be in denial. If she was, she thought, she'd rather stay in it than think the worse.

Jazz didn't watch much television, but when she went into her room, she turned it on anyway for the noise. It kept her from straining to hear other sounds in the rest of the house.

Cleo was happy to stay, and it made Jazz feel better to keep her there. She debated on whether or not to close the door, but in the end, she did. She didn't want Billy and Candace to feel the need to tiptoe down the hall when they got home.

She stared absently at the program playing, paying no attention to the actors but comforted by the glow of the screen.

Drowsy, she curled up and cuddled with the dog.

Jazz began to fall, and she smelled the dank, dark hallway.

Fuck.

Somewhere in the distance, she heard Cleo whining, and before she could pull herself back, she found she was running again, and from far away, the small window lit by the streetlight beckoned.

Jazz tried to wake herself up completely, but a wave of lethargy swept over her, and she fell back into the nightmare, alone with the damned.

Her breath was loud and heavy in her ears, and the sounds of footsteps racing behind her caused her to stumble on the floor covered in shards of glass.

Run faster.

The conscious part of her knew how this ended, but the part of her that was locked in the asylum in her dream always hoped she was going to escape before *it* got her.

That same conscious part of her always knew it was futile. Her life had been irrevocably changed that night.

And she'd been living with the consequences for the last thirteen years.

Chapter Three

Jazz was sitting at the breakfast table with Billy when Candace came in. She looked terrible, her red-rimmed eyes and dark circles seemed out of place. Jazz had never seen her look anything less than impeccably groomed.

"Good morning, beautiful," Billy said.

"Back at you, gorgeous," she said with a weak smile.

"Rough night?" he asked.

"Bad, bad dreams." Candace ran a hand through her tangled hair.

"Tell Uncle Billy about it." He placed a glass of orange juice in front of her.

"It…uh…was horrible. I was lost in some kind of abandoned building. I kept running and turning corners but always ended up in the same place. I was being chased, and it sounded like whoever *they* were, consistently stayed two paces behind me."

Jazz stiffened in her seat. It was the same nightmare she'd had the previous night. She listened with horror and played hers concurrently with Candace's. *I rounded the corner into an old operating room.*

"Then I ran into an empty room with an old-fashioned hospital table."

And the windows started rattling.

"When I turned," Candace said, "all the glass

started shaking."

And shattered.

"Then just burst out of their frames."

Billy's gaze went from Candace to Jazz. She wondered if her alarm was visible.

"I finally turned and saw a crazy old woman."

Jazz covered her mouth and left the room before she gasped. She slammed the bedroom door and stood in the middle of the space. "You fucking bitch."

A knock had her spinning toward the door, ready for battle when it opened.

"I'm sorry—" Candace began.

"Oh, no, it's not you," Jazz said. "I apologize for leaving so abruptly." She had no idea what to say that wouldn't make her look batshit crazy or worry Billy.

"It was just a nightmare," he said.

"No, it's not," Jazz snapped and was instantly sorry for it.

"What?" Candace asked. "What are you talking about?"

Jazz didn't want to scare her. Hell, if she'd heard her own story, it would freak her out.

"How did you sleep?" she asked Billy.

"I'm still up, more or less," he said.

Jorge appeared behind Candace, his hair sticking up in all directions with a bad case of bed head. "What's going on and who are we calling a bitch?"

Jazz had to grin at him, she couldn't help it, and it deflated some of her anger. "It's nothing. Come on, let's go back to breakfast."

Candace looked unsure, but Jazz motioned her out. Alone, she looked around her room again. "Get the fuck out." But she knew, *knew* it was only going to get worse.

She willed herself to calm down before she went back to the kitchen. "Where's Candace?"

"She'll be fine," Billy said. "She's going to a cattle call today for a scream queen."

"I feel bad. I shouldn't have…"

"She's fine," he repeated. "I didn't tell her anything."

"Tell her what?" Jorge asked with wide eyes. "Tell me."

Billy turned to Jazz, graciously changing the subject. "What are you doing today?"

"I have the day off."

Jorge tapped the table. "I know you're avoiding the question, but I refuse to feel insulted yet. I have clients today, thank you for asking."

Billy looked positively gleeful. "If they see you like that, they'll never let you touch them again."

"Like what?" Horrified, Jorge put a hand to his head. "Omigod, I ran out when I heard you scream."

Billy made a kissy face at him as he ran back down the hall to the master suite.

Jazz laughed. "He's adorable, you should keep him."

"Thinking about it, we'll see." He looked thoughtful for a moment while he started clearing the table. "I don't have any clients today. Let's say we blow this Popsicle stand and get out of the house."

Jazz gazed with longing at the pool. She'd been looking forward to spending the day next to it doing absolutely nothing. But now, she didn't want to be alone with her racing thoughts.

Billy must have misunderstood her silence for an excuse to beg out because he began whining. "Come on," he urged. "I'll take you on a cheesy Hollywood tour, then we'll go have lunch and make fun of the ladies' shoes."

Tickled, Jazz nodded. "God, I love you. Let's do that." She wouldn't be insulting any footwear, but it was hilarious when he did. When your best friend had idolized Joan Rivers and agreed with most of what she'd said, lunch conversations could be the funniest part of your day.

Billy whistled while he finished the breakfast dishes. If the nightmares continued to affect people in the house, she'd have to move. She didn't want any of them to get hurt.

Take me down to the Paradise City.

She smiled at the ringtone. It was her father's favorite song, and every chance he got, he sang about the grass being green and the girls being pretty.

"Hi, Dad."

"Good morning, Jazzy." His voice boomed over the tiny speaker.

"You're sounding chipper this morning."

"Oh, I keep forgetting that you're three hours behind me. It's noon here. I've already gone to a meeting, had coffee with my cronies, and—never mind."

Jazz grinned. "Is Bea there?"

"Yes. Anyway, how's it all going with you?"

"You know me, inciting riots, conquering small planets."

He chuckled. "Never expected anything less from my little girl."

"I know you've told me everything has been fine since I left, but I want you to be truthful, it's important. Has anything happened to you in the last few weeks?"

"No, baby," he said.

"You're not lying to me, are you?"

"Not in my program today."

"Really?"

"Jazzy, stop it. Nothing has gone on here, I promise. But now that you keep asking, I'm worried about you."

"I told you, everything is fine."

"Don't bullshit an old bullshitter."

"I'm fine."

"Why is getting anything out of you so freaking hard?"

Because I'm used to taking care of myself. For years, he hadn't been lucid enough to solve or help with any of her problems.

The silence over the line told her that he was thinking the same.

"I'm sor—"

"Please don't apologize," she interrupted. "I had a nightmare last night."

"The usual?"

"Yes."

"I don't know what to say to make it better, honey. I'm at a loss here."

"I don't either. Hopefully, it's a lingering leftover thing."

"Have you found a new counselor?"

"No. I'm done telling my drama to other people. They never believe me anyway, want to convince me I have sleep paralysis, or give me drugs for the voices."

"That's bullshit."

She smiled. "I know." At least he had always believed her.

"Doesn't California have all those New Age hippie-type people that can help?"

"I'm sure they do, but as I said, I haven't gone

looking for anyone. I hadn't had any problems until last night." *Much.*

"Will you promise me that you'll try talking to someone? I worry about you."

"Maybe I can ask Billy if he knows someone or someone who knows someone who can help."

"Come again?"

Jazz laughed. "That's how it works here. It's a huge network. Their people have people who know people who know someone else that might be able to help."

"Sounds confusing."

"It is, and someday, I might get used to it."

"Hmm. What are you going to do this weekend?"

"I'm sure Billy has some cheesy tourist thing planned." She heard Bea in the background ask him who he was talking to because they were late for the car show. Since they'd gotten together, he was busy all the time, and Jazz was glad for it. She took the opportunity to get off the phone first. "I have to go now," she said. "Call me later? Let me know how the old Ford does in the contest."

"Of course."

"I love you, Dad."

"I love you, too, Jazzy. Bye."

❧ ❧ ❧ ❧

Gypsy looked over the ocean and watched the morning come to life in the brilliant colors of a painted sky and tried to shake the nausea still churning in her stomach.

Who wouldn't have their share of nightmares in her line of work?

But they had never, ever been this intense where she felt actual pain upon waking, and the sequence of events continued to loop in her mind.

She was aware of being lost. She'd called out and heard it echo down the hall. No one answered, but she *knew* she wasn't alone. Something lurked behind her, no matter which way she turned in the dark, it was there, just behind her shoulder.

Her heart had tripped as she looked down the hall of closed doors. She tried turning a few of the knobs, but even as some crumbled in her hands, none of them opened.

She could hear it, breathing still, even over the knocking of her heart in her ears.

She'd wanted out. And a voice in her head screamed, "Run!"

And she did—even as she knew somehow something else kept pace with her, she'd heard rapid thumps where her leading foot had just been.

She'd run toward the light the little window provided under the exit sign.

When she'd burst out into the night, lightning struck the streetlight, it burst in a flash, and shards of glass shattered around her.

A sheet of rain made it impossible for her to see where she was going, and there was no way in hell she was going backward. She'd seen the shadow out of the corner of her eye; it grew bigger than she could have imagined and blocked out the light of the moon high in the sky.

The cold had sliced her to the bone, and she'd fallen to her knees in the mud.

Claws reached for her, and she screamed as unimaginable pain tore through her.

Her world went black, and she'd woken cold and clammy. Fear had held her hostage as the sun streamed in her windows.

When she'd gone into the bathroom and looked in the mirror, her face was white, her eyes dull and glassy, and if that weren't bad enough, and it was, she registered she was soaked through. Her hair and clothes were wet, and her skin was goose bumped and frigid. The sense of impending doom left her shaken.

Gypsy turned the hot water on in the shower and set it to boil.

She turned away from the window, grateful it had washed away the oily residue of the nightmare. After she poured another cup of coffee, she went back to her room, grabbed her journal, walked into her office, and sat to write it out.

☙☙☙☙

Midway through her workday, Gypsy felt a sharp jab in her side. "What the—?" She turned to see Tangie standing next to her with her mouth wide open.

"Two o'clock, hunky carpenter."

"Oh, for goodness sake." Gypsy spared a glance and felt her own eyes widen as she noted details in shorthand.

Dark hair with platinum streaks, short with bangs that she expertly flicked out of her eyes with a little nod. A white sleeveless tank that revealed sharply toned muscles tucked into carpenter jeans. Wide shoulders tapered down to a slim waist and rounded out to a perfect—

Gypsy stopped herself.

The woman wore work boots, but she would be

taller than her, which was rare since she'd left the tribe of gazelles behind in the fashion world.

When she turned, her back muscles rippled with the movement.

"Yummy," Tangie whispered.

She must have felt them staring at her. She twisted back around, saw Gypsy, then *her* mouth dropped open. It was almost comical.

The carpenter dropped the hammer she'd been holding onto her foot.

Gypsy had a chance to register brandy-colored eyes, kissable lips, and high cheekbones. The camera would love her. It was second nature for her to notice such things.

"You're straight," she hissed at Tangie.

"Yes, yes, I am, but I'd have to be dead not to notice that." She pinched herself. "Nope, still kicking. That woman has pheromones oozing out of her pores. And oh, boy, did she notice you. Go see if she's okay." Tangie gave her a little push.

"No. You go." Gyp looked back at the woman who'd already picked up the tool and appeared to be trying very hard not to look as if she were staring at Gypsy, who was still trying not to look at her.

Mmm. She might have gone over, maybe, but she'd have to explain the reason to Rhiannon, who would tease her about her current dry spell.

Gypsy certainly didn't feel dry right now. *Oh, you wicked, wicked girl.*

Sadly, she refused to let the thoughts carry out to the deed; she was far too busy to pursue anything. What a shame, she thought, tool belts are hot. She'd like to think it let her know a woman knew how to handle things.

When she reached makeup, Rhiannon was tapping her foot impatiently on the floor. "I saw that."

"What?" Gypsy feigned innocence.

"That." She pointed out the hunky carpenter woman and fanned herself. "You're blushing."

Gyp laughed. "Not. I don't have time to pursue anything."

"Well," Rhiannon said. "You could make some."

Hopefully. "Not now, maybe later," she said and changed the subject. "Let's go, Mom's waiting for us."

"Let's talk about Tusk instead and his latest fiasco."

"What did he do now?" Gypsy loved her older brother, and with his job as bartender to the stars, the stories were legend.

They left arm in arm, and though Gypsy looked as they passed, hunky carpenter wasn't in sight.

It wouldn't hurt to take a walk over to the set the next day.

Gypsy may not have much time in her life for something serious, but she didn't want to live without regrets, either.

And it looked as if there were a lot of things about her Gypsy wouldn't regret seeing.

⚜ ⚜ ⚜ ⚜

Distracted, Jazz didn't even think to bitch about the snaking metal river on the way home as she replayed the chance meeting.

She hadn't been thinking of Billy's puppies and rainbows, but the Universe had been smiling on her.

Lucky didn't even begin to describe the shock to her system when she saw *her*. She barely felt the hammer blow as she'd dropped it. Good thing she wore steel-toed boots. She'd been too astonished to feel stupid about it when *she'd* smiled at her.

Jazz would have walked over to her, but her boss motioned her over after he saw her drop the hammer, and she had to follow him.

By the time she convinced him she'd be fine and not to file an incident report and then returned to the spot, she'd been devastated to find them gone.

When she'd reached the employee parking lot, the young woman with purple hair had been leaning against her truck waiting for her. She'd introduced herself as Tangie, Gypsy's personal assistant.

Elated but curious, Jazz had asked how she'd known which vehicle was hers. Tangie had smiled demurely, informed her that she had her ways, then winked at Jazz before snapping her gum.

She'd thought it rather charming, but...

A horn bleeped behind her, and a squeal of brakes harshly reminded her she should be paying attention to the road.

But the smile on her face refused to dim. Tangie had told her to meet Gypsy the next day at three. Before she could ask how she knew what time she got off, Tangie walked away.

Jazz would never doubt Billy's positive thought energy again.

Maybe her dark days were behind her because things were definitely looking up. Along with being elated, she knew she'd be a nervous wreck until then.

When she finally, *finally* pulled onto her street, Jazz parked behind Billy, who was just getting out of his sporty red car. She jumped out of the truck, ready to share her exciting news, and reached him as he inserted the key into the lock.

"Hey, Jazzy," he said. "Perfect timing."

She bumped his shoulder with her own. "You're never going to believe—" She cut off abruptly as they were met with a foul odor.

Rotten meat, spoiled fruit, and milk that smelled as if it were a month past its "use by" date. It wasn't anything fastidious Billy would have on hand.

His shock and disgust mirrored hers, and he raced to the kitchen with Jazz gagging right behind him.

They spun around together when they heard Cleo whining in her crate behind them. The dog huddled in the back, shivering and making tiny distressed noises in the back of her throat.

Inexplicably, the smell stopped abruptly. Billy cuddled the dog close to his body. "What the hell was that?"

Jazz shook her head. "We both know."

"No, I won't believe that. This was to be your sanctuary."

"I know." Jazz was disappointed beyond belief because she knew the entity's antics would progress until she called uncle and moved. "Realistically, how long are you going to let this progress until you see I can't stay here?"

He turned away from her, went into the family room, and cuddled with Cleo.

"Billy," she began.

"No, I refuse to discuss this on the basis of a bad odor that went away. Cleo and I are going to meditate. I suggest you do the same."

She was tired, she couldn't disagree. As much as she wanted to argue with him, she knew that when

Billy dug his feet in, there was no way around it. "All right then."

"Good," he said, then took Cleo down the hall and shut his door.

Jazz looked longingly at her comfortable bed. A short nap sounded wonderful, but anxiety had creeped in. How stupid was it, she thought, that earlier she'd only been nervous about meeting Gypsy the next day.

Jazz looked at the bed again. It couldn't hurt to lie down for a few minutes in broad daylight.

She was wrong.

God, she could still smell the place, a sense memory that never went away. The ever-present scent of a derelict building mixed with madness.

Her thoughts were in direct contrast to the beautiful day outside her window, and once again, she felt stifled in the ever-present darkness that surrounded her.

What had she been thinking? That moving to California would stop the persecution? It had worked at first, and she'd been drawn into complacency. Now she worried Billy and Candace were threatened by her personal nightmare.

She'd have to go.

Again.

If she'd been trapped all night so many years ago, would she be dead? Would she have brought home even more bad energy?

Sometimes when she didn't feel there was a way out—when hopelessness overcame her, like now—she couldn't help but think that death would be the only way out.

But fuck if she would give the bitch what she wanted.

Some of the hag's words from the past echoed over and over. *Kill yourself, go ahead, you know you want to. This will all go away if you want it to.*

Everyone around you would be better off. They suffer only because they know you.

"Fuck off. I'm not going to the dark side, bitch."

Still, Jazz wondered how much longer she'd be able to fight her. How long until she gave up and did exactly what the entity wanted?

How long could she put the night terrors into a box during the day and fight all night? Thirteen years and counting so far—how long would it go on until she broke?

How many more people would she have to push away for their own safety? Candace had already seemed to have an experience.

Billy was putting up a brave front for her, but she would never forgive herself if anything happened to him.

Jazz hated feeling sorry for herself, but hadn't she earned a pity party now and then?

She caught it and shook her head to negate the progression.

Oppression was sneaky like that; if you were already on an emotional downward spiral, you gave *it* an in—and *its* thoughts could take over your own.

Jazz lay still on her back and began one of the meditations she'd been given to help fight the thing no one had ever managed to get rid of.

She started imagining a big ball of golden light representing the divine universe and protection forming on the ceiling and dropping down to her, starting at the top of her head and ending with her toes, until she was entirely covered with the energy.

If she tried really hard to hold on to the picture, sometimes it worked enough to cut her a break. Connecting the divine, as she was taught, was the only defense she had.

None of the churches, none of the religious doctrines had accomplished anything.

It changed her entire perception of the world.

The only thing that helped was making the divine bigger than God could ever be on paper, written by misogynistic men colored by their perceptions of the world at that time.

She stopped herself there. It would only piss her off and ruin what she was trying to accomplish.

Concentrate.

When she felt somewhat remotely safe, she let her eyes close.

Just for a minute, she promised herself.

❧❧❧❧

Jazz heard mumbling voices in the dark, but it felt as if she had cotton in her ears and couldn't make out the words. Jazz slipped out of bed quietly and tiptoed to the door before she yanked it open.

The hall was empty, but she was met with a cold wind that blew past her and into the bedroom.

She wanted to drop to her knees and cry but knew it wouldn't do any good. This time when hope died, despair convinced her she would never be free.

Jazz left the door open, walked slowly back to the bed, and waited for the attack she knew was coming. All the signs were present.

She would come.

A hand grabbed her ankle and pulled her awake.

Panic rose in her chest like foam from a shaken champagne bottle. Her vocal cords froze, making her incapable of making a sound to protest her fear or the weight on her chest.

Her eyes were the only thing she could move, and she looked around the room to see where the attack would come from next.

The entity was in her head. *You thought you could run.*

She could see the black shadow from the corner of her eye, but she couldn't move her head to make it out.

Her limbs were leaden, her muscles strained against the feeling of being held down. The choking sounds she was capable of emitting weren't loud enough to attract any help. The sound of maniacal laughter alone would have paralyzed her if she weren't already.

You're mine.

If she could've talked, she would have had plenty to say about that.

Jazz felt the entity's thighs straddle her hips and used its knees to pin her wrists, unnecessarily as she couldn't move anyway.

She didn't care how many times this happened to her, she would never get used to it, and she would never stop trying to fight it.

She wanted to close her eyes before she saw its face, but she was denied even that.

The wild, tangled long black hair was the first thing to come into her line of sight, followed by the dark, fathomless evil-shadowed eyes, the crooked nose, and sneering mouth with sharp teeth.

She waited for spittle to spray her cheeks and

pointed claws to scratch her.

Jazz's eyes snapped open, she threw the blankets off, and checked herself for marks but found none. Slowly, she became aware of muffled voices in the dark. With a creepy sense of déjà vu, she again tiptoed to the door but this time, opened it quietly.

No cold wind greeted her, and the voices were coming from the kitchen. She leaned against the frame and took two deep breaths. A nightmare about a nightmare? Just freaking awesome. She wondered if the shaking in her limbs was relief instead of fear. Probably a little of both.

Her throat felt like sandpaper. She needed something to drink, but she looked down to realize she'd fallen asleep in her crumpled work clothes. She should take a shower but needed the comfort of her friend more.

Jazz made her way to the kitchen and found Billy and Jorge at the table with dinner in front of them. She'd assumed it was the middle of the night but now realized it had only been a couple of hours since she'd lain down.

Billy looked up. "Hey, Jazzy, come to join us?" He studied her face and got up. "You look like death warmed over."

"Gee, thanks." She grabbed a bottle of water from the fridge, plopped down in a chair, and plucked a cherry tomato from his salad. Instead of eating it, she rolled it under her palm on the table. "I'm fine."

"No, you're not."

"I had a nightmare, okay? According to your Law of Attraction theory, the more I talk about it, the more I'll draw them to me, then spread the curse vicariously to you, and that makes me worry *for* you."

"Bullshit," Billy said. "I don't care about that. What happened?"

Jorge, who she noticed had been looking back and forth between Billy and her, looked completely exasperated and threw his hands up. "Could somebody please tell *me* what's going on? What curse?"

Jazz picked up Cleo, who'd been pawing at her ankles, and covered her face with kisses. "Aw, thank you, little one."

"She's a good mommy," Billy said. "So are we going to give him the whole story? I haven't told him anything."

"Even though I sleep with him," Jorge muttered.

"Hey!" Billy said. "Sisters before misters."

Jazz managed to laugh. "It's a long, long sad story."

"Apparently, I have time," Jorge said. "We're here for you."

"Well then." Billy got up. "I'm getting a round of drinks."

Jorge's expression remained open and friendly. Maybe talking about it would help. After being ridiculed for so many years, it had been a long time since she'd told anyone about what happened to her. Jazz slipped Cleo a treat and let her settle onto her lap. Petting her was comforting and somehow made her anxiety a bit more tolerable.

Billy came back with a bottle of wine and three glasses. "Go ahead, hon, we're listening."

"I thought you knew the story," Jorge said.

"I do. But I haven't heard it in years."

"You always refuse to listen," Jazz pointed out. "And that's just as well. You probably wouldn't have invited me if you knew the entirety of it."

"Having you live with me is never going to be something I regret. I just want to know how to help you fight it."

"Fight what?" Jorge's tone was impatient. "I can't be part of the conversation if I don't know what the hell you're talking about."

Jazz took a deep breath, then another. "Could we turn on another light, please? I keep thinking I see shadows."

Jorge spun around to look. "There's nothing there."

"I will," Billy said, then leaned over to flip the switch.

"Thanks. Okay, Jorge, you asked for it. Thirteen years ago, I was working at a famous asylum. Though when it was in use, it was called a sanitarium."

"Like where they sent tuberculosis patients?" Jorge asked.

"That's a sanatorium," Billy said. "People that were sick."

"Okay, for clarity's sake, we'll continue to call it an asylum," Jazz said.

"For crazy people." Jorge nodded.

"I'm not even going to play semantics right now," Billy said. "People that were not wanted for a variety of reasons."

"Okay," Jorge said. "Go on."

Billy interrupted. "They were horrible. The owners gave haunted tours of the building, they faked a bunch of shit, and the employees were hired to help perpetuate the lies."

"As I was saying—"

"She didn't want to, she needed the job." Billy sipped from his glass. "Go ahead, honey," he said and waved his fingers.

Jazz smiled inwardly and waited a beat. He wouldn't be able to help himself.

"Fakers." Billy knocked on the table. "Even though they didn't need to, that place was frightening as hell. I would have piddled if Jazz hadn't told me some of the stuff was staged."

She rested her chin on her hand and sighed.

"Then they locked her in with the crazy ghosts."

Jorge looked confused as he looked back and forth between the two again.

"Well?" Billy demanded. "What are you waiting for? Tell the story."

"When you're finished," Jazz said.

"Don't you get saucy with me, girl, go on."

Jazz laughed. "Did you really just say that?"

"I've been saving it for you." He grinned back at her.

"Pulease," Jorge said. "Can someone continue? I can feel the gray hair growing."

"Don't be such a drama queen."

Jorge shot him a look. "You weren't arguing about that earlier."

"All right," Jazz jumped in. She had no desire to get into their sniping or their sex life for that matter.

"I had been working in the basement, graveyard shift. I didn't know it, but the person who was supposed to pick me up bailed early, and I fell asleep waiting for him." She looked warily at Billy to see if he was going to interrupt again, but he was uncharacteristically silent, so she continued. "Long story short, I was locked in."

"In the dark?" Jorge put a hand over his mouth.

"Yes," Billy said. "With the freaking ghosts."

"I thought you said they faked them."

"Of course they did." Billy took a sip of his wine. "But there were real ones, too. In that place, where so many atrocities were committed, how could there not be?"

"Yes, there were real ones," Jazz said. "To get back to the story, I ran to the exit doors, but they were locked."

"And that's when the entity grabbed her neck."

Jazz skipped her response to that comment. "My phone, which I was also using as a flashlight, died."

"Omigod," Jorge said. "What did you do?"

"She beat her hands bloody on the glass." Billy touched her arm. "Poor baby."

"You must have been terrified." Jorge's sympathy was obvious but not at all condescending.

Jazz appreciated him for it and nodded.

"I understand if you don't want to relive it," he said.

"Nutshell," Billy blurted, "is that Stacy, her girlfriend, woke up, got worried, and called Eric, her ride. After finding out he'd left early, she called me, and we burned rubber out to the cursed place. I looked in the window at the main entrance, and all I could see of her was her shoes because Jazz was curled next to the door and not moving. We called 911, who called the owner, who called the security guard to unlock the door, and sent an ambulance."

Jazz cringed at the memory but smiled for Billy's sake and nodded to agree with his staccato version of events.

He grinned back, then turned to look at Jorge. "Wait until you hear what *that* bitch did. But that was later."

"Who?"

"Stacy, my ex-girlfriend," Jazz said. "She wasn't a bitch, Billy. She was scared and left." And didn't that bring up a plethora of insecurities? The circumstances and her abandonment had colored every relationship Jazz had been in since.

"She should have stuck by you."

"Well, she didn't," Jazz said. "But you did."

"Of course I did. You're my best friend. But *she's* still a bitch, and we hate her."

"Yes, of course we do." Jorge nodded.

A laugh escaped before she could swallow it. Leave it to Billy to offer some comedic relief from an experience that had ripped her up emotionally. "Her exit was the very least of my worries."

Jorge's eyes widened. "You should go on that show *Paradigm*."

Billy slapped the table. "That's what I said."

"No." Jazz stood. "Final answer." Cleo barked. Jazz weighed her decision to tell them about her chance meeting that afternoon, not because she didn't want to share, but because of the thousand questions that would follow.

"Hey, one more thing," she said. "You know that woman that I saw at the mall? She works at the studio and I believe on that show you just mentioned."

Billy put a hand over his heart in mock reverence. "Gypsy Tanner? Oh. My. God. That's what I call burying the lead."

"Sorry. The nightmare I crawled out of took precedence over my hormones."

"She's an exquisite creature," Jorge said.

"That she is." Jazz agreed. "And…" She paused.

"And what?" Billy asked. "Tell me."

"I have a date with her tomorrow afternoon."

Billy gasped. "A date date? Already?"

"Actually," Jazz said, "it's more of a let's meet after work and get to know each other."

Jorge laughed wickedly. "Sounds just like ours, babe."

"Shut up," Billy said, then laughed. "It *does.*"

"You know she's a supermodel, as well, right?" Jorge asked.

Jazz's stomach tingled. "I can believe it."

"How could you not know that?" Billy hit her arm.

"Please," Jazz said and tossed the tomato into the sink. "Score. Do I look like I read or keep up on fashion?"

Billy pursed his lips and stayed silent.

"I have to take a shower."

"Just leave us hanging," Jorge said under his breath.

"Will you be okay?" Billy's voice was full of concern. "All joking aside, do you want me to sleep with you?"

Was it any wonder she loved him? Years ago, he had done just that when she was afraid to be alone. She leaned over and kissed his forehead. "I'll be fine, but thanks for the offer."

"I'll leave my door open, shout if you need me."

Jorge rose and hugged her. She really liked him. No silly suggestions such as sleeping pills and no probing for salacious details had earned him her respect, too. Even so, she'd left a great deal of the story untold.

"Thanks, guys." Jazz left, and Cleo followed her down the hall, ran up the little carpeted stairs at the far side of the bed, and jumped onto the mattress.

"Guess I'll have company after all," she said to

the dog. As if a five-pound ball of fur could protect her.

Yet she was comforted nonetheless when she returned from her shower and the dog was still there. She lay next to her and relaxed bit by bit, thinking of the exotic Gypsy until she drifted off to sleep.

Only to drop into her ordeal yet again, watching the story repeat from the point her shift ended, the experience relived from hindsight and toxic clarity.

When the lights went out, the dark invaded, shutting off her breath while her heart stuttered and squeezed, pain became agony.

An icy wind numbed her skin as she tried to crawl away, but she didn't move a foot from where she'd landed after being thrown, trying to run through the locked doors. She felt something scratch her neck, down to her spine, and screams were torn from her throat.

Voices frantically called her name and shook her.

From her perspective on the dirty floor, she could smell blood and wondered if any of it was hers.

Billy's pale, wide-eyed face appeared inches from her own. She gripped his arms and tried to speak, but the words wouldn't force past her chattering teeth.

Jazz turned her head and saw Stacy and the night guard, Vince, in front of the open steel door, and she crawled toward it.

"Hey, hey," Vince said and attempted to help Billy lift her, but Jazz kicked and scratched them away, and didn't stop until she was on the grass in front of the hospital.

Jazz felt the tears on her face before she woke.

Telling Jorge had opened the can of worms, rekindling the beginning of her personal hell. She knew he could only understand the surface. Unless you'd been plugged into that level of terror, there weren't enough words to convey it accurately.

Just when the memories started to fade, the visitations would begin again.

The nightmare that had become her life lived on.

Chapter Four

Gypsy nearly dropped her coffee when she felt the poke. "Tangie, you've *got* to stop doing that."

Snap.

"Sorry." Tangie grinned up at her. "For both."

"There are better ways to get my attention."

"Any-way," Tangie said. "I got the skinny on the carpenter."

As efficient as she was, Gypsy hadn't expected anything less. "Of course you did."

Tangie feigned nonchalance. "If you're not interested…"

"Gimme," Gypsy said.

"Okay, you've twisted my arm. Her name is Jazz, and don't ask me how I got it, but her last name is Miller, she's just turned thirty, and…" Tangie trailed off.

"And what?"

Snap.

"And she's single."

Gypsy tapped her fingernail against her cup. "Is that so?"

Tangie agreed with enthusiasm.

"I'll bite," Gypsy said when Tangie didn't offer more. "How do you know that?"

"I hit on her."

Gypsy sputtered. "What?"

"She turned me down."

Snap.

"Are you crazy, what were you thinking? You're engaged."

"It was my way of finding out if she was a lesbian."

"How's that working for you?" Gypsy bit the inside of her mouth to keep from laughing. There was nothing wrong with her gaydar.

Snap.

Tangie stared at her.

Gypsy stared back.

Snap.

"This is ridiculous," Gypsy said. "Stop it with the damn gum. I have to get ready for an interview."

"With Jane Boren, the demonologist."

"Yes, and I'd rather go to the dentist."

"Okay," Tangie said and began inching away. "I told Jazz you'd meet her at craft around three. That's… that's when she gets off." She ran toward the set.

What? Gypsy felt as if she'd asked that question a dozen times this morning. Gypsy's hand went automatically to her hair, her pulse picked up, and she felt the pleasurable stir of butterflies low in her belly.

It had been a long time since that happened. She didn't know how she would handle Tangie for throwing her out—*ha ha*—like that, but she'd think of something. She was kind of glad she had.

It was kind of a date.

But first, she had this bit with Jane Boren to get through professionally and gracefully. And God, who was it that told Gypsy she couldn't act?

Gypsy worked to keep her expression neutral yet interested, even as she knew Jane had terrified the Edgar family. She wasn't supposed to judge, that wasn't her job. She was here to listen and prompt the guests when needed, making comments, asking questions.

Never mind that this woman had taken two steps inside the family's doorway and loudly announced it was a demon that haunted them.

Whatever terms she used, it was something this particular woman told every family she visited, and using the guise of help—and Gypsy used the word loosely—scared the hell out of them.

Forget that she also told them moving wouldn't do any good because a creature from hell would stalk them.

Gypsy wanted to slap her. She'd seen the abject terror this woman provoked this family to feel.

An entire generation had been traumatized by the movie *The Exorcist*. The special effects of the day might seem silly by today's standards, but time did not erase all the fear the original movie inspired to impressionable young people.

And she felt this woman and her late husband took advantage of them for personal notoriety and book deals. Still, Gypsy nodded and continued to appear attentive to Jane's experience at the Edgars'.

To be fair, though she didn't want to, maybe this woman believed her own hype. She'd been doing it for forty years.

But even that, in Gypsy's opinion, didn't make what she did excusable. When the editing was finished with this particular episode, it would intersperse this interview with clips from Jane's walkthrough of the house, which Gypsy had already seen this morning.

And as predicted, Jane dramatically pronounced the home was infested with evil entities.

If that was so, Gypsy wondered sarcastically,

maybe evil mothers-in-law had a patron demon they invited in to manifest and have a little fun.

Stop it.

What got her, what really got her, was that Jane made these announcements, then left the home with no resolutions. Just that she'd get back with them in a few weeks while she tried to convince church authorities.

The family wasn't even Catholic. On top of that, she claimed the process took months.

If Jane *was* psychic, she didn't appear to feel Gypsy's derision. Jane sat back with what Gypsy thought was a self-satisfied smile when she was finished.

Gypsy pulled her thoughts back and put on her game face. "Thank you so much, Jane, it's been a pleasure talking with you." There, she spit out the pleasantries despite her genuine dislike of the woman.

"Thank you for having me." Jane smiled, and it looked so completely genuine, and Gypsy immediately felt bad for her mean-spirited thoughts.

Right up until Jane grabbed her hand. "There is darkness around you, dear." Her tone was downright spooky.

Gypsy tried to extricate her hand politely, but Jane had an iron grip for an old woman, and her nails were sharp and digging into her skin.

"You have an attachment, I can feel it. There is darkness coming."

As much as Gypsy wanted to call bullshit, she did feel a chill on the back of her neck. Power of suggestion, it must have been.

She tugged harder, and Jane let go.

Tangie pushed between them, took her arm, thanked her for coming, and firmly led Jane away.

Bless you, Tangie.

Gypsy stood where she was, but Jane continued to look over her shoulder at her.

What the hell was that? Gypsy wiped her arm several times and tried to erase the creepy feeling Jane's hand had caused.

But the impression of her grip remained.

☙ ☙ ☙ ☙

Now that Jazz knew to look for her, she caught glimpses of Gypsy throughout the day. She'd come into work wearing jeans and a ponytail. Next time she saw her, it was one of those sexy bohemian outfits with a flowy skirt and blouse, and the last pass, Gypsy wore a black power suit. She looked gorgeous in all of them, and what was it about those high heels that turned her to jelly?

Jazz had woken earlier than her alarm and over her first cup of coffee used the time advantage to look Gypsy up on the internet. Even if she'd had a week, she'd never have been able to visit all the links devoted to her.

It was a good thing, she thought, that she wasn't insecure about her own looks, or she'd never have planned on keeping the date with the intimidatingly gorgeous Gypsy.

It was her own baggage she was concerned with.

At precisely two fifty-nine, Jazz walked over to craft and positioned herself to watch for her arrival.

Not that she'd miss her; Gypsy had more than enough gorgeous about her to stop traffic, and she was sure to see heads turn in her direction.

When she spotted Gypsy approaching, still in her power suit, Jazz felt something inside her clutch and release, along with a surge of happy anticipation she'd been missing for a long time.

Not that she knew she'd been missing it—realization had come just at that instant.

As she'd predicted, heads turned in her wake, but Gypsy's gaze held Jazz's own the entire walk over.

Her mouth went dry, then she smelled her. An expensive scent that provoked thoughts of summer nights that Jazz knew would now forever be associated with Gypsy.

She wasn't at all shy and stepped right up to her. "Hi."

"Hello," Jazz said and held out her hand.

"Oh, I think we can dispense with that, don't you, Jazz?" Gypsy kissed her cheek.

"Mmm." She searched for the emotion she felt. Thunderstruck, yes, perfect.

"Since my assistant pimped me out."

Jazz laughed. "Was I supposed to pay her?"

Gypsy looked at her from under her lashes. "You're so striking." She paused. "But you know that."

"Back at you." Jazz was grateful for the auto response that came naturally. She was still trying to get her feet under her after Gypsy's lips brushed her skin. She knew she was nervous, but this was what swept away must actually feel like.

God, she was full of clichés today.

Gypsy continued to stare at her with big green eyes. Jazz had missed those on her first sighting. *Uh-oh.* Her lips had been moving. "Excuse me?" Jazz said.

"Did you not hear me?" Gypsy asked.

"Apparently, I'm still trying to crawl out of the cave I was born in."

"That's a new one. Inventive too." She grinned.

"I asked if you wanted to take a walk, I've been inside all day."

Jazz looked down at Gypsy's feet. "You want to stroll in those?"

She sighed, twisted her leg, and stared down. "They're great, aren't they? After the runways, I could run a 5K in them."

"In that case, I'm right behind you."

Gypsy took a few steps forward and then looked over her shoulder. "Just checking to see if you were following."

"Where else would I be?" Jazz loved a confident woman, and Gypsy had it in spades.

They walked through the studio and out before skirting the crowds and obvious film extras.

Gypsy led her down a street where they sat on the stoop of a façade of a brownstone. "I checked earlier, and this set isn't being used today. We could have gone to a bench in Central Park, but that's a longer walk."

"It's so realistic. I don't remember watching any movies and thinking, 'Oh, that's a movie set used a thousand times.' It looks different empty and with the camera rails."

"It's been a long time since I've noticed that," Gypsy said. "What's really jolting is actually going to New York and seeing this same street, or one like it, teeming with people who are not actors. And in reality, to catch one of those"—she pointed at a yellow cab—"can be difficult."

"Doesn't everyone use Uber now?"

Gypsy shook her head. "I'm too used to the taxis. When I heard a few stories about people impersonating drivers and committing crimes, I refused to use them. Most of the drivers in New York are too jaded to be star-struck, as well. It's more comfortable for me."

Jazz startled when she heard gunfire and pulled Gypsy down to cover her.

"Hey." She laughed and sat up. "It's okay. It's one of the Wild West shows they do twice a day."

"Well, now I feel like an idiot," Jazz said.

"You're new." Gypsy smiled at her. "And how gallant are you trying to protect me?"

"There's a word you don't hear every day." Jazz wanted to change the subject, she hated feeling stupid. "I Googled you," she blurted.

"Well then, not only do you have me at a disadvantage, you've seen me naked before our first date."

How to be diplomatic? "Hmm," Jazz said, then grinned. "Your naughty bits were covered."

Gypsy coughed, her drink splashed. "I'll guess we'll save that for our second date then."

Jazz handed her a napkin. "The gods have spoken." She grinned. "How about we get to know each other a little bit first?"

She looked at Jazz thoughtfully. "It's been a while since anyone wondered if and what was behind the face. It's…uh…unusual."

"I'm not going to lie. You might be one of the most beautiful women I've ever seen. Makes me wonder if you're an alien."

"I'm surprised and delighted." Gypsy snorted, which made them both laugh.

The charge of electrical attraction was impossible to ignore, and Gypsy's bare shoulders tempted Jazz to run the back of her fingers along the tan skin to see if they were as soft as they looked.

Gypsy's hair blew across her face in the soft

breeze, and Jazz wanted to move it in an irresistible call to touch her. She'd waited too long, and the moment passed. Gypsy's eyes held her captive and immobile.

The knowing look Gypsy returned told her she was aware of it and returned the favor.

Jazz swallowed. "You make me nervous." She tried to cover the hitch in her voice by taking a sip of her water.

"You don't look it."

"Yeah? What do I look like?"

Gypsy paused for a second. "Interested."

Jazz sputtered and sprayed water. "Oh, God, I'm sorry." She grabbed a napkin and dabbed at Gypsy's chest. "Ah, here."

Gypsy took it and slowly wiped instead.

Jesus.

"What?" Gypsy asked.

"Did I say that out loud?"

The air turned combustible, as if a mere spark or slight touch would engulf them in flames. But *no*, she'd spit water at her. It was mortifying.

Dumbass.

Jazz desperately needed to talk, to get her mind off the fact she wanted to—

Stop it! She wasn't a hormone-driven adolescent boy.

"So," Gypsy said. "Where are you from?"

Jazz was desperately grateful for the reprieve. "New York, State not City."

"I know, isn't it funny how people think the whole place is the city? Rural New York is beautiful."

"If you like snow, maybe."

"I do love the California winters."

"Totally what I'd love to get used to living here."

"This is home and where I always come back to."

"Is your family from here, too?"

"Yes, third generation. My grandmother was on contract right here at Universal."

"Show biz family?"

"Yes. Interesting story. Her name was Irma. Maybe that's why she chose unique and unusual names for her kids."

"Such as? Tell me about your family," Jazz said.

"Well, you've met Rhiannon, my sister. My mom is Janis, as in Joplin. That's actually how she introduces herself. Janis as in Joplin. Mom loves and absolutely adores Stevie Nicks, hence Gypsy and Rhiannon, after two of her popular songs. She figured she'd keep up my grandmother's habit of naming after rock stars. My uncles are Jimi, with an 'i'—"

Delighted, Jazz finished, "As in Hendrix."

Gypsy grinned. "Yes, exactly. And there's Uncle Mick."

"Not a nickname for Michael, but Mick as in Jagger."

Gypsy laughed.

"How cool is that?" Jazz laughed with her. "I suppose it's a good thing that you don't have a brother named Tusk, after another Fleetwood Mac song."

Gypsy stared, then blinked.

Jazz couldn't hold in the strangled laugh. "You don't!"

"Do."

"Oh…um…I'm sorry." *Foot in mouth. Again.* "Did he have a rough time growing up with the name?"

"No, he was blessed to be super popular. No one would dare."

Jazz hoped she hadn't offended her. But really,

Tusk? She didn't know how to get past her faux pas, so she took another drink of her water.

Gyp laughed. "You look so uncomfortable—it's okay, really. We're used to it, and my brother loves his name. He says it made him tough. Anyway, he's good-looking and athletic, the girls loved him, the boys wanted to be him."

"Or want him." Jazz grinned. "What does he do now?"

"He's a bartender for an exclusive caterer that the top event planners use for their big Hollywood social scenes."

"Ah," Jazz said. This was all so foreign to her. Like landing on a different planet not knowing the language or social standards.

"He has some stories, let me tell you. It's a good thing he has so much integrity—what he could sell to the tabloids is lethal."

"I'll bet."

"He makes crazy tips. And you know the old adage that your bartender is a psychologist?"

Jazz nodded. She'd unloaded some secrets to various barkeeps over the years.

"It's true. Get a few drinks in anyone, and they start talking buckets."

"I'll bet you have a few stories of your own."

"I do. The modeling world is a hotbed of scandals and trysts, and for now, my lips are sealed. To protect the innocent from the guilty."

"Your life sounds so interesting." Nothing Jazz had done could ever compare.

"It was—is. How about you, what about your family? All we've done is talk about me."

Gypsy herself was—at this moment—Jazz's

favorite subject, and she sure as hell didn't want to talk about her life. "Only child, raised by my father."

"Can I ask about your mom?"

"She left us." Another short answer.

"I'm sorry."

Jazz didn't want her pity. "It was a very long time ago."

Her questions and Jazz's clipped responses put them at an impasse, and the pause became awkward silence.

Gypsy stood and brushed the back of her skirt after checking her watch. "It's later than I thought. I still have a few hours left here, walk me back?"

"Of course." Jazz picked up her empty water bottle and joined her on the sidewalk.

"I'm sure you have all kinds of interesting facets under all that stoicism." Gypsy batted her eyelashes.

It was, Jazz knew, a deliberate change of subject, and Gypsy meant to lighten the moment.

She'd take the out. "Maybe I can show you a few," Jazz said. "Lunch tomorrow?"

"Bet you could." Gypsy winked as she smiled. "Show me a few moves, that is. And yes, I'd love to."

❧ ❧ ❦ ❦

Gypsy admired Jazz's easy way—so different from the frantic pace she was accustomed to.

After they reached the stage door and when she glanced back, Jazz had been standing with her thumbs in her front pockets, letting the crowd pass to either side of her, grinning back at her.

"Oh, yeah," Gypsy murmured, "definitely going there." She knew there was a great deal more under the surface.

Her heart did a little happy dance in her chest, and she felt like a teenager after a first date, though that had been a million years ago, right? How long had it been since she'd had that skip in her step?

And all they'd done was talked for the better part of an hour. She called herself all kinds of a dumb fool, but it didn't diminish what she felt.

Of course, she thought, when she saw Tangie and Rhiannon waiting for her. They were going to pounce for information.

She didn't have much to tell them. Before Jazz left for the parking lot, she'd held Gypsy's hand in her warm calloused one and asked to meet her for lunch the following day to which she readily agreed. She didn't care what she had scheduled. Tangie would have to put them off for an hour.

She mentally prepared herself for the barrage of questions and approached them.

Tangie jumped first. "How was hunky carpenter girl?"

"Her name is Jazz, and you know it."

"Hey, I was—"

Rhiannon cut her off. "Jazz then. What did you talk about? Do you have another date? Is she all looks, no substance?"

"Slow down," Gypsy said. "What is this—the Inquisition?"

Snap. "Well, yeah." Tangie smiled around her gum. "I've known you for close to three years, and I've never seen you like this."

Without really knowing why, Gypsy felt a little defensive. Or maybe it was because she didn't want to share yet. So many people around her expected to know every detail of her life.

Rhiannon must have caught her thoughts as she waved a hand. "We're going to back off for now."

"Why?"

"Because," Rhiannon said.

Gypsy felt bad when she noticed the hurt on Tangie's face and softened her voice. "I'm pretty sure we're going to meet for lunch tomorrow. Could you please check my appointments and arrange that?

Snap. "Sure."

"Thank you. I appreciate it. That's all for now."

"She's young," Rhiannon said after Tangie left.

"Or we're old." Gypsy sighed. "Really, there isn't much to share."

"Other than the fact your hormones are leaking all over the place."

Gypsy smiled. "There is that."

"Come on back, we'll get you ready for your next interview."

They turned to go to makeup, and Rhiannon shot Gypsy a sly look. "And where I can fix the lipstick that's all over your chin."

"No." Gypsy put a hand to her mouth.

"Ha. I knew it."

"You're devious," Gypsy said, then laughed. "And it didn't happen."

"There's always tomorrow."

She felt that pleasant kick in her belly again. "Yes, there is."

Later that night, after she'd poured wine and was drinking it on her back deck, Gypsy read her schedule for the next day. She wondered why Jazz. Why this woman and this time and this moment of her life.

She'd been attracted to a few women—okay, if she

were to be honest with herself, she'd admit to several since her breakup. She'd enjoyed their company.

But that initial jolt she'd felt seeing Jazz for the first time? The elation? That was something rare for her.

Was it timing? Or something more along the lines of fate?

She was still mulling that over when she changed for bed and snuggled in.

Gypsy was aware she was dozing, just on the edge of sleep but not quite over it. It irritated her, she had an early call in the morning.

Frustrated, she turned over. The comforter had become suffocating, and she scissored her legs in an attempt to extricate herself.

She heard a thump coming from the left side of the room.

Gypsy.

She opened her eyes, then doubled her attempt to get free. Shaken, Gypsy finally untangled herself, sat up, and wrapped her arms around her torso.

Because she wanted to, she persuaded herself she had fallen asleep after all, and since she was up anyway, Gypsy got up to use the bathroom. On her way back, she checked the air conditioning and turned it up against the chill.

Gypsy Ann.

This time, the hiss was coming from the hall.

No one had used her middle name since elementary school and only when she was in trouble.

She moved quickly to the doorway and leaned out. The motion sensor lights hidden in the baseboard came on, and when they did, there was no one and nothing to be seen in the hall. *She* was the one who tripped them.

Gypsy backed away and to the bed again just as the lights turned themselves back off and wrapped up tightly. By the time she felt warm and relaxed again, she'd convinced herself it had been nothing and let herself relax back into her pillows.

She knew she was dreaming when she found herself in a dark and what felt like an abandoned hallway.

She wasn't scared—she knew it wasn't real.

A sick yellow light appeared in the distance, a minute before a thick fog passed in front of it. At the same time, she heard whispers behind her.

She spun toward the voices—the conversation was indiscernible but creeped her out at the same time.

She chose to move forward toward the light, and in her dream, she noticed herself walk faster.

A body huddled under the light, the voices faded away as she became aware of the sobs that shook the woman's shoulders. Compassion compressed her heart as she crouched to help her.

The body uncoiled faster than a rattlesnake, hissed, and fangs protruded from a hideous mouth as it began to strike.

Gypsy stumbled back and landed on the floor, the fog swallowed the woman but began to choke her. That part of her that was lucid and awake acknowledged this was a different kind of nightmare, and now, she *was* scared.

"Help me!" Gypsy managed to crab walk backward and screamed when a hand landed on her shoulder.

There is no way out.

She pushed away and grabbed a doorframe to

help herself up; there was nowhere to run, she felt unseen danger on each side close in on her as the mist wound itself higher around her legs.

Wake up. Wake up.

Gypsy's eyes snapped open. She reached over to turn on the bedside lamp and searched every corner and every angle of her room.

Nothing.

"Hello?" Even as she said it, she felt a thousand times stupid. Disgusted with her reaction to a nightmare, even as bad as it was, she turned the light back off and flopped back down.

God, she was tired. Her mind was playing tricks on her.

She didn't have to be up for a couple of hours, and she really wanted some restful sleep before she started the day. Gypsy reached down for the comforter, then noticed it had slipped halfway down the bed.

Oh, hell no.

Momentarily paralyzed, she watched as it was whipped down to the foot of her bed two seconds before she felt the grip on her ankles. She kicked and thrashed against the downward force and hit the floor.

And woke up.

"Jesus fucking Christ."

Goose bumps raced from head to toe and covered her in places she didn't know they could form.

Had the whole experience since she'd gone to bed been one long nightmare? She checked the clock and realized it must have been. It was nearly four a.m., and since she knew she wouldn't sleep again, she got up.

Logically, they came with the territory, and it was the price she paid for doing business on her show.

It wasn't her first or even her hundred and first.

Unfortunately, she also knew it wouldn't be her last.

Gypsy made herself a cup of coffee, and in her robe, sat outside on the deck while she tried to shake the slimy anxiety she'd been left with.

Jazz walked down the busy street and descended into the stairwell. Her stomach turned while the ever-present fear of the dark cloaked her, restricting her breath as she continued through the turnstile, down another flight of stairs, and waited on the white-tiled landing.

Her skin crawled as the crowd jostled her, and she bit her lip when the overhead lights blinked as she got on and the train pulled out.

She must have dozed because when the train jolted, the screech of brakes woke her up with a violent start and body chills set her spine to tingling as she looked around the empty car.

The buzz of the lights was loud and eerie in the silence as she picked up her backpack.

Where was she going?

Better yet, why was she here?

Normally when she went to the city, the commuters were packed in like sardines. How long had she been sleeping? How had she even managed to?

Panic married confusion as the double doors hissed open and nearly stopped her heart. She couldn't see the station platform, and her fists tightened on the straps until her knuckles ached.

When the doors slammed shut and opened again

with force, she couldn't keep the scream in her throat from escaping, and it echoed back to her from the tunnel.

The car shook from side to side and trembled, as if it wanted her out and off. The poles squeaked and shuddered, threatening to snap when the roof began to cave in around her.

She was thrown from the seat and onto the filthy floor. Through her terror, she tried to hold on to her sanity and convince herself it wasn't happening.

It's not real.

The door continued to slam in its frame as Jazz desperately tried to hold that thought. She frantically crawled out toward a single light in the distance and toward it, dropping to the dirt of the tunnel, ignoring the shards of glass and rocks that ripped through her jeans and dug into her knees and palms.

Terror clogged her throat, and warm blood ran down her legs.

She heard a crack, a rock fell from the ceiling, and it slammed her in the head.

The train shot down the tunnel and left her in the dark.

The dark.

Jazz's eyes popped open, and she knocked over the water on the nightstand while trying to turn on the light to pierce the darkness the nightmare left in her mind.

Knees to her chest, she rocked until her pulse slowed.

She was at home, in her own bed, and hadn't been on a subway train in years.

She didn't want to think about it.

Inexplicably, thoughts of her mother intruded.

Now *that* was a road she definitely didn't want to travel, either.

She wiped a hand over her face and longed for something she'd never felt, not really.

Normality. Normal people slept. Normal people weren't haunted.

And normally, mothers didn't abandon their daughters.

Jazz groaned. She was an adult woman. Grow up, for fuck's sake, she ordered herself. The clock was shy of four a.m., but getting up was a given. Her mind was racing too fast to go back to bed. It was nearly time to get ready for the day anyway.

Her legs still shook as she walked quietly toward the kitchen to start the coffee.

She pressed the light on and lost ten years off her life when Billy screamed in her face.

She'd been too surprised to scream herself. Instead, she leaned against the wall and slammed her hand to her chest. "Jesus, you scared me."

Billy was as pale as she'd ever seen him, and his movements mirrored her own, his fingers pressed to his heart.

The house ticked around them in the silence while they each attempted to gather their sanity.

"Good morning?" she finally managed.

"Fuck me," Billy said.

Jazz lifted a brow.

"Oh, you know what I mean." He snarled.

"Whoa." Jazz put her hands up in mock surrender.

"Sorry." Billy rubbed his mouth. "Sorry, bitchy."

"What are you doing up at o dark thirty?

"Nightmare," he said.

Jazz stiffened. "Billy," she began.

"Oh, stop it," he snapped. "It isn't always about you."

"What?" Cautious now, Jazz slipped around him to get a mug out and noticed he'd already made coffee, apparently in the dark. "Okay."

He took a deep audible breath. "Halls of our hallowed high school. James."

Understanding his short-speak, she nodded. "The Hulk?"

He nodded. "Bastard. There I was again, fourteen, hanging by my tighty whiteys on the doorknob of the history class."

"Oh, honey," she said.

Billy waved her off. "God, it was so long ago, you'd think I'd have outgrown the stark terror that boy inspired in me."

"Since I saw him before I left, I can tell you he's now feeding a ginormous beer gut, bald, and unemployed, reliving his football glory days down at Snuffy's."

"God can be kind sometimes," Billy said. "I hate that he still has power over me like that."

"Try picturing Homer Simpson because that's who he is now."

"Truly?" he asked. "Hope springs eternal?"

She nodded. "And you've kept both your hair and your girlish figure."

"I am pretty, aren't I? There is that," he said. "Thank you."

Jazz smiled. That was her story, and she was sticking to it till the day she died if it made Billy feel better. In truth, she hadn't seen James, the Hulk, in years, but it *could* have happened just that way.

They sat at the table and took their first sips of

coffee.

"What happened with you?" he asked.

"Lyn Cody," she said, referring to another of their high school tormentors.

"Nuh-uh," he said. "The beanpole and her sidekick who threatened to drown you in the toilet?"

"Not that they would have been able to follow through with it, but yes."

"Bullshit. Now you're lying to make me feel better."

She nodded. "May they get what they deserve."

"Amen."

They sat in comfortable silence before Billy got up for more coffee. He gestured toward the machine. "Another?"

"Sure."

After pouring more for both of them, he sat back down. "Tell me about your Gypsy." He laughed. "I can't say that now without thinking of the song."

"Which one?"

"Don't play dense, you know it's the one Stevie Nicks sings."

"Her mother was a fan. Her sister is Rhiannon and brother, Tusk."

"Nuh-uh," he said. "Really?" His face lit up.

Jazz nodded. "Cool, right?"

Billy nodded. "I'm going to need more coffee."

Chapter Five

Gypsy had the perfect spot to watch Jazz while she was working.

Jazz was on a ladder, and a line of sweat darkened the collar of her shirt. Add the belt on her slim hips and a dangerous tool in her hand, and Gypsy fanned herself. Lust played a fancy tune in interesting places.

And when Jazz turned and smiled at her, it did all kinds of wonderful things to her nervous system.

Jazz climbed down, and Gypsy crooked a finger.

"Good morning," Gypsy said.

"You smell fantastic."

Jazz had leaned into Gypsy's personal space and flustered her. "Thanks."

"Never underestimate the power of the perfume. I've thought about you all night." Jazz reached out and rubbed a strand of hair between her fingers. "And this. All of this."

"You did?"

"Uh-huh."

Gypsy told herself to get a grip. She'd been complimented before. She swallowed nervously. Jazz's voice was rough and incited some additional sparks.

"And again, that sexy little smirk, there, that one."

Now Gypsy couldn't remember why she'd called Jazz over to begin with. She made her dizzy. Time to get some game of her own into the mix. "I've thought about you, too."

"Yeah?"

Gypsy nodded. "I've come over to give you a proper hello, Hollywood style."

Jazz looked puzzled.

Perfect, Gypsy thought. She didn't want to be the only one unbalanced. She stepped forward, angled her head, stopped a whisper away, and pressed her lips against Jazz's cheek. When she went to kiss the other, Jazz turned her head and met her lips instead.

There was no awkwardness or hesitation. Gypsy melted against her and marveled at how warm her lips were.

Jazz's hands were on either side of Gypsy's face and held her while she kissed her jaw and grazed her teeth against her neck.

Gypsy felt a sharp pain in her stomach and stiffened.

"Shit, oh, sorry." Jazz stepped back. "At the risk of sounding horribly cliché, yes, I'm very happy to see you, but it's actually my hammer."

"Good to know." Gypsy laughed.

"I have to go…" Jazz motioned back to the set.

"I know. I'll see you at noon?"

"Oh, yeah." Jazz smiled and backed away.

Gypsy watched her turn, and the sight of Jazz's tool belt swinging against her ass became incredibly erotic. Who knew?

Holy mother of god. Gypsy needed to sit. She looked around, decided this wasn't the place, and headed toward wardrobe on legs that were decidedly unsteady.

If a quick hurried kiss felt this shattering, what on earth would happen when they were alone?

Snap.

Awesome. "Good morning, Tangie."

"Saw that. Mucho hot."

Instead of being annoyed, Gypsy laughed because, really, wasn't that one of the traits she loved about Tangie? That she was close enough to monitor what she needed? "Seriously hot."

Snap. "You're blushing."

"Am I?"

"Yes. I've never seen you this flustered. Cool as a cucumber, that's you."

"Been a while," Gypsy said.

"She sure doesn't look like that singer you dated or the actress." *Snap.* "The accountant."

"Tangie." *Did she remember everything?*

"What?"

"You make me sound like, I don't know, a floozy."

Her eyes went wide. "I didn't mean—" Tangie looked mortified.

"I know, it's okay." Gypsy wanted to snicker at her reaction but didn't.

"None of them were good enough for you."

They reached makeup and wardrobe. "You sound like my sister."

Rhiannon turned as they approached. "What'd I say now?"

"We're talking about Jazz and the hot kiss in the corner."

"Slow down," Rhiannon said. "What?"

Gypsy didn't mind talking with them, but she was still reeling from that kiss and really just wanted to get her feet back under her. "It was kind of an accident."

"Didn't look like one." *Snap.* "Has she ever acted star-struck around you?"

"No." But Gypsy sure saw some stars of her own.

Rhiannon picked up a comb and started on Gypsy's hair.

"I ran her last night," Tangie said.

Gypsy turned sharply to look at her. "Ow."

"Stay still," Rhiannon said. "I'm trying to get this up the right way. I have some fabulous earrings for you to show off. I don't blame her. I would have done the same thing had I thought about it. What did you find?"

"You're not in law enforcement," Gypsy said. "How did you manage that?"

Snap. "I put her name in one of those online thingys." *Snap.* "In my defense, it's not the first time I've run women who want to get to know you."

"What?"

Rhiannon popped in. "We're just looking out for you."

"You're in on this?" Save me, Gypsy thought. "And what came up?" *Please say nothing.*

"Nada, zip, zilch. Clean as a whistle, unless you want to count a speeding ticket or two."

Gypsy breathed an internal sigh of relief. "Rhia, if you keep pulling at my hair, you're going to slant my eyes."

"What? Oh, sorry." She handed her the earrings to put on.

"It's okay, and it looks great." Gypsy smiled at her in the mirror. "Tangie, what's my next appointment?"

Tangie turned to Rhiannon and whispered loudly, "She doesn't remember because Jazz just kissed her stupid." *Snap.* "It's Roger."

Awesome.

❧❧❧❧

Because she was on the other side of the lot, Gypsy met Jazz at the cafeteria. She spotted her right away, watching the crowd and wasn't that fun? To see her fresh reactions to the various people.

You could run into anything or anyone, from aliens to zombies and everything in between.

When Jazz's glance finally landed on her, Gypsy waved, pleased to see the absolute direct attention in Jazz's eyes as she was spotted in return, making her feel as if she were the most important person in the room.

"Hey," Gypsy said, then kissed her on the cheek.

"I could get used to that," Jazz said. "Is that a Hollywood thing or just me?"

"Just this minute? Both." Gypsy grinned.

"Good to know."

Giddiness threatened her composure. What was that about? Gypsy rarely lost it.

"Um, do you know what you want?" Jazz pointed at the buffet.

"Now that's a double entendre if I've ever heard one." Gypsy would have smiled, but she was already doing so. Her cheeks felt as if they were busting.

"I meant for lunch."

"I know. The pasta looks good."

They got in line. Gypsy studied Jazz's hands while they slid their trays down. Long fingers and she knew from holding her hand yesterday, work callused. How would they feel in the dark, sliding down her bare skin? She grabbed a salad and tried to squelch the thought even as she shivered.

Jazz bumped her hip. "How was your morning?"

"Started out fabulous." There, Gypsy thought. That half smile again. It was connected to her libido.

Dangerous.

"Hey," Jazz said. "Mine too." She pulled out her wallet.

"No, my treat. I'll use my card." And because she saw the immediate negation, she put a hand on her arm. "Please, you can get the next one." She looked down and saw the goose bumps form where their skin connected. It was nice to see she affected her the same way, and in her mind, it evened the playing field somewhat.

Gypsy led them to a table overlooking the lot's gardens. Some people recognized her, but thankfully, none of them approached. There were far bigger fish that came in here. Although not always obeyed, there was an unwritten rule of etiquette to let others dine in peace.

"How is it that you're single?" Jazz asked.

"I could ask the same thing." Gypsy speared her salad and took a bite.

"You can, but I asked you first. I just moved here." Her tone was smooth, curious.

When Gypsy didn't answer right away, Jazz fidgeted. "You're not involved, are you?"

"No, not even a little. I'm sorry, still chewing here."

"Good, because that would be downright cruel." Jazz pointed with her fork.

"I kissed you this morning," Gypsy pointed out. She paused and flashed a quick dimple. "I devastated you."

Jazz wagged her fork again. "I can say with utter confidence, it was pretty mutual. And I don't know if I'll ever get used to cheek kisses. You caught me by surprise."

"I agree. But on to your question, it's been about eighteen months since I've been in a serious relationship. You?"

"Longer than that."

"Jazz," she said. "You really have to quit going on about your life. You're embarrassing yourself."

Jazz laughed as Gypsy had hoped she would. Her expression was open and kind. "Not used to it."

"Perfect opening. All right, we'll start there. Past relationship. Go." Gypsy could find out a lot about a person by how she talked about her ex.

Jazz's forehead creased. "Do you really want to talk about this?"

"I'm curious. How long?" She crossed her legs, pleased to note that Jazz noticed, as well.

"Since I was seventeen."

Gypsy nearly spit out the crushed ice she was sucking on. "How old are you now because that seems like a long time. Was she your first love?"

"Just turned thirty. And yes, she left me."

"Why?" The pain in Jazz's expression told Gypsy it must have hurt deeply.

"She didn't love me enough, I guess." Jazz stared down at her glass, and Gypsy regretted she'd even asked. "Stacy had her reasons." Jazz's bangs hid her eyes for a moment before she flipped them back.

"Mmm," Gypsy said. "Such as? Are you violent?"

"No. Jesus." Jazz's eyes widened, telling Gypsy what she wanted to know.

"Cheater?"

"No." Jazz laughed. "But I'll be honest and tell you I haven't been in a relationship long enough to matter since then."

Change the subject. "Why are you so serious?"

Gypsy asked. Something was under that stoic manner.

"Okay, honesty again. I can't stop thinking about you. You're under my skin, and every time you cross my mind, butterflies tap-dance in my stomach."

"You're so good at that." Gypsy smiled.

"What?"

"Flirting. Making me feel special."

"You are special."

"Why so soon?" Gypsy asked. In her experience, the fast and furious attraction burned out quickly. Something in her didn't want that to be the case here.

"Okay." Jazz took a deep breath. "The first time I saw you was at the mall. You came down the escalator and took my breath away."

"Really? How come you didn't approach me?"

"I was loaded down with shopping bags and waiting for Billy outside the restroom."

"Billy?"

"My best friend and roommate. Anyway, you disappeared so fast, I didn't know where you'd gone."

Delighted, Gypsy smiled. "You would have chased me?"

Jazz looked anxious. "Not like a crazy stalker or anything. God, is that how this sounds?"

"No," Gypsy said. "I've had stalkers." Remembering that threatened her good mood. She considered carefully. Unless Jazz *was* one of the crazies who wrote her letters and followed her. She instantly dismissed the thought. Her excellent instincts told her Jazz was genuine, though definitely hiding something.

"Your turn." Jazz pointed the water bottle at her.

She had, rather astutely Gypsy thought, changed the conversation back. "Okay then," she said slowly and sat back in her chair. "Last serious relationship,

Marky, and we broke up about a year and a half ago."

"Why?" Jazz asked.

"She didn't love me enough," Gypsy said, repeating back Jazz's words. "I deserved better."

Jazz looked surprised. "How could she not? You're smart, interesting, and beautiful."

"Thank you." We traveled round the world together, but when we moved back and semi-retired—"

"She was a model, too?" Jazz interrupted.

"Yes. When we got back," she repeated, "things began to change, and in short, I wasn't enough for her anymore." Underneath her quick explanation, there was a twinge of sadness. Gypsy always considered herself a confident woman, but for that period of time, Marky had done everything she could to chip away at it.

"Unless you're an uber-bitch in disguise, I'm having a hard time with that. Could you expand a bit?"

"Okay, but tit for tat." Gypsy leaned forward. "If you do." She couldn't read Jazz's expression but continued her story after her quick nod of assent.

"Keeping it brief, you understand, she picked at me about my hair, my clothes, and my career. Marky climbed on a hypocritical soapbox, decided she was better than me and my fake Hollywood lifestyle. She insulted my family, my friends, and so on. She accused me of being a vain, selfish, shallow creature."

"She said you were shallow?" Jazz's tone was sharp.

"No, she implied it. But when she left for South America, she left a note saying that if I wanted to give up my little fake life, I was welcome to join her."

"You didn't."

"Hell no." Gypsy laughed. "And I like where I am

this moment very much."

Jazz finally smiled. "Me too."

"Your turn. How do you like working here?"

"View's nice."

Gypsy blinked twice. "How many more teeth do I have to pull to get you to speak in complete sentences?"

"Thirty-one."

"Smart ass."

Jazz smiled. "What do you like to do for fun when you're not working?"

"Sometimes, I'd like to know that, as well," Gypsy said. "My schedule is crazy busy most of the time."

"Doesn't leave you much time to date."

"No. Why?"

"I'm wondering how far down the line I have to go to get some of that valuable time."

"I'm pretty sure you've jumped to the front."

"Have I now?"

"See? You keep answering my questions with a question."

"I'm nervous. In case you haven't noticed, I'm eating lunch with the most beautiful woman in the room. And back to your first question. In a complete sentence even, as I've said, it's been years since I've been serious about someone."

Curious now, Gypsy put down her fork. "Why?"

"It's complicated," Jazz said.

"Aren't they all?" Gypsy countered. Though Jazz was fidgeting, her smile distracted Gypsy, and she lost her train of thought. Jazz was proving to be dangerous to her libido.

"How do you like living in Los Angeles?" Jazz asked and jolted Gypsy back to the conversation. "It seems very...busy."

"Bright lights, big city," Gypsy agreed. "I've been fortunate enough to travel extensively around the world. But for me," she gestured toward the window, "it's always been home. And you?"

"It's been interesting so far." Jazz brushed her fingers against Gypsy's. "And getting better all the time."

Definitely a major zip.

Flirting was easy and proving effortless with Jazz. She had an easy charm.

Gypsy's phone buzzed on the table. "Excuse me, I hate it when people do it to me, but I have to check." She looked at the screen. "It's my assistant. I'll get back with her, lunch is almost over."

"The charming, gum-snapping Tangie?"

Gypsy laughed. "The very one. We're working on a case right now." She stopped and considered. "I think it's related somehow to my nightmare last night." She glanced up to see the color drain from Jazz's face. "What? What's the matter?"

Jazz shook her head. "Nothing. Just curious. So," she asked. "Why the paranormal? Do you have…um… spiritual gifts?"

Interesting, Gypsy thought, another deflection.

"For a long time, I thought it was my imagination. Another perk from growing up in California is that eccentric or pure batshit crazy isn't even a blip on the normal radar. Let's just say I'm open to it and have had validation pertaining to my humble talent. I've adjusted to having a little buzz now and then. It's not anything I talk about or expand on because in my line of work, I'm afraid of losing objective credibility." She kept her eyes level with Jazz's and paused before speaking again. "I can tell you have some intuitive gifts, as well." Gypsy took a bite of her salad and looked around the room.

In her opinion, Jazz's expression didn't show any surprise or negation; she appeared to be too controlled.

Crickets, Gypsy thought. You could hear crickets in the silence.

"In any case," she said. "I learned to trust my guts—they're rarely wrong."

Jazz leaned closer. "What do they say about me?"

"I'm incredibly drawn to you, but there's something under it."

"Yeah? What's that?"

"Danger."

"Gypsy!"

She startled. "Tangie. Don't mind her," she said to Jazz. "She has a fetish about scaring me."

Snap. "No, I have an emergency. Hey, Jazz."

Jazz nodded. "Hello."

"Sorry to interrupt, but I got an urgent call from Alayna." Tangie turned to Jazz. "Client from our last show."

Gypsy went cold. "What happened?"

Tangie looked around the room. "Do you want me to tell you here?"

"Yes, damn it."

"The enti—she was thrown…she had an accident."

"Oh, no." Gypsy stood. "I hate to leave you this way." She leaned over and kissed Jazz. "I'm sorry, I have to take this, it's urgent."

"Of course. I'll see you later."

"I hope so."

Jazz watched Gypsy leave. She couldn't say she didn't enjoy the view.

If the turn in the conversation had left her jittery, the word entity had left sweat pooling at the base of her spine.

Oh, Tangie had stopped herself, but Jazz knew what she was going to say.

The clatter of dishes around her reminded Jazz lunch was over and it was time to clock back in. She gathered their dishes and trays, dropped them off, and headed back to work.

Her mind replayed their conversation. Gypsy mentioned a nightmare, and though she hadn't described it, Jazz was left with a sinking feeling it might be related to her own.

It was close enough to her past experiences to be anything else, but it had never affected someone this *fast*. And she knew Gypsy could sense something. She was connected to the paranormal, worked closely with it.

And damn it, the more she was near Gypsy, the more Jazz wanted. She began to crave her touch, her words. The stuff Jazz imagined being normal in a new relationship. She craved the bliss of normality.

She hadn't yet had the nerve to watch any of the *Paradigm* shows. What if doing so would jinx Gypsy further?

A tiny whisper in the back of her mind asked, "What if she could help you?"

But another, more reasonable and experienced voice finished with an inquiry of its own. "What if she ran away, too?"

Jazz wanted this connection. After hearing about Gypsy's nightmare, she knew it could be dicey, and she may be lying to herself, but she didn't want to give up. The hag hadn't come back, not really. Could she herself have created the situation in her head because she'd been looking and waiting for it to happen? The dread of anticipation was a formidable enemy.

God, she hoped so. It had been so easy to put the night terrors to rest during the day since she'd moved here. Some of that, she knew, was Billy, some because she didn't want to believe the entity had followed her.

All of it could threaten her new life here.

She tried to tuck the bad thoughts away and dared herself to give it a chance.

A pretty little blonde in a pirate costume and several in a horde of female zombies smiled at her. As they passed, she heard one of them say, "Nice ass."

Jazz looked down at her carpenter jeans and felt heat rush to her cheeks. She still hadn't gotten accustomed to people being so free with their sexuality on the West Coast.

It was pretty freaking cool.

❧❧❧❧

It was becoming regular, this meeting at the same time in the driveway. Jazz liked it when she and Billy walked in together, though it hadn't been so pleasant the last time.

They were met with a blast of frigid air.

"What the hell?" Billy asked. "Who turned the A/C down to Antarctica?" His hand clamped to her arm when they heard voices.

Despite the shiver down her spine, Jazz kept walking down the hall. "It's Candace and someone else," she whispered.

"Okay then." He let her go and followed her into the living room.

Candace and another woman were sitting on either side of the coffee table.

"Hey, guys, this is Laura. Laura, this is Billy and Jazz."

When Laura moved to look at them, the center of the table was exposed, and Jazz saw what was on it.

Billy squeaked with alarm. "What the hell are you doing with that in *my* house?"

Candace appeared genuinely shocked. "What do you mean? Miss Laura brought the Ouija board. I told her I was seeing shadows and having bad dreams. She's here to find out why."

"Are you kidding me?" Jazz assessed Laura, who'd stood and smirked. She hated smug people, especially those who acted as if they knew everything. She knew from personal experience most had no clue about the terrible things that could be unleashed by amateurs. Or even worse, fakes.

"I know what I'm doing," Laura said. "There is something horribly dark here. And if you want me to get rid of it, I'm happy to help." She paused.

"For a price, I assume," Jazz hissed.

"I'm sorry, sweetie," Billy said, "but you have to get that out of here immediately."

"Of course," Candace said nervously, her glance going back and forth among the three of them.

Laura picked up the board and started to put it into her large bag.

Jazz was pissed. "Had you made actual contact?"

"Yes," Laura snapped. "I'm a channel for spirits."

She was so snotty, Jazz wanted to slap her. "If—and that's a big if—you had knowledge, did you close the door you opened?"

"What are you talking about? I'm confused."

Candace stood.

On the miniscule chance Laura had been successful, she had to say it. "You have to say goodbye and close the window you opened."

"Do it," Billy ordered Laura. "Right now."

"You're playing with shit you have no business fucking with." Jazz despised Laura's haughty posturing. "How much did you pay her, Candace?"

Now she blushed and looked at the floor. "I don't want to say."

"Close the fucking door," Jazz demanded and watched Laura carefully as she did or pretended to do with her dramatic posturing. "Now get out."

"No refunds," Laura said. "You don't have to be rude about it."

"Rude would be dragging your raggedy ass to the door, which I'm about to do," Billy said. "And I think you'd better leave before I do just that."

"Still, no refund."

"Whatever, get out."

"I didn't know, Billy. I'm so sorry." Candace crossed her arms over her chest.

Jazz followed Laura to the door and stayed until she drove off while Jazz hoped like hell she didn't leave anything nasty behind or give a freaking GPS signal to the entity that haunted her.

When she returned, Candace was crying.

Billy came in from the kitchen with a glass. "Here, drink this."

"What is it?" she asked but took it, downed it, and coughed.

"Whiskey, cures everything." He took the empty glass and went back for more.

"Eww. I don't want anymore," Candace said

when he poured another jig.

"The next is for Jazz," he called back.

Jazz held steady, but inside, she felt as if she were trembling. "With all the information out there and horror stories, how could you not know how utterly dangerous those boards could be?"

"I've never heard anything about them," Candace said defensively.

God, save me from idiots. Jazz decided to cut her a break—maybe Candace was that naïve, despite her profession—and took a deep breath. "What's been happening to you?"

"Well, you already know about the nightmare. Two nights ago, I could swear I saw shadows going up and down the hallway. At first, I thought it was the champagne from my…um…date earlier. Then I thought I saw a woman in the bathroom."

"What woman?" Billy asked. "Dear lord, now I need whiskey." He left again.

The front door opened, and footsteps came down the hall. Jazz held her breath.

"What's up, buttercup?" Jorge asked, then looked around before putting a hand to his cheek. "I smell whiskey, and you two are both pale as sheets—oh, lord—who died?"

Billy came in, saw Jorge, and turned around.

"Now where are you going?" Candace asked.

"To get my man some."

Jorge shook his head. "I'm so confused. Some what?"

"Whiskey," Jazz and Candace answered in unison.

"I hate whiskey," Jorge said.

"Trust me," Billy handed him a glass. "You're

going to need it."

"Go on, Candace," Jazz said. "From the beginning."

Jazz's phone rang. She didn't recognize the number, but it had a local area code. She thought about letting it go to voicemail but it might be something about work. She excused herself and went out into the hall. "Hello?"

"Jazz?"

That smoky voice. "Gypsy?" She felt a funny flip in her stomach. "Not that I mind in the least, but how did you get my number?"

"Tangie. Don't ask. She's a whiz at things like that. I just wanted to apologize again for leaving so abruptly."

"Okay. Is everything all right?"

Billy came up behind her and interrupted. "Is that Gypsy?"

She nodded.

"Invite her to our pool party this weekend."

She mouthed back. "What party?"

"Just do it."

"Billy wants to know if you'll come over this weekend for a pool party."

There was a moment of silence, and Jazz wondered if she was thinking of refusing.

"What day?"

Billy could obviously hear Gypsy. "Saturday," he said. "Six o'clock."

"I'll see what I can do."

"Awesome."

"I should be back home by then. I'm going out of town for work."

"Yeah? Where?"

"San Francisco."

Jazz felt the silence hang. Did she even want to know why she was taking a trip given she knew it had something to do with spooky shit?

"Okay," Gypsy said. "Since you aren't asking, I'll tell you anyway. I have an interview with the Edgars' son, Junior. But we can talk about it when I get home."

Deflect again. "I'm looking forward to seeing you," Jazz said.

There was a sigh over the line. "Me too. I'll talk with you later, okay?"

"Okay."

"And, Jazz?"

"Yes?"

"Now you have my number. Bye."

Jazz took the phone away from her ear and stared at it before turning back to Billy. "How come I didn't know we were having a party?"

"I just decided."

"You have two days."

He shot her his "honey, please" expression. "I'll manage. He yelled over his shoulder, "Jorge, babe? We're having a little get-together Saturday, make your calls."

"Ooh," Jorge exclaimed. "A party." He rubbed his hands together. "Two days to make an event happen. I can do it."

Jazz shook her head but had no doubt they could pull it off.

She went back into the living room to talk with Candace, but she must have slipped by her in the hall when she was talking with Gypsy. She didn't want to know but needed to find out what she'd been talking about when she said she saw a woman in the bathroom. A lady was one thing. If Candace had seen what haunted

Jazz, she'd be stark raving hysterical about it.

Billy motioned her into the kitchen. "It's not all bad, Jazz," he said. "She said it was only shadows, a few voices, but that could be anything, right? From what I could find out, Laura the fake overheard her talking to someone else and approached her. It's not like she sought it out. For all we know, Candace even said it herself, she could have been slipped a hallucinogenic from one of her…"

"Dates," Jazz finished his sentence. Though she hoped not, the entity could be toying with her, playing hide and seek around the edges of her mind until it either had enough energy to attack or wait until her guard was lax. Maybes aside, it wouldn't do to skip her vigilance. She'd keep an eye on Candace, Billy, and now Jorge.

And if she had anything to say about it, she'd keep a quiet vigilance on Gypsy, as well.

Jazz wanted to believe it was over. Sometimes, here in sunny California with her best friend, she could believe it was done.

Almost.

Chapter Six

Gypsy pulled up behind Rhiannon's car in her mother's driveway. Either her brother wasn't here yet or wasn't coming. It was not unusual for him to be called out to sub for another bartender.

A warm feeling of nostalgia brushed over her as she stared up at the house. She'd lived here as long as she could remember and had in fact since the day she'd been brought home from the hospital.

At one time, three generations of women had lived here.

After hearing of Jazz's mother's abandonment, Gypsy thought of the constancy her family had given her. A strong foundation in this land of illusion she was sure kept her from burning out a long time ago.

Gypsy had her key ready. It had taken her forever to train her grandmother to lock the doors, but her mother had drilled it into their heads from a young age.

She dropped her Coach bag in the entry and was caught by a large picture hanging in the hallway. It was one of her swimsuit covers, she remembered it vividly, and shivered with sympathy for her younger self. It had been freezing that day while the photographer circled around her clicking shots, telling her she was sexy while she was purple and covered in goose bumps.

She didn't miss stripping in front of strangers, though it was impersonal, clinical. Simply put, they were mannequins for hire. Well-paid ones, but mannequins nonetheless.

Next to her picture was an almost identical one of Rhiannon taken a year later and a professional headshot of Tusk.

Not for the first time, she wondered how a family of blonds and blues produced her, the only brunette and green of the bunch. When she was younger and asked her mother about it, she'd laughed and promised Gypsy she wasn't the product of an illicit affair with the mailman. It had taken her two years to research her genealogy, and she finally found the great-times-two aunt she resembled and inherited the dark-haired DNA from.

She chuckled on her way to the kitchen where she could hear happy laughter, and called out, "I'm here."

Her mother and sister came out, still chattering to each other.

Gypsy tried but had a hard time centering herself to enjoy their conversation for more than a few seconds. She went to the edge of the deck, looked out at the view of the hills, and thought about Jazz.

She'd thought more about being lonely in the last week than she had when Marky had been escorted out or, so she thought, left. It depended on who was telling the story.

In either case, Marky was off in some jungle battling mosquitoes the size of Chihuahuas. It was mean of her, but Gypsy unashamedly hoped she ran out of bug juice.

Her mother patted her leg. "Honey, where are you?"

"In LA."

"Mom, you should see the butch candy sis has

been canoodling with." Rhiannon's eyes twinkled.

"Really?" Her mother drew the word out and looked at her with curiosity. "Canoodling?"

"Oh, don't pretend you haven't heard about Jazz. I know damn well Rhiannon calls you every day with the latest gossip." Gypsy pointed at Rhiannon. "I do not canoodle, who came up with that stupid word anyway?"

Her mother snickered. "I wouldn't have to listen to gossip if you'd told me yourself."

"One, I haven't had time, two, there's not a whole lot to share about yet, three—"

"Not true," Rhiannon interrupted. "I've seen them together. Raw, sexy vibes fly all over the place." She swatted the air.

Gypsy pressed her lips together to keep the chuckle from escaping. "Three, I'm still trying to figure things out and not get ahead of myself."

A look of understanding swept over her mother's face. Gypsy had been raised by two very intuitive women. Both her grandmother and mother were gifted, or cursed as they sometimes put it, with empathy. "It's headed toward something serious already?" she asked.

Gypsy shrugged. "Looks like, feels like. She's interesting, funny, and smart."

"Bzzt," Rhiannon said, batting the air again. "And hot."

"All that," Gypsy agreed. "And I think a lot more."

Her mother tucked a strand of her hair behind her ear and touched her cheek. "Then I'm happy for you, baby," she whispered in her ear, then raised her voice. "Rhia, help me get dinner and let's set the table up out here."

"But…"

"Now, sweetie. Gypsy will tell us more when she's ready."

Rhia looked back over her shoulder on her way into the house. "Later," she said. "Tell me later."

Gypsy smiled back at her and nodded. It wasn't as if she didn't want to share with them *exactly*. They usually told each other everything eventually.

Hadn't she been just fine? Plenty of social interaction, a job she loved, and her treasured privacy at home?

A home she'd worked very hard for. Some people might think modeling and being a television personality to be easy and glamorous. Reality was early calls, terrible hours, headaches, starving herself, and constant vigilance against the backbiting of cutthroat competition that could smell blood in the water any time your guard was down. Gypsy had accepted there would always be someone prettier, thinner, and younger behind her ready to take her place.

Wisely, Gypsy made sure all her eggs weren't in the same basket. She had investments and high-paying odd jobs to keep her image out there—the only real things she splurged on were her house and personal vacations since she'd retired from the runway. She craved new experiences and wanted to live with no regrets.

So far, her biggest mistake had walked out the door.

And after Tangie's little list of Gypsy's hook-ups, even if they had given her a much-needed boost to her fractured self-esteem, she could admit to herself she might have gone a little over the top.

And if she were to keep being honest with herself, if Jazz's allure had been purely physical, she wouldn't have had a problem following through with it.

But she knew underneath that, it wasn't just her hormones tap dancing around, there was *interest*.

Hadn't she been hoping for that little extra in the women she'd previously dated?

Sex with them had been…nice. "Nice" was okay, but underneath, Gypsy longed for that bodice-ripping, up-against-the-wall sex.

And really, what was wrong with that?

Nothing.

Gypsy hadn't been able to pry much out of Jazz, but her instincts were rarely wrong, and she knew that underneath Jazz's appearance was an intelligent person.

She was fine alone, she really was. But at times, she missed coming home to a face she loved every day; she missed the lazy Sundays in bed, the walks along the beach, drinking wine and toasting the sunset.

Being half of a whole.

But that had been the problem, hadn't it? Being the bigger half of a couple. The one who shifted and put aside her own needs to make the other happy.

Codependency, anyone?

Hell with it, Gypsy thought. She deserved some fun and strong arms to wrap her up in the middle of the night.

Maybe some good old-fashioned panty ripping while she was at it. Yes, she definitely deserved that.

❧ ❧ ❧ ❧

Jazz kicked back on a chaise by the pool. Despite the warmth of the evening, she shivered. Someone walking over her grave, her father would say. Funny how she remembered childhood superstitions so readily. Maybe because tonight, the adage hit a little too close to home for comfort.

The Ouija board incident weighed heavily on her mind. What, if anything, had that fake unleashed? Did she have any more to worry about? Or had Laura been as incompetent as she seemed and only pretended her skills to bilk Candace out of her money? She voted for the latter but hoped she was wrong about a door being opened and having the entity come through like a demented open phone line.

Shit, she had enough to worry about.

On the heels of those thoughts, loneliness peeked around a corner in her mind to see if she were paying attention. An enduring emotion she hadn't paid much attention to since being reunited with Billy and the introduction of Jorge and Candace into her life.

Now with Gypsy in her life, with some regularity she hoped, and the presence of friends, she realized she could let a great deal of that go.

Some of the pressure on her chest lifted. She tried not to think about what she referred to as her curse or the idea of having to explain it to Gypsy.

Because a curse it was, and it hadn't caught up with her.

Yet.

Nightmares and PTSD aside.

Ice clinked in her glass, and she got up to refill her sun tea. The real stuff. Billy would have had her head if she'd brought home one of those gallon jugs from the store.

She passed him in the family room on her way to the kitchen.

"Oh, no, you don't," he said and grasped her

arm. "Girl, how long have we been friends?"

Jazz wondered where this conversation was going. "Um, almost twenty years?"

"That long?" Billy darted a glance into the large mirror and patted under his eyes.

"I saw that." Jazz laughed. "You're looking to see if the time-bitch has called."

"Jesus," he said. "Enough about that. You've yet to sit down and give me deets about your Gypsy."

"Where's Jorge?"

"Don't change the subject, Jazzy." He pointed to the stool. "Sit."

She sat and sighed.

"Why don't you want to talk to me?"

He looked hurt, and that more than anything prompted her to. "It's not that, sweets." Jazz shook her head. "We've been a little busy."

"We should never be too busy to catch up."

"Agreed," she said. "It's been weird. I've got Gypsy and all the wonderful possibilities on one side and all the crap that's haunted me for so many years on the other. I feel split, as if I'm trying to function in two separate realities."

"Honey," Billy said, "stress will do that to you."

"That's me." She nodded. "All stress, all the time." Jazz ran her finger down the condensation on Billy's glass. "I'm afraid the two worlds will collide and leave me shattered on the floor."

Billy's eyes welled up. "What can I do?"

She forced herself to smile. "Being here for me is enough."

"Let me ask you something."

"Shoot."

"What if these two parts of your life were meant

to crash? What if moving here and meeting Gypsy was like fate or something?"

She opened her mouth to argue, but he cut her off.

"You've been fighting an entity of sorts. You've met someone you want to be with who happens to have a show about the paranormal. This *is* happening. But you don't want to believe it is somehow meant to be? You can't have it both ways."

"Looking for rainbows, Billy?" She heard the snarl in her voice and ashamed of it, softened her tone. "I don't know. Maybe."

"As far as I'm concerned, it's more than coincidence."

"Here's the thing, you moved away years ago. You weren't there for the majority of the attacks. This entity, this hag, has hurt everyone I've loved in one way or another. You've witnessed it."

He nodded and patted her arm. "I have."

"Didn't it cross your mind, even for a second, it might happen here?" She held out a hand to stop him from interrupting. "It would destroy me inside if I were to be responsible if you or someone you loved were wounded in any way. I would be devastated if something happened to Gypsy. I'm finding it so damn easy to fall in love with her."

"Now you listen," he said. "I had a choice, and it *was* my choice. I'll take full ownership of it. I do know what happened, I have full disclosure, remember? We're going to get through this together, honey." He got up to leave, shook his head, and turned around. "Wait. What did you say about Gypsy?"

Jazz gave him a Cheshire cat grin. "Caught that, did you?"

"I'll be back," he said. "And you'll tell Uncle Billy all about it."

❧❧❧❧

Gypsy felt a tap on her shoulder and turned. Rhiannon leaned in for a hug.

"Here's your kit for the trip." She held out a case. "I wish I was going with you. It's been a while since we tore up San Francisco."

"How long has it been?"

"Since we took the world by storm? Drinking the wine, partying on the yachts, and being the sisters that the photographers adored?" Rhia sighed. "I don't know, honey, I hardly think about it."

Gyp laughed. "Yes, you do. At least we can still drink wine. Tell Mom I'll call when I get there."

Rhia walked away muttering something about Greece in the summer.

On her way to the airport, Gypsy replayed some of those memories. Nostalgia for those days came seldom now, but Gypsy still occasionally felt wistful.

"Penny pincher," Gypsy said under her breath after she reached the ticket counter. She didn't want to be a snob, she really didn't, but she'd been flying first class for more than a decade. Roger had already booked them on a dinner flight, with no food service.

He had knocked her down to coach behind her back after she'd told him she wanted Tangie to come with her.

She calmly asked the ticket agent to wait a second while she searched for her business expense credit card and making sure it was the correct one.

It was.

"Please upgrade us to first class."

"Yes!" Tangie fist pumped the air beside her.

"You're in luck, we have two left."

"Thank you so much."

"And thank you for flying with us, Miss Tanner."

That felt good, Gypsy thought. She would justify her expenditure by having Tangie stay with her—the room had two beds anyway. Problem solved. She turned on her thousand-watt smile as they slid into the seats in front of Roger.

The look on his face when Tangie finger-waved to him was worth any headache he may try to give her later.

Gypsy turned to avoid him further and leaned back. Tangie's fingers flew across the keyboard on her tablet she was never without right up until they were told to turn them off.

"Take a breath, grasshopper."

"What?" *Snap.*

"Never mind," Gypsy said. "Something my mother used to say."

"Oh-kay." Tangie didn't look convinced.

Gypsy let it go. Tangie bounced and fidgeted in her seat. It had to be because being unplugged must be driving her crazy, Gypsy thought.

And damn it, she was making her want to twitch and beginning to have second thoughts about giving her the adjoining seat. Then she felt small for thinking it; she adored Tangie, and at least she'd stopped snapping her gum every seven seconds.

Thankfully, it wasn't too much longer, and they were in the air. When the stewardess came by, Tangie ordered a drink.

Good, Gypsy thought. Maybe she'd mellow her

little ADD self out a little. Thank the friendly skies for small favors.

She reclined her seat, took the offered tiny blanket, and quickly dozed off.

She must have fallen into a deep sleep because when Tangie shook her, Gypsy was surprised to find they were already descending.

The pressure had her ears popping, and she yawned to clear them. Tangie offered her a tissue.

"Why are you giving me this?" Gypsy asked. "Oh, please don't tell me I was drooling." She pulled out her compact and checked her face. 'You didn't put me on Instagram, did you?"

Tangie laughed. "Maybe."

"You didn't!"

"No," she said. "But I thought about it. Just think of all the people who think you're perfect. Don't you want them to know you're human?"

"By showing them my mouth hanging open and drooling? Absolutely not." Gypsy took a long drink of water.

They went through baggage claim, gathered the crew around to wait for the courtesy van from the hotel they'd chosen, then waited again as Gypsy signed autographs. She was never too busy, nor would she want to be, to interact with fans. After four seasons, she still appreciated each and every one.

"I'm hungry," Tangie said.

"I'm ordering a fat dripping pizza without my sister or mother making a fuss about it."

Tangie smiled. "A rare treat for you. I'm going out for the crew's free dinner, and I'm going to order steak."

Crap, now she had to let Roger off the hook

because he'd planned to take care of them despite the coach seats he'd booked. "You do that, sweetie. I'm getting into my pajamas before ten."

"Another rare occasion. Are you sure you don't need me for anything?"

"Nope, you enjoy yourself, but don't let Bruce and Leo talk you into a drinking contest."

"As if they'd win." Tangie brushed her shoulder. "I won't be in late."

"I'm so tired, even if you did, I'm sure I won't stir."

Tangie freshened up while Gypsy unpacked her bag and made good on her promise to be ready for bed.

She turned on the television while she ate the promised pizza, but it was only to cover the noises of the hotel. She'd never had a hard time sleeping away from home, as she'd been doing it since she was fifteen. Sometimes, it did her good to remind herself in the beginning of her career, it had been hovels and hostels, where the new models were packed in like sardines, she could only be grateful she was a long time and a long way from those days now.

Her mother would freak out if she knew where her daughters were when they were on assignments in far-off locales.

So in honor of her mother's sensibilities and the love she had, she'd never tell and knew her sister wouldn't, either.

Gypsy bounced on the plush bed and tried not to think about how nice it would be to roll around on it with someone she really cared about. This moratorium had lasted way longer than she'd ever expected.

The scars Marky had inflicted weren't as easily dismissed. Sometimes, they itched and burned when she'd least expect them to.

Gypsy's lovely mood was threatening to dive by remembering the hole Marky had left.

She ordered herself to fill it up again before she brooded much longer. Gypsy hated, absolutely despised, feeling sorry for herself. If Marky had been too stupid to realize how awesome she'd had it—screw her.

There. That felt better.

⁂

Candace appeared at the sliding door. "Good night, guys, I'm off."

"Like a bad prom dress?"

"Ha ha." Candace laughed sarcastically.

"Aw, you know I love you, Candy-girl," Billy said. "But it was right there, a little escort humor."

"Be careful," Jazz said.

Candace smiled. "Always am." Her heels clicked down the hallway and then back again. "Have either of you seen my keys?"

"If you've lost something, you only have to remember they're always right where you left them," Billy said.

"You're just a barrel of laughs tonight, aren't you?" Jazz asked. "Where do you remember leaving them?"

"I always put them in the basket in the entry or on my dresser."

Jazz got up. "We'll help you find them."

The three of them looked in all the obvious places. It wasn't until Jazz knocked a necklace off Candace's bureau and she bent over to pick it up that she spotted them under the bed. They were far enough back that even with his long arms, Billy had to stretch to get them.

"Oh, god," Candace said. "I can't even think about how they got there, I'm late." She ran out of the room.

As they walked back down the hall, Jorge walked in the back door, and Billy went over to greet him.

"Hey, buddy," Jazz said. "I'm going to make it an early night. You all behave now."

After going to her room and lying down, Jazz squinted in the dark, tired but nervous about going to sleep.

She let out a strangled gasp when the comforter moved and shot up straight in the bed.

Cleo's tiny head popped out from beneath the covers.

"Fuck me." Jazz jumped and immediately felt horrible when she saw her shout had Cleo trembling. She picked her up and cuddled her on the pillow next to her. "You know," she whispered to her, "I love that I'm not sleeping alone."

Big brown eyes stared into hers as she continued. "I'm glad I have a sympathetic ear tonight, no fear of anything being repeated, and no judgment or well-meant sarcasm from you, huh, little girl?"

"Okay, here we go." Jazz snuggled deeper. "On one hand, Gypsy, she's every woman's dream. On the other, she's into the paranormal. I know, I know, I should tell her about my," she searched for a word to describe her situation, "stuff," she decided. "But we haven't had much luck in the past doing that, have we?" She checked Cleo's reaction. She kept eye contact and appeared to be riveted, so Jazz continued. "If your daddy Billy really knew everything that happened since he moved away from me, he might not think that meeting Gypsy was fate. There are things I've never told a living soul."

Jazz knew with certainty what was happening here. As much as she wanted to believe Candace knocked her keys off the dresser and under the bed, she didn't, and the alternative was real.

All these events were adding up. Yes, they were.

⚜ ⚜ ⚜ ⚜

Gypsy felt disoriented and rubbed her eyes. It must have been the recall she'd had last night of how she'd spent the early part of her career that was the reason she woke up in the hotel room and thought she was on assignment. Unfortunately, it brought up uncomfortable memories of what had been under the surface and behind the glamorous lifestyle.

The constant insecurity, the unmerciful bullying to lose weight, as if being almost six feet tall and a size two was a bad thing. She hated the industry for that alone.

At least she'd had her sister to lean on during that time, and her mother, being a former model herself, had been a constant positive force, reinforcing they were so much more than the way they looked. Blessed DNA shouldn't affect how they saw and acted in the world. Even if the critics and press could and did rip apart anyone who appeared less than perfect, her family kept her grounded, and she'd never believed her own hype. It wasn't how an individual looked that determined what kind of person they'd be.

Gypsy pulled the blankets off her legs and got up

to take a shower. But the memories continued.

She still did occasional runway shows for a designer or charities, even though every time Gypsy stepped back in the game, she was hit with the backbiting chaos and grateful she no longer felt she had to be a twig to be accepted. She wanted and did tell the up-and-coming models that those five to ten pounds they were always trying to lose were going to mean so little in the long run.

And boy, Gypsy thought, she loved to eat. No more celery sticks and lettuce as complete meals for her.

She loved her career and silently thanked Crawford, Klum, Banks, and numerous other supermodels who built empires after they retired. It was because of them and their trailblazing Gypsy felt she could do the same.

She brought herself back to the present just as she finished her hair and makeup, then stepped out of the bathroom where Tangie waited with a big to-go cup. "An answer to a prayer, as always, my faithful friend," Gypsy said with a smile. "Thank you."

"No prob. The car is downstairs."

She checked her watch. "Damn, I thought I was doing well on time. How do you look so put together and I didn't even hear you do it?"

"Youth is a wonderful thing." Tangie grinned.

"Now I hate you."

She laughed. "You do not. Drink the coffee and get the cranky out."

"Mmm," Gypsy said. "Did you have fun last night?"

"Unfortunately not. I didn't get into that drinking contest because you asked so sweetly, Mom."

"Stop that." Gypsy laughed. She tossed her lip gloss back into her bag and made sure she had what she needed for the day. She looked for her little velvet bag that held her protection crystal, herbs, and talisman but couldn't find it. After a few minutes, she gave up. She hated to be late. "I'm ready, let's go."

The black car stopped at the street, and after Gypsy got out, she looked up to see a well-maintained charming row house that showed pride of ownership.

Gypsy looked up at the third-story attic window and saw something blur past the glass. The file said he lived alone, and no one had said anything about Junior's house having any weird paranormal activity. Mild anxiety tapped her nerves when she recalled she'd left her talismans at the hotel. She hadn't thought she'd need them.

The interior camera caught her entrance into Junior Edgar's house. He took her jacket and bag, and then directed them to sit in the living room while the cameras shifted for their new scene.

The hair tingled on the back of her neck, but Gypsy kept a cool demeanor, for both herself and the cameras.

"Ouch!" Tangie hissed. "Something pinched me."

Gypsy went to her. "Where?"

Tangie pointed to the inside of her thigh.

"She likes those the most because they hurt so much," Junior said.

"Why me?" Tangie asked. "I'm not even a part of this."

"You should go, Tang."

"I will not, and I am also not dropping my pants for the camera. Get away from me, Bob." Tangie walked to the microphone and muttered expletives into the microphone. "There, you can't use that, either."

He laughed. "You know we can edit that out, right?"

Tangie sneered at him and snapped her gum for effect.

Gypsy closed her eyes for a moment. "I was not informed of probable paranormal activity before the interview."

"My grandmother showed up a couple of days ago."

"Wonderful," Gypsy said, her tone dripping with sarcasm before noticing how pale Junior was. She didn't know how he normally appeared, but currently, there were deep bruises under his eyes, and her heart immediately went out to him. "I apologize."

Junior nodded.

"Gypsy?" Bob prompted.

"Yes, sorry. Let's go outside."

They set up chairs in the courtyard in the center of the house, and Gypsy looked around. She could see the dining and living rooms and the little window above the sink that looked out over the lovely flowerpots lining the bricks, and she couldn't help but love this particular architecture she'd found in San Francisco, especially because in this area, it was usually quite chilly and foggy.

The mics died. Now that she'd felt the energy, she wasn't at all surprised, and she despised those shows that showed the hunters freaking out every time it happened to them. It was a common occurrence when dealing with the paranormal and happened more often than not.

When the crew finished taking care of that little problem, she leaned back in her chair. "Thank you,

Junior, for having us." Reading his body language, she could tell he was nervous but trying very hard not to be.

"I'm not enthusiastic about sharing my story. I feel it leaves me open to ridicule, but I want to make sure this is told from our point of view. I want to help my parents put this to rest, and I worry constantly about my mother and what she's going through."

"I understand, and I want to reassure you we're going to do all we can behind the scenes to get resolution," Gypsy said.

"That's why I was willing to let you come and do this."

"Can you start from the beginning?"

Junior nodded. "It began when we moved in. I don't remember what it was like when I was a baby. I only know the stories from my parents on what it was like for my mother when she lived with Grandmother. And she made me say it just like that—grandmother. No grandma, no nana, it had to be formal and clipped. Never to be said in public."

"I can't imagine what that must have been like. I have wonderful memories with mine," Gypsy said.

"Well, you're lucky. I have no good memories of her. She was horrible to me, and I had no idea that it wasn't normal until much later, when I had a chance to see my friends' interactions with their grandmothers. There were no cookies or milk with her, no loving hugs. As far back as I can remember, only cruelty. Though I do want to point out emphatically that my grandfather was a very good man, and I never felt as if I were unloved when I was with him."

"Did you ever talk about it with him?"

"There came a point when I stopped. I don't

know if he stayed because he was in severe denial or that it was because he was from a generation that didn't divorce. I do remember making the decision to stop telling him of her behavior when I was old enough to discern the pain on his face. I didn't want to hurt him, I mean Jesus, what she must have put him through, you know?"

Junior's voice had become hoarse and he seemed to be struggling. Gypsy gave him a moment to gather himself before she went on with the interview.

"After Grandpa died, my dad would make an effort, even though in my opinion, Grandmother didn't deserve it. I stopped going over because, really, I felt no loyalty and also felt I was old enough to make my own decision about it. Thankfully, neither he nor my mother pushed me.

"After Dad inherited the house, I hated the thought of moving into it, but my mom jumped right into redecorating and remodeling. I didn't blame her, not one little bit. I was happy to see her stand up to the old bat and get rid of her things, even if calling her that makes me seem ungrateful and horrible."

Gypsy smiled. "It seems applicable from what you've all told me."

The hinge on the boom slipped, and Junior barely got out of the way before it crashed next to him. "See?" he said. "You can't even talk about her." He looked around the room quickly, as if judging what else could fall on him.

Gypsy turned to Leo, the sound man. "Are you okay?"

"Yeah," he said and began putting it back together.

Junior still appeared nervous and shaken.

"Let's take a break," Gypsy said.

When the crew was done setting up again, Gypsy looked into the camera. "Welcome back. As you can see, we are having numerous technical difficulties." She turned back to Junior. "Could you tell us how the activity started after you moved in?"

"Immediately, I had the feeling of being watched. No, it was more like something invisible was screaming in my face all the time. I was always on alert. Does that make sense?"

"Yes," Gypsy said.

"In the middle of the night, something would hit my bed, like they rammed their knee into the side of my mattress. It would wake me up, and after I checked, nothing was there. It was always around three in the morning."

"That seems to be the haunting hour." Gypsy had heard it a hundred times, had been through it herself.

"Yeah," Junior said. "I used to think it was bull… baloney. But when it happens to you, it sure opens your eyes to the possibility."

Gypsy nodded. "It does. And not easily dismissed."

"Right? Anyway, I knew Mom was worried about something, but she wouldn't talk about it. I know now it was because she was scared and didn't want to frighten me. At the same time, I didn't tell her anything of my experiences for the same reason."

"When did you start talking about it?" Gypsy relaxed into the interview. Junior was making it easy for her to guide the story with short questions.

"I told my father first," he said.

"It sounds like you're both very protective of her."

"My mother is an awesome person. Kind, sweet, considerate, always helping others. She's never hurt anyone in her life, and it straight pisses me off at what's going on."

"After having met her, I can see why. Your mom is a lovely woman."

He nodded. "Inside and out. She didn't deserve this crap when the witch was alive, and she surely doesn't deserve it now." He sneered. "Grandmother," he said sarcastically, "was a narcissist when she was alive, and death hasn't changed her one bit."

"Why is that, I wonder?" Gypsy asked. "You would think it would change when they move into the light."

"They say," Junior said, then rolled his eyes. "But she was stubborn. I don't know if she was afraid of her consequences for being so rotten—likely not—or now she can torment my mother as she likes because Dad wouldn't tolerate it from her before. The first time she slapped her—"

"Wait," Gypsy interrupted and checked her notes. "She hit her? I didn't hear anything about that." She scribbled in the margin of her sheets.

Junior nodded. "She came downstairs and her cheek was red, and I could see the fingerprints on her face. I was shocked and thought my father did it, but of course, he reassured me he would never strike my mother. I knew that, he adores her, but I continued to rationalize it. How else could it have happened? They sat me down and finally told me what she'd been going through."

"Your family's experience was bad enough with what you've told me. But I've never heard any of this. It takes this to a whole new level," Gypsy said. "Do you have any pictures?"

Junior pulled his phone out. "I think Mom didn't

tell you because she was afraid you might not help, that maybe you would become too nervous, and with how credible she believes your show to be, she wanted you specifically."

"This is vicious." Gypsy looked at the screen. "Is your mom the only one who's been attacked?"

"Straight up vicious," Junior said. "And no, Mom wasn't Grandmother's only target. Dad has been scratched, and I've been pinched."

Gypsy was surprised and looked up. "Like Tangie was before we started." She turned to camera two to explain. "My assistant." To continue with the interview itself, she then looked back to camera one for Junior's answers. "I apologize for the interruption," Gypsy said. "Was there any kind of pattern to this behavior when she was alive?"

He nodded. "Anytime I did anything she perceived to be naughty or unacceptable. By the time I'd go home after a visit, I would have bruises."

Gypsy hated this woman, and she'd never met her. "Did you tell your parents?"

"Um, no." Junior blushed. "What adolescent boy is going to yank his pants down in front of his mother?"

"I suppose not many," Gypsy said.

"And because she's started up again here, at my home, the same rule applies as an adult. I'm still not going to drop my pants to show them."

"Is that why you originally moved out?" Gypsy redirected. She wanted to know more about Eunice's new attacks but knew the final show wouldn't have the time. She might push to do a follow-up segment in the future.

"As soon as I was able, I moved into the dorms, and was subsequently left alone."

"You mentioned attacks on your father."

"I've seen scratches on his ribs and back." He tapped his pad again. "I took some pictures of his injuries he didn't want Mom to see."

Gypsy studied them, letting Doug catch a close-up.

"I only agreed to talk to you because of my parents. I want someone to exorcise that bitch out of our lives." His eyes went wide, and he covered his mouth. "Sorry, do we have to do that again because I swore?"

"It's perfectly understandable," Gypsy said. "We'll bleep it. Thank you again for talking with us."

Junior leaned forward and put his hands on his knees. "I appreciate your gratitude, but what I really want is your help."

"We'll do our best." Through his desperation, she discerned a sliver of hope. Gypsy ended the interview. "Cut."

She wanted to promise him but didn't dare. Even though her intentions were always good, sometimes they didn't win, and she'd broken her vows unintentionally. It was those cases that kept her up at night.

Junior stood. "And if you're thinking about sending another person like the last, don't dare to bother."

Jane Boren. Gypsy took off her mic and motioned him to do the same. When the assistant came over, she waved him off and stood closer to Junior. "I was overruled on that for ratings."

"She scared the holy hell out of my mother. I was livid when she called me in hysterics."

"I'm truly sorry for that," Gypsy said. *Damn Roger.* "And I can promise you Jane will not be back."

"I've watched your shows, and I know you don't televise the actual blessings, cleansings, exorcisms, or whatever. Sorry if I'm skeptical, but how would I know? I'm hoping you don't leave my parents hanging."

Gypsy patted his forearm. "I won't, and the reason I don't let them film is that I believe whichever method is used should be kept private, and well, *sacred.*"

Junior nodded. "I'm counting on you. I may need one of the aforementioned rituals myself if the bitch, sorry, my grandmother," his lip curled, "doesn't leave me alone."

"Again, I'll do my best," Gypsy said.

And meant it.

After Junior went back into the house, Roger came up to her in the courtyard. "That was some good stuff."

Ass hat. "And yet horrible to live through. I'm sure they don't think it's good stuff." She said the last two words with as much sarcasm as she could muster.

He managed to look chagrined. "No, of course not. I meant…"

"I know what you meant," Gypsy said. "It's good television, right? They're living in hell, and we're using it for entertainment." She decided to be frank with him. "Something about this case breaks my heart, Roger."

"I know," he said in a rare moment of sympathy. "Mine too." He turned away and missed the look of utter shock on her face.

"Crap, the beast has feelings," Tangie said.

Gypsy flinched.

Snap.

"You could have done that before you snuck up on me." Gypsy held a hand over her heart.

"Sorry. I just wanted to let you know that the

flight home has been confirmed."

"All right." Gypsy gathered her notebooks. "I feel the need for another shower."

"I gotta say, me too." *Snap.*

"Tangie, please, the gum. My nerves are raw right now."

"Okay." She took a tissue from her pocket and wrapped it up. "Can we get out of here now?"

"I'll be out in a minute after I say goodbye to Junior."

When Gypsy got to the car, Tangie was going to town on her tablet, already chewing another stick of gum.

Gypsy was still seething over Roger's decision to send Jane into the Edgars' home. They hadn't needed her opinion or her egotistical scare tactics.

The *Paradigm* crew's two-day investigation had collected more evidence than any ghost hunter could dream of.

Other than her segment dealing with scrutinizing the collected evidence with the family, experts, and skeptics, her job and this case were officially over.

Unofficially, she wouldn't leave them high and dry without help in the aftermath.

Gypsy would make sure she found guidance.

Legitimate help.

Chapter Seven

To Jazz's utter amazement, Billy and Jorge had accomplished what she'd thought to be impossible.

The last two days had been an insane flurry of activity but totally worth it. The patio area was festive with lights and torches waiting for nightfall, and scattered flowers and floating candles filled the pool.

Neighbors and friends arrived with platters of food she'd never heard of, and drinks were constantly being refilled at the bar Billy had provided.

Even Candace had taken the night off and seemed to be enjoying herself.

Billy had thrown a welcome home party when she'd arrived, but this, this was Hollywood style and a different dog altogether.

Happy anticipation for Gypsy's arrival had caused the butterflies in her stomach to kick into high gear. Yet under that was a low-level buzz of the constant strain of anxiety.

Put it away.

Jazz was taking a sip of her drink when she saw her.

Her mass of hair was loose and flowing around her shoulders. She wore a turquoise wrap low around her hips and a matching camisole with what appeared to be a bathing suit top underneath. She looked as if she had strutted straight out of a magazine.

Gypsy's gaze zoomed straight to hers and zeroed in, as if Jazz were the only person at the party. Jazz's ears buzzed. She pounded on her chest in an attempt to dislodge the piece of ice she'd nearly choked on.

"I can say that's the best reaction I've ever had when I walked into the room." Instead of her usual cheek greeting, Gypsy kissed her full on the mouth, then stared into her eyes. "Hello, you. How's it going?"

Jazz smiled. "Embarrassed, but hi."

Jorge came over and held out a hand. "Gypsy, it's so good to see you."

"Hi, Jorge, it's been a while."

"You two know each other?" Jazz asked. "You never told me."

"Honey," he said. "This is Hollywood. We're all connected by six degrees of Kevin Bacon."

"Huh?"

"I'll explain later. For now," Billy said, "introduce me to this lovely creature."

Jorge put an arm around him. "This, my pet, is Gypsy Tanner, supermodel, queen of the runway, and formidable threat to things that go bump…"

"Enough, stop it." Gypsy laughed and handed him the festive bag she'd been holding.

"Ooh, classy wine. Thank you. It's so nice to finally meet you. I've heard so much about you."

"Really?" Gypsy drew the word out. "All good, I hope."

"You have no idea," Billy said. "Jazz has been my sister in every way, well, except the DNA part, for, well, ever."

Jazz elbowed him. "Go play with your guests."

Gypsy widened her eyes. "Afraid he'll tell me secrets?"

"Actually, yes," Jazz said.

"Let's go, Jorge. Apparently, it's Miller time."

"Ha." Jorge laughed. "I get it. Jazz—Miller—time."

"Mission accomplished," Billy said.

Jazz ignored the giggling they left in their wake. "Billy planned this party just to bring us all together and meet you."

"Aw, that's so sweet." Gypsy flashed a killer smile in his direction. "I'm flattered."

Jazz put an arm around her waist. "I'm so glad you came."

"Me too." Gypsy turned and fit her body against Jazz's so they stood eye to eye before she nuzzled her neck. "You smell fantastic," she said. "What are you wearing?"

"Um, I have no idea. It's the body wash Billy put in my bathroom."

"Hmm. Sexy and fresh."

"I'll buy a case tomorrow." Jazz's nerve endings snapped and sizzled. "Hell, I'll buy two."

Gypsy smiled again and brushed her lips over Jazz's. "After I get a drink and we mingle for a while, want to sneak into your room and neck?"

"Wow. Why wait?" Jazz tightened her hold, lifted Gypsy a few inches, and took two steps backward. She made a sound that was half purr, half laugh, and all take me.

"Uh, yeah. Here. This is Dan, and he's our bartender for the evening."

"Hey, stranger," Gypsy said. "How's life treating you?"

"You know him, too?"

"We all run into each other at one time or another," Dan said. "I work with her brother sometimes. You tell your mama and sister I said hello."

"Will do."

Bob slid a glass to her and turned to help another guest.

"Let me get this out of the way because I should have said it the second I saw you," Jazz said. "You look stunning."

Gypsy smiled. "Thanks. You look nummy."

Jazz felt her cheeks heat up and tapped a finger on her temple. "And you're stuck in here. I can't stop thinking about you."

"I'll raise you and justify that by answering I feel the same."

"Well then, aren't we both lucky?"

"Extremely." Gypsy took a sip of her drink. "Let's try the get-to-know-you-more conversation. How old are you again? I was too busy looking at you to recall."

"Thirty, and you're thirty-one. And please, don't be impressed. Remember I Googled you."

"That makes you younger than me." Gypsy smiled. "Younger women are sexy."

Jazz nearly spit her drink out. "Cute." She reached and tucked a strand of hair behind Gypsy's ear and tapped her dangling silver earring. She felt a small rush of intimacy at the gesture, and it left her with the sense of knowing everything about her. The one where you met a stranger and knew, just knew, deep down you'd met them before without ever having done so. It had been the same way when she'd met Billy so many years ago. The coming together that told you *there* was a kindred spirit. There was tribe.

"Can we sit down somewhere?" Gypsy asked.

Jazz had a wicked comment about her bed in the house on tap, but even in her head, she knew it sounded juvenile. "Inside or out?"

"Wherever."

"Okay, are we going to talk or—?"

"I'm hoping a little of this and a little of that." Gypsy looked up at her through her lashes.

Jazz wanted to fall into her eyes. "I'm sorry, what did you say? My IQ is sinking by the second." Jazz took her hand, soft and warm in her own, and led her to the living room. The sliding doors were open to the pool, but as soon as they walked in, she noticed there would be little privacy. Ditto in the kitchen and dining room. She gestured. "Ah…"

Too late, she realized. Gypsy had been swept away into the crowd of people who all seemed to know her or wanted to. She looked back helplessly at Jazz as they surrounded her, and followed it with a shrug that seemed to say, "What can you do?"

Jazz stepped back and let her socialize. She felt there would be plenty of time to talk later. And truthfully, she was just as happy to watch her, the way her face lit up and her hands moved animatedly when she was excited. She kept a careful eye on poachers, not that she was the jealous type, but ready to extricate Gypsy if she needed to.

She did, however, waylay the exhibitionist neighbor before she reached the clutch of guests surrounding Gypsy. Jazz steered her, and quite skillfully she thought, back outside and pointed her without a twinge of guilt to another group she could crash.

Gypsy flashed her killer smile from across the room, and Jazz's heart fell at her feet. She hadn't realized her emotions kicked in right along with the insane attraction.

Liar.

It had happened the first moment she'd seen Gypsy in the mall. That click, that knowing she'd been waiting for her. What Jazz didn't know was how long she'd be able to keep her.

The party morphed into night, and the game became about those long glances across the crowd. Subtle touches and the way Gypsy leaned against her when they managed a moment together.

After a guest interrupted them yet again, Jazz excused herself and took a moment to escape into her bathroom.

She'd already kicked a couple out of her bedroom. What was it about people? Why didn't they ever consider it might be rude to go at it in a stranger's bedroom without permission? She'd never even consider it okay. At least they hadn't gotten to the deed yet, or she'd be changing the linens.

Gross.

She pushed the incident out of her mind and brought Gypsy back instead. After such a long drought, God knew Jazz herself was due for a little passion.

But because she admitted to herself she already felt that little bit more, things could become complicated quickly.

The last time she'd remotely felt that ping, it had ended badly. She'd give anything to not have seen her last girlfriend look at her with such abject horror when she'd walked out.

The door slamming and the squeal of her tires as she'd fled.

If that had been a ping, what Jazz felt for Gypsy now could already be compared to a sonic boom. If it was only physical and sweet Jesus, it was that, too, she'd take her to bed, and they could have an affair to remember.

But that would deny the deep pull. That feeling of wanting more before she'd even had a little.

Scary stuff.

Jazz took a quick glance in the mirror and twitched, thinking there was a shadow behind her. After a closer look, the anomaly disappeared, and she breathed a sigh of relief. Thinking of the past had her imagination going into overtime.

Or was it guilt?

Anything but the reality, she thought.

A knock on the door *did* startle her, and she stifled a gasp. The noise of the party filtered back and now had her attention. She opened it to yet another couple and sternly pointed to the guest bath at the other end of the hall.

Jazz ran her fingers quickly through her hair and left to go find Gypsy. She was tipsy enough to not let it bother her and figured she could stress about the implications of the hag's appearance later. As much as the threat worried her, she knew she was past the point that she would refuse to see Gypsy at all. Then again, Jazz rationalized, she might have seen her because she'd been thinking of that past relationship.

Maybe.

She went back to the party and leaned against the wall to look at her, thinking she should be embarrassed about her puppy-dog crush.

No, Jazz didn't want to take a step back.

Hell, not even an inch.

When she got her attention, Jazz wove her way through the crowd, using Gypsy's smoky sexy stare as a beacon to get to her side.

"Save me," she whispered into Jazz's ear. "Where's your room?"

Jazz hesitated and weighed her conscience. She thought she'd just seen the apparition, but the idea of having Gypsy to herself overshadowed her reluctance. But that didn't mean she wasn't cursing herself for being selfish. She squeezed Gypsy's hand. "Follow me." She picked up two drinks from the tray Billy was circulating and ignored his winky-wink facial expression.

The small of her back instantly heated where Gypsy laid her hand. It calmed her even as it lit her from the inside.

They stepped up to the door, and Jazz gestured. "Can you open it? My hands are full."

Gypsy brushed against her, and the swell of her breast touched her own and she bit her lower lip.

Once inside, Jazz bumped the door closed with her hip.

"It's cold in here." Gypsy hugged her arms. "There's something…" Her voice trailed off.

No, Jazz thought. It's too soon to tell her. She was afraid to ask but had to. "What?" Her body tensed.

Gypsy stared at her and shook her head. "Nothing, it's just chilly in here."

"Do you want a sweatshirt?"

"No, I'm fine."

"Good, the Universe loves me because it would be a shame to cover you up." Jazz picked up a glass to give her and when she touched her hand, she felt the sharp static charge.

"We seem to make a habit of that." Gypsy smiled and sat on the side of the bed.

"Excuse the blankets," Jazz said. "I just kicked

out a couple of busy bunnies a few minutes ago."

"Really?" She laughed. "Some people can be so rude."

"That's what I'm saying. Hang on." Jazz crossed the room, then locked the bathroom door. "Jack and Jill," she explained. She surprised herself with her easy tone and effortless flirting. Underneath it, she was scared something would happen and Gypsy would never see her again.

Thinking of that, and though her need for physical contact edged toward actual pain, she sat in the armchair across from the bed.

Gypsy patted the space beside her; Jazz shook her head and watched her eyes widen.

"Why?" she asked.

"Oh, I really want to lay you down on that bed right now."

"And the problem?" Gypsy appeared slightly confused.

Jazz gestured toward the party in high swing outside her window and the yelling in the pool and lowered her voice. "Because when I take you? The only screams I want to hear are yours."

She heard the sharp intake of Gypsy's breath.

"Is that so?"

"Absolutely." It took all Jazz had not to lunge at her. Not to react to Gypsy's near feline expression.

"This is our third date, don't you remember the unspoken rule?" Gypsy patted the mattress again.

"Pardon me?" Jazz laughed and thought about it. "Oh, if you count the afternoon, the lunch, and now, I guess it is, but I've never followed the rules. Do people still go by that?"

"It's a good thing I'm not generally insecure or

I'd wonder if your reluctance toward my second offer was my fault."

"Gypsy," Jazz said. "You leave me breathless." She took a sip of the drink she no longer wanted to steady herself.

"Well then, how can I argue with that?" Gypsy clicked her nail against her glass. "I guess we'll have to talk instead."

The action drew Jazz's attention to her long fingernails and the fact they were painted blue to match her outfit. God, she loved female rituals. The perfect way she was put together. Jazz had always been confident in her looks, but an intruding thought asked her if Gypsy might be out of her league. She wanted her more than she'd ever desired another. But what *right* did she have to bring Gypsy into her personal nightmare?"

"Jazz, where did you go?"

Damn, her worrying must have been obvious. She leaned forward in the chair. "I'm right here."

"I guess we really will talk instead." Gypsy crossed her legs.

The gesture caused her skirt to reveal more of her golden thigh, and Jazz's mouth went dry as yearning battered against her willpower. Why again wasn't she kissing that skin yet?

"You certainly chatter on and on," Gypsy said.

Amused now but still struck mute, Jazz nodded. "Uh-huh."

"Okay. Aren't you going to ask why I became a television host?"

"If I do, will I have to answer your questions?"
Deflect.

"We'll get there," Gypsy said. "I like to talk.

That's why, by the way. Do you want my opinion about you strong silent types?"

"Please." Jazz was easing in and enjoying the banter. "Let's hear it."

Gypsy smiled. "Since you insist. I think when you do finally want to talk, you'll mean what you say and say what you mean."

"Pretty much."

Gypsy sighed. "I do this interviewing thing for a living, so you may just as well give up."

"I might, if you're always this persistent." Jazz deliberately smirked.

"Let me see." Gypsy tapped her lower lip. "Okay, here goes. The rapid-fire version. Ready? What's your favorite color? Do you read? Do you like sports? How about the ancient alien theory, do you believe it?"

"The color you're wearing right now, yes, yes, and I haven't decided."

"See?" Gypsy put down her drink and rubbed her hands together. "You're beginning to crack. Did it hurt?"

"Just a little. I'm out of practice having personal conversations."

"Aha," Gypsy said. "There's a deeper answer, one with a story behind it."

The question came too close to Jazz's secret. She'd never hated the entity more than she did right this second. She didn't *want* to be guarded and careful with Gypsy. If she didn't care, she would have already jumped at her offer. "A tale for another day," she said finally.

"Cryptic answer," Gypsy pointed out. "And a hell of a challenge for me."

"It's complicated."

"You can't leave me there." Gypsy's gaze searched

hers.

Jazz pointed to herself. "I'm right here."

With a thoughtful expression, Gypsy nodded. "Will we matter, Jazz?"

"You already matter to me."

Gypsy stood. "Let's try this." She stepped up to the chair, leaned over, and brushed her mouth against Jazz's.

The gentleness of the gesture nearly undid her. Gypsy pulled back slightly to look into Jazz's eyes again and kissed her once more.

Jazz tugged at her hips, and she tumbled into her lap. When their lips met again, her tongue slid against her with an excruciating slowness. Gypsy's hair fell around them, and Jazz's heart did a slow roll in her chest.

She melted into the chair. Jazz's hands swept along Gypsy's hip, waist, and the curve of her breast before she caught her face to look at her. "You already matter to me," she repeated.

Someone banged on the door, and they both twitched. "They'll go away," Jazz said.

Gypsy withdrew and shivered. "It just got freezing in here. Can't you feel it?"

Jazz shook her head. Of course she did, but over the years, she'd gotten used to it.

"I'm not imagining it." Gypsy stood and held out a hand for Jazz to get up. "I'm sorry. I have to get out of this room."

The chill Jazz felt had nothing to do with the sudden cold. She got up and walked to the door, opened it, and ushered her out. "I probably shouldn't keep you all to myself anyway."

Fuck. She'd forgotten Gypsy told her she was

gifted. If she had any desire to take this relationship forward, and god she did, she was going to have to tell her about what haunted her.

And she was going to have to do it sooner rather than later.

⁂

The party had gone into the early morning, and Gypsy tried to remember the last time she'd walked in her door at that hour.

Jazz had politely sidestepped her invitation to go home with her.

Gypsy's body burned where Jazz had touched her, her lips felt full and tingled long after their goodbye kiss had ended.

It was tough not to be frustrated when she felt like a kid in a candy store who'd only been able to lick the wrapper after her chocolate bar had been taken away. On top of that, she couldn't recall a woman telling her "no" once she'd turned on the charm.

Okay, she admitted to herself as she walked up the stairs, that thought edged toward conceit. Gypsy stripped, then turned on the shower while she ordered herself to bring the flipside to the forefront.

Jazz's reasons to keep her at arm's length that night were valid, and she herself wouldn't normally jump someone at a party. Gypsy felt she'd been caught up in her spell. The way Jazz carried herself, smiled, smelled, her style, heat, and the damn challenge of her enigmatic personality. Definitely something hidden deeper there.

And hadn't it been stimulating to feel as if Jazz looked past her physical appearance?

As she stood at the counter and braided her wet hair, the lights went out, then on before turning off again. The cold tingle on the back of her neck was overshadowed by an icy breeze that blew through the bathroom.

Gypsy stood frozen in the doorway when she heard a strange ticking sound that appeared to be coming from the far corner. She walked over and opened the door to her walk-in closet.

The hangers were clicking together as they moved side to side.

Despite the fear that tap-danced on her spine, she slammed the door. The only possibility she could think of was maybe she'd brought home something from Junior Edgar's house. She knew there had been something off about his place.

She let go of most of her anxiety. Wherever the unwanted energy had come from, she was well versed on how to get rid of it or at least move it along. Gypsy had her own ritual. One she felt covered all her bases, created by culling pieces from several religions until they fit together, and she could stand with conviction because it conformed to her beliefs. She'd learned to trust her instincts.

She wasn't worried. It had always worked in the past. When it was done and she felt comfortable again, she slipped between the cool sheets, curled up, and let her thoughts wander where they would.

Of course, they turned to Jazz. Look at me, Gypsy thought, all gone over the sexy new girl in town on her way to being seriously swept off her feet. She even loved the way their names sounded together. Gypsy and Jazz, she said to herself five times fast. Her stomach jittered as she chuckled at how silly she sounded.

And as she admitted she *had* fallen for her, she drifted into sleep.

Gypsy dreamed of tunnels and people crying in the dark. The air around her had been cold and dank, and a lucid part of her mind had wondered if it were a memory. That she'd been there before, maybe on an investigation.

She felt a whisper along the back of her neck. *Get out while you can.*

Gypsy heard a whimper, realized it was hers, and turned to find the path behind her was as dark as the one ahead.

She shivered under the covers while the voice slithered in her ear. *Stay away.*

She turned a circle in the tunnel and looked for a way out.

Run, Gypsy, run.

She sat up in bed and tried to shake it off while she remembered she'd had a version of that dream before when she'd seen a woman crying in that hallway. And that had been after her interview with Ted and Alayna.

Since the nightmares seemed to appear right after she'd interviewed any one of the Edgars, it must be leftovers from the parasitic visitor she seemed to pick up when around them.

The nightmare had been uncomfortable but completely explainable.

She would talk to Rhiannon about it. Her sister was great at interpreting dreams. Just a little Freudian slip is was what she'd tell Gypsy.

Feeling better already, Gypsy had just covered herself when she realized the voice telling her to flee sounded as if it could be Jazz's.

As the thought came, she became aware of what

had been picking at her consciousness all night. In hindsight, and taking her raging hormones out of the equation, Gypsy realized the emotion she'd felt from Jazz was—fear.

Of what?

Jazz stumbled on her way to the bathroom and went down on one knee at the door. She didn't want to get up, so she crawled on her way to the toilet and gagged repeatedly.

When she felt she could stand, she leaned on the sink to rinse out the tequila and broken intentions she'd been left with.

That fucking bitch.

Gypsy had floated into her dreams, and at the foot of her bed, she'd pulled a pink dress up, and in one motion, revealed herself.

Exquisite in the moonlight, her mass of curls spread around her, vivid against the white sheets, and her eyes glowed with seduction.

She'd wrapped Jazz up, tangling her legs, and rocked against her, igniting heat inside and out.

Jazz's pulse seemed to race faster than her heart. Joy became equal with her need, and passion climbed higher and higher still. The taste that was Gypsy became forever etched into her memory as she lay over her.

She cried out when Gypsy's nails scored her back violently. Jazz looked up and saw the fire circling her bed while she was trapped in the center. Confused, her first reaction was to cover and protect.

Flames licked closer, and she felt Gypsy's body

shift and change beneath her. When she tried to get up, she was unable to move, and she watched her long beautiful hair morph into a brittle tangled mess.

Laughter rose up and around her until her eardrums threatened to pop, the arms around her so tight, her ribcage compressed.

Terrified, paralyzed, and revolted, Jazz screamed at herself to wake up.

Wake the fuck up.

Hands pinched her cheeks, forcing her to look at the grotesque face inches from her own, staring into empty black holes.

"Give us another kiss, sweetheart."

At that point, it had been too much to bear, and Jazz blacked out. The second her eyes opened, she ran to the bathroom to wash her face and waited by the sink until she was sure her stomach wasn't going to revolt again.

There was no explaining this away, no room for a sliver of doubt anymore.

The nightmares were real and back in full force.

The entity had found her.

Chapter Eight

Jazz walked in the front door, and the smell of cheap whiskey assaulted her.

She put down her bag in the hall and started toward the kitchen. It had been a long day full of job interviews, and it was time for her to make dinner.

"Jashmine, ish that you?"

Her father's words were slurred, and she knew he must be on his second bottle of the day. The first one went down like water for him.

"Jasshy." Dad was sitting at the small table in the kitchen still in his rumpled pajamas, and she felt the familiar despair and heartbreak she always did when she came home and found him in this condition.

She stepped around the door and gasped. The cupboards and drawers stood wide open. Silverware, broken dishes scattered on the floor, and cans were still rolling across the scarred linoleum.

Jazz glanced to the right and wanted to cry. Peanut butter had been smeared on the counter and appeared to be melting down the front of it. The jelly jar looked as if it shattered in an explosion of red goop that covered the walls.

Shocked didn't cover what she felt right now.

"Daddy? What have you done in here?"

He looked up at her, his hair stood in tufts, and his eyes were wide and glassy. When he grabbed for her hand, she couldn't help but notice how badly he was shaking. "I was jusht shtanding at the shink and it...it..."

Impatience needled her skin, and she flicked away from his grip. "This did not *just* happen," she snapped. "What were you thinking?" She stomped across the room and started picking up the shards of glass. "It looks like you had a drunken fit, goddamn it."

"I shwear." His shoulders slumped, and fat tears ran down his unshaven face.

"Save it, Dad." She threw the broken pieces in the trash, and when she reached down to pick up more, she glanced under the table and was horrified to see the bloody gashes on her father's swollen feet.

Her anger instantly drained, replaced with pity and a sense of hopelessness. "Oh, Daddy, what have you done?" she repeated.

"It hurts, honey." He looked down. "It really hurts."

Jazz woke with tears on her cheeks. She still felt awful about the pain she must have caused him on that first of many horrible days. She'd discounted him, and she'd never forgive herself for it.

After she rolled over in the bed, she curled up and rocked back and forth against the ache, wishing she'd believed him.

After a couple more hours of sleep, Jazz stood at the coffeepot and willed it to go faster. She heard Billy's door open down the hall and pulled down another mug.

A chair scraped, and at his heavy sigh, she turned to say good morning. Billy sat with his head in his hands, and his foot bounced up and down.

Instantly concerned, she went to him. "Honey, what's wrong?"

He lifted his face, and his red-rimmed eyes let her know he'd been crying.

Tears pricked at her own because she knew he'd had a nightmare, as well. "Tell me." She brushed a hand over his hair.

"Coffee first."

She filled their cups and sat across from him, needing to hear but nervous about the details.

"Thank you," he said. "It was horrible." He wrapped his fingers around the mug and simply held it, as if warming them. "I was in junior high again, not dreaming of it, but actually *in* it. I could smell it, I could feel it, standing at my locker, thinking of the fight I'd had with my mother the night before. The evening she told me she'd rather I was dead than be gay. Remember that one?"

She nodded. "I do." At the time, she was horrified a parent could even think it let alone say it. Her throat closed because she remembered that day.

"Anyway, Ape came up behind me, smashed my face into the metal door, and I felt it. I freaking felt my nose break, the feeling of blood running down my face. It was real all over again. The humiliation of being picked up by the waistband of my pants. My shame because I couldn't stop crying." He paused after his voice broke. "As if that weren't bad enough, and it fucking well was, I saw my mother's face after I told her, the disgust evident on her face when she told me I deserved it because I was a fag."

"That's the first night you spent at my house," Jazz said, and her heart broke again as it had then. Jazz dropped to her knees in front of his chair and rocked with him as he cried.

The sounds of chattering colleagues rose around Gypsy as they began arriving for the day. Still reeling from a brief but knee-knocking kiss in the corridor, Gypsy watched Jazz walk away.

She mentally fanned herself. If it weren't for moments like this over the last several days, she might think Jazz was avoiding being alone with her. She stood in stasis, not exactly going forward, but at least not moving back.

At least they had long phone conversations about everything, including music, books, and family. No, Gypsy corrected herself. They talked about *her* family. She knew Jazz was interested in what she had to say but didn't reciprocate much regarding where she came from.

Aside from that, they laughed and got to know each other. There were breaks, lunches, and those scorching, what felt like stolen kisses. They did everything but dig deep. Gypsy's schedule was hectic, the days ran into each other and blurred, but it wasn't as if she hadn't invited Jazz over but she always had excuses and changed the subject. It was obvious she wanted her, but to Gypsy, they seemed to be moving slow as molasses.

Yes, it was important to be friends first, even excellent ones, but the sexual tension was a living, breathing thing between them, but...

But she was frustrated beyond belief, that's what.

Wanting Jazz was simple, but there was nothing simple about Jazz.

Whoever said sex wasn't a huge portion of a relationship wasn't getting any to begin with. Gypsy longed to slide against her hot skin, share heated breath, and wrap her up for the night. She wanted to find out about the haunted, wounded look in her eyes that she saw when she thought no one was looking. There was so much more—she wanted to know everything. She wanted more of Jazz, what made her *her*. She wasn't just sexy—she was interesting. She had substance.

Gypsy didn't want to take it slow. She wanted to jump in and feast.

She longed for intimate touch, the delightful anticipation of discovering each other's hot spots, the moves that made her sigh, and the ones that made her stop breathing altogether. The touch of skin not seen every day—the ease of laughter and taking down the wall of separation.

The spirituality of the experience.

"Boo."

Gypsy screeched and turned. Tangie was standing behind her with her clipboard, laughing.

"Wow." *Snap.* "Didn't think it would actually scare you. What were you thinking about?"

Gypsy put a hand at the wall separating her stage from Jazz's set and sighed. "Nothing."

⁂

Jazz watched the excruciatingly slow clock and waited for the next break when she'd have more time than for a thirty-second kiss. She had a constant urge to see Gypsy and ached when she caught the scent of her perfume where she had passed in the hall.

She settled for the calls and texts but went out of her way during work to catch a quick glance.

Jazz burned for her as she had no other and

thought more about Gypsy than…

Than, she admitted, she did about the dreams and activity that had increased in the house. Those instances became hazy when faced with Gypsy's beauty, wit, style, and lovely, lovely skin.

Or what she imagined it to feel like since she'd yet to act on the heat between them.

What a dumbass.

That Jazz had fallen was a given, and she had to do something. Jazz cherished her company, and even though the right thing felt wrong, she wanted and craved everything Gypsy had to offer.

But could she have it?

Jazz was constantly waiting for the fall.

Gypsy walked around the wall, and Jazz was surprised. She'd been thinking so hard about her, the time had passed without notice.

"Hey," she said. "Now that we have more time to talk, sorry I missed your call last night." Jazz didn't want to tell her Billy had had a priest over blessing the house after having yet more nightmares over the last week.

"It's okay. Production was a bitch, and I got home late anyway."

"Doesn't make me less sorry." She turned to put her tools up, and Gypsy came up next to her and turned Jazz to face her.

She heard Gypsy's quick intake of breath before brushing her lips against hers. Just a little taste, she told herself. Solid ground turned to water as she sank into the kiss, the silky slide of her tongue and lips, her drugging scent, and the small sound of pleasure in the back of her throat.

After pulling mere inches away, she

metaphorically got her feet underneath her and rested her forehead against Gypsy's. "God, you're good at that," she whispered and drew back a little more. Damn, she'd nearly backed her into a storage closet full of construction supplies. "I am so sorry. This is totally inappropriate."

"I'd say it was amazing." Gypsy laughed.

"Hey." Tangie popped up from nowhere.

Jazz froze, though the blood still roared in her ears.

"I know you do it on purpose." Gypsy managed to stay cool and amused at the same time. "See you later."

Snap. "You want me to go away?"

"Yes," they said in unison.

Jazz was only grateful it had been Tangie interrupting instead of her boss.

After she left, Gypsy gripped Jazz's hands. "It's Friday. Come to dinner. Please come and be with me."

Jazz, awash in her feelings, nodded slightly.

"Seven o'clock?"

Jazz nodded again as she backed away and watched Gypsy disappear around the corner.

Jazz hated herself.

She could hardly wait.

❧ ❧ ❧ ❧

Jazz checked the number on the house. It looked simple from the front, smaller, and less flashy than she expected being right on the road.

She parked and got out. Gypsy opened the door before Jazz got to it and was framed by ocean behind her. But holy crap, Jazz thought, who could think of anything else when Gypsy was right there?

"Wow, I have to tell you how fabulous you look."

Gypsy wore a silky blue dress, legs and arms beautifully bare. Jazz handed her a bouquet of wildflowers.

"Thank you, they're beautiful. You didn't have to do that."

"Yeah, well…I would have bought roses, but that seemed too obvious." Now that she was actually here, she was nervous.

"You're looking very fine, as well."

Relief was a rush. She'd never dated someone with so much style, never wanted to impress so badly. Shut up, she ordered herself. "I'm so afraid I'm going to say the wrong thing."

"You haven't so far."

"The night is young."

"Aw," Gypsy said and let her in. "You give yourself too little credit for your charismatic charm."

"See? You say that with a straight face, and I'm lost. You dazzle me, Gypsy."

She looked at Jazz from under her lashes, and the sexual jolt kicked up to an almost unbearable need, and she didn't think, she reacted. Jazz stepped up to her, slammed her hands against the door to balance herself, then crushed her mouth to hers, a hot and demanding kiss. She wanted to taste, feel, and inhale her essence in one greedy bite.

Gypsy matched the pace she set beat by heart-thundering beat against her as Jazz slipped her hands under her skirt, skimming the material along smooth thighs to the swatch of lace covering her heat.

She gasped at the contact, and the sound shot through Jazz with a lightning bolt, causing acceleration to an already desperate need.

Gypsy's nails lightly scraped her shoulders, then moved down to her stomach, and the sting of her teeth scraped along her throat.

Jazz had a bad moment when the memory of her nightmare surfaced, but she shoved the similarity down and away from her consciousness. Heat and hunger overwhelmed the momentary chill.

"Hurry, hurry, oh, god." Gypsy fumbled with Jazz's waistband before cupping her hand over her sex.

Their suppression of lust fired up a fast and furious coupling of emotion, and passion filled up places in Jazz's mind and body she'd forgotten existed. Her kisses ignited a burn within.

Time was nonexistent, sensation took her over, and their lips fused as she matched the rhythm of her strokes to Gypsy's.

Ragged breaths filled the entry, and Jazz couldn't tell her own from Gypsy's over her thundering pulse. Her orgasm shattered inside her seconds before Gypsy came. She shuddered with the power of it while they were still pressed against the door.

Jazz reluctantly eased back and brushed Gypsy's hair from her face. "So not the welcome I expected but totally amazing."

Gypsy laughed weakly. "I had a plan."

"For sex in the entry?"

She blushed. "No. Dinner and drinks on the deck watching the sun set, then whatever came next."

"All sounds good." Jazz slid a hand down Gypsy's thigh, smoothing her skirt down before stepping back to button her shorts, and she looked down. "Um, oops."

"You ripped my panties."

"I'm sorry."

Gypsy laughed. "I'm totally not. I have more. All kinds of colors and styles."

"Yeah? Oh, well, hmm." Jazz felt the blush creep into her cheeks. Then she turned, and the entire back of the house opened to the beach through the wall-to-wall windows. Jesus, she thought and pointed. "There are people down there."

"And I have not a single regret." She smiled at her. "Let me show you around."

Suddenly, Jazz felt like the small-town girl she was. The front of the house had seemed unimposing and didn't reflect the inside. From the entry, two steps down into an open living room. The muted colors were a perfect backdrop against Gypsy's vividness. The furniture was white with pops of teal blue against the walls of soft gray, reminding Jazz of early morning fog.

To the left, a kitchen with what looked like an acre of granite counters and shiny stainless steel appliances, and to the right, a dining table that took advantage of the awe-inspiring view.

The deck was a room itself, beautifully furnished and with a clear railing leaving no obstruction of the image of rolling waves.

For Jazz, being here with Gypsy was like taking a small step into what heaven might be like. She wanted to be here with her but was afraid, so afraid of what might happen if she let her all the way in.

Gypsy directed her to sit on one of the several wooden rocking chairs painted in different colors and plopped down next to her.

Jazz took the offered wine, and Gypsy toasted her. "To us," she said.

"To us," Jazz repeated. She'd hold on to every moment she could grasp.

Until she had to leave to keep Gypsy safe.

❧❧❧❧

"I can't cook, and I'm not at all ashamed of it." Gypsy took a foil-covered pan out of the oven and tapped the paper instructions on the counter. "Warm and serve."

"I can't look past you just yet, but I can cook."

Gypsy put a hand to her heart. "Inside, I'm doing the happy dance right now." For that, Gypsy thought, and the panty ripping she'd imagined previously, looked forward to, and gratefully received. That also deserved a mental cartwheel.

"It's a little premature for all that," Jazz said. "I'm sure Hamburger Helper isn't on the menu."

"Seriously?"

Jazz laughed. "Not lately. But there were plenty of times it was."

"Are we going to talk about that?" That was a good as time as any, Gypsy thought, and a great lead-in.

"Now?" Jazz looked around the room.

"Does it hurt that much?"

"Do you really want to know?"

"Of course." Gypsy laid a hand over hers. "Isn't that what this was about? Getting to know each other and creating new memories?"

"I thought it was about sex." Jazz winked. "Kidding. Go ahead then."

"What's your real name?"

"That's an easy one."

"Just warming you up."

"Jasmine Rochelle Miller."

"I can understand the nickname, though I thought it might be because your parents liked the genre."

"Ha, nice segue."

Gypsy smiled craftily. "I do this for a living, remember?"

❧ ❧ ❧ ❧

"Dinner smells good."

"And…" Gypsy drew the word out. "She changes the subject again. Okay, we'll go with that. I'm so glad you wanted to stay in."

"Feels funny not taking you on a real date. I would love it."

Gypsy looked out the window. "Clubs, bars, movies, restaurants, I'm usually recognized, you haven't seen the paparazzi part of my life, and it's nice being here with you."

"How can I argue with that? Especially after such a nice greeting."

Gypsy felt herself blush. At this point, she didn't care what Jazz shared, only that she would. Something, anything that would quiet the unrest she felt emanating from her.

Instead of filling the silence as she usually would, Gypsy focused on her plate, hoping Jazz would open up.

It worked. Jazz put down her fork and dabbed her mouth with a napkin.

"The past is just that," she said. "I don't know why you'd want to know my sad story."

"See?" Gypsy asked. "That's where I think you're missing the point. The past is what defines us, makes us who we are today. And besides that, Jazz, I'm hungry to know. You said that we, as a couple, are going to matter. I'm as open as a book, but you've yet to trust me with even a piece of yourself. It makes me think you're hiding something."

"First, you have to understand it's not that I don't want to talk. It's that it's ugly. I look at you, and all this…" She gestured around the room. "Beauty and I don't want to bring it here or to you."

Gypsy shook her head. It was a rare occasion she didn't know what to say. When Jazz pushed her plate, she picked them up, and began clearing the table. Maybe if she wasn't staring at her, she'd find it easier to talk. She heard Jazz's sigh behind her.

"Where do you want me to start?"

The dishes clacked as Gypsy loaded them into the dishwasher. "Wherever you want." She hadn't meant to make such a big deal out of it, but now she wanted to know. Identify those bits and pieces of Jazz that made her unique. "Wherever you feel you should."

Gypsy turned from the sink and looked at her.

"I was a normal child who grew up in a working-class neighborhood."

Gypsy smiled. "I can work with that. Were you a good student?"

"Average," Jazz said. "I was better at sports."

"Consider this my surprised face."

Jazz smiled without humor as she shredded her napkin. "That all changed when my mother left. I came home from junior high school one day calling out for her. When I didn't see her in the living room or kitchen, I looked for a note. She never left the house without writing one. I went to their bedroom, and it looked as if a tornado went off. At first, I thought she'd been hurt, and I called my father at work to come home."

"That must have been terrifying for you."

Jazz shrugged, and Gypsy's heart cracked. She could clearly see it affected her deeper than the nonchalant cloak she wore over it.

"Anyway, after he got home, we realized she'd packed her clothes and jewelry. Stuffed everything in a suitcase to go, as we found out later, to 'find herself' because she hadn't been happy."

The cracks grew wider, but before Gypsy could offer any condolences, Jazz continued.

"When it became clear she wasn't coming back, after receiving no letters and no phone calls, my father broke. That's the only way to describe it. He began drinking heavily until he was a full-blown alcoholic."

The cracks became grief for the young girl Jazz had been, and Gypsy realized there had been no mention of herself; she'd skipped right over how it had affected her. "I can't imagine how it felt for a young girl on the verge of transitioning to a teenager. How difficult it must have been for you."

"I dealt with it. Taking care of my father was a priority. His home life sucked, as well, and he helped me through most of it, especially when I realized it was the cheerleaders I was more interested in than the star football players. It was amusing the situation was reversed." She laughed. "What a pair we made."

It explained their deep bond, Gypsy thought. And time to break off this conversation on a high note. It was enough. "Then I think you were both lucky to have each other." She crossed back to Jazz and hugged her from behind. "Thank you," she said softly.

Jazz rose and wrapped her arms around her. "Kind of killed the mood, huh?"

"I certainly hope not." Gypsy untangled herself and walked backward. "I have big plans."

"Yeah?" Jazz grinned and followed.

"Uh-huh. Now *this*," Gypsy said and tugged her upstairs and into the bedroom. "May hurt." She strolled around the room and lit several candles, filling it with scents of seduction.

Gypsy looked back at Jazz sitting on the bed and was struck with a feeling that this was important. She wanted this to happen with this woman in this moment in time. She wanted to touch every curve, every inch of her skin from taut muscles to her softness.

She wanted all of her. She cupped Jazz's face and laid her lips softly against hers. Once, twice, before tugging the hem of her shirt, skimming her fingers along her back as she lifted it up and over her head while Jazz slid her shorts off.

Gypsy ran her nails lightly along the inside of Jazz's arms, and she shivered with the contact. "Cold?" she asked as she stripped her own tank.

After a long exhale, Jazz shook her head. "Hot as Hades." She pulled Gypsy even closer and untied the straps holding her dress, and the material flowed down like water. Jazz kissed her stomach before leaning back, and they tumbled to the bed.

Finally, Gypsy thought. Finally, they were skin to skin, heat against heat. She arched up and reveled in the feel of Jazz's hands against her breasts, her work callouses rasping againt her nipples.

Her body rolled against hers, wave over wave in sync with the sound of the ocean crashing on the beach below them.

Jazz flipped her onto her back, and Gypsy cried out, appreciating the artistry of pleasure and emotion it elicited.

Whisper-soft kisses along her inner thighs became insistent fingers and the nip of teeth, and Gypsy quivered under the sensual onslaught as they rolled together. Hands and lips were greedy for more as Gypsy didn't know where she began and Jazz ended.

The passing of time was measured by sensation. Jazz reared up, and the sight of her silhouetted by the candlelight would forever be seared into Gypsy's mind to be synonymous with passion and pleasure.

Overwhelmed, she reached and touched Jazz's cheek. Jazz turned her hand and kissed her palm.

Gypsy's throat tightened with endearment even as her body reached for its peak and completion of her fall.

Feeling Jazz's orgasm above her and looking into her eyes pushed Gypsy to the edge and over. They held each other while the aftershocks continued and shook them within and without.

Jazz's heart thundered against her own, her ragged breath against her neck. Gypsy ran her hand lazily over her back.

"I'll get off in a minute," Jazz murmured. "When I can move again."

"You're fine." Gypsy laughed weakly; it was all she could manage. She watched Jazz's pulse beat madly in her throat, happy to know she caused it. "We're going to kill each other."

"Thank you, God." Jazz sighed and rolled off.

Gypsy leaned up on her elbow. "Are you thanking me or praying?"

Jazz grinned. "Both."

Candles flickered across the room and reflected off the mirrors. Gypsy untangled the blankets to cover them, curled against Jazz's side, and wrapped her legs around her.

Jazz kissed the top of her head. "Gypsy?"

She'd just begun drifting. "Mmm?"

"That didn't hurt a bit."

Chapter Nine

Jazz heard a bloodcurdling scream, shoved upright, and struggled to see in the dark. It took a split second to realize she was at Gypsy's, and the scream had been entirely in her own head.

During the night, Gypsy had shifted and taken the blankets with her. Apparently, she wasn't a light sleeper.

Thank God. Jazz tried to let go of the nightmare, relaxing her muscles one by one, evened out her breathing, and let the rhythm of the breaking waves lull her back to sleep.

Her eyes snapped open. Jazz was flat on her back being pushed into her mattress, trapped with her arms by her side. The angry buzz of pissed-off wasps filled her ears, and she was unable to protect herself as they viciously stung every inch of her skin. Paralyzed, she could only move her eyes from side to side.

She immediately tried to see Gypsy, but she remained outside her vision. Jazz prayed she was spared the onslaught she knew would follow.

The wasps became an electrical surge, and Jazz heard tapping on the sliding doors.

Though she knew it was futile, she tried to scream, but her lips were sealed, and not even a whimper could escape.

The scant moonlight was cut off as a shadow passed between the bed and the window. The noise of hell surrounded her, the moans and screams of tortured souls filled her ears.

Another shadow broke out of the dark, and a cold wind preceded her stark terror as it walked in a mad, disjointed stride toward the bed with a dread-inducing clicking noise.

Time warped in and out as it approached. First the entity was five strides away, then one.

Jazz wondered if *this* was the visit that would break her sanity. Directly under that question was the hysterical panic it might affect Gypsy, and she hadn't warned her. She'd been selfish to keep her.

What had she been thinking?

Then she couldn't contemplate at all as the hag had jumped onto her chest, causing what felt like a rib-breaking pressure she was almost sure would push shards of bone into her heart and lungs.

The bile-inducing sight caused her stomach to turn, and she struggled to breathe.

Mine.

Jazz heard the word echoed until she thought her mind might explode from the deafening roar.

From the depths of her psyche, Jazz gathered what strength she could and screamed internally.

The darkness beat and grew around her, then her world went black.

❧ ❧ ❧ ❧

Gypsy woke when the morning light streamed through the bedroom. She turned to see Jazz in a ball on the other side of the bed. She carefully got out and draped the sheet she must have kicked off during the night. Jazz didn't appear to be a bed hog, and that earned major points in her book.

She felt loose, limber, and wonderful as she slipped into the kitchen to make coffee. She appreciated the view as she rarely saw it, having to be at the studio early in the mornings. She would have to go in later at some point to make up for it.

"Hurry up," she ordered the coffeepot. "Before she gets out of bed." Gypsy had all kinds of interesting ideas of how to wake her.

Finally. She poured both mugs, then walked back to the bedroom where she put them down to gingerly sit on the bed.

In her absence, Jazz had curled even tighter around herself, and her knuckles were white against the sheet. Had she been cold?

Gypsy lightly touched her shoulder and was thrown on her back in an instant. Jazz pinned her and snarled into her face. Gypsy could see she was far away.

"Jazz, honey, it's me."

She saw the realization hit Jazz's eyes before she twisted off and away from Gypsy and covered her face with her hands.

"Oh, fuck, I'm so sorry. I'm so sorry." Her shoulders shook.

Gypsy climbed over to her. "Hey, it's okay." She rubbed Jazz's arms, tried to pry her fingers away.

"I have to go. Right now." Jazz tried to sit, then attempted to crawl away to the other side of the bed.

Gypsy was having none of that. It took all her strength, but she managed to keep her on it. "Oh, no, you don't. You tell me what's wrong. You don't get to shut me out."

Jazz stilled but kept her back turned.

"Did you have a nightmare?"

"Something like that." Her voice was hoarse and cracked.

"It's okay now." Gypsy pressed her body against Jazz's back. "I'm here. It's going to be all right." She felt some of the tension release across her shoulders, and Gypsy kissed the nape of her neck. "I'm not going anywhere."

"Gypsy, you have no idea how fucked up I am."

"You aren't fucked up, as you so eloquently put it. Let me be my own judge." Gypsy let her hands roam over Jazz's breasts and her fingers trail along her stomach. "Besides," she said and gently but insistently pushed her down. "Don't argue with me when you're naked. You won't win."

"Yeah?" Jazz asked. "Prove it."

Gypsy smiled down at her. "Why don't I?"

Afterward, Gypsy lay depleted next to Jazz, and watching the rise and fall of her chest, knew she'd proven her case after all. "Better?" she asked, feeling breathless herself.

Jazz laughed weakly. "Fantastic. You win."

She turned toward her and leaned up on her elbow. "And don't you forget it."

"You may have to remind me again," Jazz said.

"Anytime. Your coffee is cold."

Jazz pulled her back down. "I can live with that. Then again, we can heat it later."

Gypsy laughed. "If you insist."

❀❀❀❀

After a long steamy shower together, they finally made it back to the kitchen where Gypsy ordered Jazz to sit and began pulling items out of the fridge and cupboards and gathering them all on the counter.

"Wow," Jazz said. "I wouldn't think that you'd eat pancakes."

Gypsy looked over her shoulder and grinned. "Oh, I think we've burned the calories already, don't you?"

Jazz felt her cheeks burn.

"Aw, that's so cute."

"What?" Jazz looked behind herself.

"You're blushing."

"Nuh-uh." She paused. "Well, maybe a little."

Gypsy chattered while she cooked, and Jazz felt bad she'd distracted her earlier with sex. Even if it was mind-blowing.

Then it hit her. What the fuck did she think she was doing? The wall she'd so carefully built to protect others was crumbling under Gypsy's extraordinary attention. She deserved to know even if it caused her to walk away.

She'd shown no fear, had in fact shown only compassion after Jazz had volatilely reacted toward her.

And Jazz wanted desperately to hang on to this bubble of intimacy, needed her more than was good for both of them. She yearned to hold on, to stretch this fleeting time with her.

"Jazz." Gypsy snapped her fingers. "Where are you?"

Her insistent tone told Jazz it wasn't the first time she'd called her name. "Sorry."

"You've barely touched your breakfast. Did you not like it?"

"No, it's not that at all." She smiled. "You filled me up."

"Good save."

Jazz knew she was going to have to tell her. She was trying to think of a good way to begin the conversation, as if there were an easy way, she thought bitterly. She'd just opened her mouth to speak when Gypsy jumped in.

"I really have to go into work today. I wish I could stay, but you're welcome to hang out on the beach or whatever until I get back."

Jazz was ashamed at the burning relief she felt. "Thank you for the offer, but I should go home and check in with my wife."

The look of surprise on Gypsy's face turned into amusement quickly. "Billy?"

"Um, yeah. Who else?"

"For a second…"

Jazz wrapped her arms around her and kissed her forehead. "I promise you, Gypsy, a solemn oath that as long as we're together, I will never cheat or disrespect you."

Gypsy's arms tightened. "I'll promise you the same." She pulled back to look at her. "And if I'd have known how fabulous being with you would be, I'd have had you naked in ten seconds flat."

A laugh bubbled out. "I already knew you'd be."

"Come on then, I'll walk you out."

After another twenty minutes at the door well spent to say goodbye, Jazz was reluctant to let her go.

And on the way home, Jazz relived every second with her. She wanted to burn them into her memory. After what happened, she couldn't lie to herself again. If Gypsy walked away, it was going to hurt.

She took that back. It was going to fucking kill her.

⚘⚘⚘⚘

Jazz flipped her sunglasses up as she got out of the truck. Jorge's car was behind Billy's. Maybe they'd be distracted with each other and not hammer her for details. She grinned as she walked up the tiny path.

Fat chance. He'd be waiting to pounce.

But the entry was empty. She'd expected Billy to hoot, holler, and demand to see her walk of shame. She was just about to yell for him, but Cleo began barking at the back of the house. A high-pitched yipping had her running toward the sound even as she heard Billy's door burst open and his footsteps thunder down the hall behind her.

Cleo was shaking in the living room, and Billy picked her up in a sweep to comfort her.

She wanted to be amused. He and Jorge were in their underwear, and by their state, she knew they'd been busy before the interruption.

But there would be no teasing now.

"Oh. My. God," Billy said, faced the kitchen, and pointed at the wall where the word *slut* was written in red. Paper towels were strewn willy-nilly. The soap canister looked as if it had been squirted around the room. Coffee, flour, and sugar spilled out of their canisters, and the chairs had been pulled from the table and jumbled together in the corner.

As they stood in shock, the fancy mixer on the counter turned on, and the beaters against the bowl in high speed caused a nerve-pinching racket. Jazz rushed over to turn it off.

Billy turned to Jorge. "You scream like a girl."

"You think?" he said. "You didn't exactly sound

like Hercules, either."

"Boys," Jazz said. They were taking this remarkably well. The first time it had happened to her, she'd shook for hours. She guessed there might be more safety in numbers.

Until Jorge gasped and his eyes widened. The red letters began to drip down the wall. "Is that blood?"

"It's ketchup," Billy rubbed Jorge's arm and turned to Jazz. "Right?"

"Probably." Jazz watched the emotions war on his face. "Of course it is."

"This was supposed to be your sanctuary."

Jazz hugged him. "I know." She knew he loved her and would want her to stay. But she could not—would not—put him through any more of this crap. She shouldn't have rationalized the signs, but she'd wanted to believe so badly they hadn't been true.

"I've never seen anything like this," Jorge said. "Billy told me a little, but I really thought he might be overdramatizing things a teensy bit."

"Wow, really?" Billy looked at him.

"Just a bit, sweetie." Jorge patted his shoulder.

"Well," Billy pulled himself straight. "I wasn't being a drama queen."

"Of course you weren't," Jazz said quickly to smooth the argument building. "Jorge, why don't you take him into his room while I clean this up?"

A door slammed down the hall, and Jorge let out a little scream as Cleo yipped. "Will it hurt us?"

Jazz shook her head. "So far, it's been only me." She didn't want to mention her father's torment.

Billy sighed and headed for the cleaning supplies. "Honey, I had this house blessed, cleansed, and whatever else I could think about before you got here.

I can do it again."

"You shouldn't have to," Jazz said.

"Wait." Billy held his hand out. "Do you think this could have anything to do with the Ouija board Candace was using?"

She thought about it for a second. "Maybe." It could be that it helped the hag find her, but she didn't in any way want to make Candace feel responsible.

"Then that's what it was," Billy said with finality.

"I know you'd like to think that, sweetie, but the odds for that are astronomical considering my past." She would have been overjoyed to think the spirit board had anything to do with this, but after what happened last night at Gypsy's, she couldn't convince herself.

"Do I have a say in this?" Jorge asked.

Jazz was surprised at the snap in his voice. "Okay, what?"

"I think we should fight the bitch. Look what it did. It's not just you now."

"You don't know what you're saying, Jorge. This is minor destruction. It can get personal."

"So," Jorge said. "It's only calling you a slut."

Billy burst into laughter. "It's not the first time."

Jazz didn't know where he'd pulled the humor from, but she'd ride with it. "Or even the second." The gleam in his eyes let her know they were okay. "Hand me a mop."

Billy turned to Jorge. "Babe, take Cleo back to the bedroom. We've got this."

Jorge set her down in a chair. "No, we do this together."

Her estimation of him climbed to yet a newer level. She was glad Billy finally found someone who cared enough to stay through the bad times. She knew from experience it couldn't get much worse than this freaky shit to test a relationship. Manic entities aside, this could make them closer.

All things considered, the kitchen was a quick cleanup. She told them to go get dressed.

Billy put Cleo's little sweater on and announced he was getting takeout. Jazz didn't blame him, she wouldn't want to cook in here, either, nor would she leave Cleo alone. Poor little thing, she thought.

She shooed them toward the door, and despite Billy's continued welcome and declaration of unity, Jazz wouldn't put him through this.

He'd witnessed activity, of course, when they were younger at her father's house, but the acceleration of events over the years made this seem like child's play.

When they were two steps from the front door, a deafening crash came from the kitchen, and all three jumped.

Jazz ran, stood at the entry, stared at the new destruction, then closed her eyes.

Every door, each cupboard, and the fridge were open. Condiments and food were thrown and splattered every surface. Dishes were strewn about in what appeared to be a toddler's tantrum and lay in shards in every corner of the room. In the silence, Jazz heard food dripping off the counters and onto the floor.

When she opened them again, Billy and Jorge held hands looking for the entire world like two little boys.

The front door opened and closed. They turned again, and Jazz held her breath waiting for the intruder.

"What's up? Why are you all just standing here?"

Candace took another step, looked behind them, and screeched at the top of her lungs.

The unbelievable volume of it had Billy steering her toward the back doors and he shoved her outside on the patio. "Shut up and stay there." He paused. "Sweetheart."

Candace stood on the other side of the glass with her mouth still open in a silent scream and wrung her hands.

A horrific re-enactment of the events in Jazz's father's house had been visited on Billy's utterly devastated kitchen.

Under the odor of the spills was a whiff of an acidic smell Jazz learned to associate with fear.

Billy sank into a chair. "Jazzy." His voice broke. "Look at what happened."

To his credit, Jorge stayed glued to his side, though if his eyes were any wider, they'd look like saucers.

"Billy," she managed. "I am so sorry." The words were barely out of her mouth when the one closed cupboard over the stove opened, then shut with a squeak.

Jorge screamed again and grabbed Billy in an embrace. "Oh, my god."

Their expressions of abject terror broke her heart. It was all her fault.

A wine bottle rolled toward her and stopped at her feet. Paralyzed, they watched it lift, then drop with a force that shattered it, spraying Jazz, making it appear as if she were covered in blood.

"That's it. That's it." Candace screeched outside. "Give me my keys. I'm out of here."

"Billy, honey," Jazz said. "Take them to her and

go to Jorge's place."

He nodded and left the kitchen, clutching Cleo and walking like an old man with Jorge still glued to his side.

Jazz would give anything, anything at all to change what had happened here simply because she loved him, and she had thought she could outrun her destiny.

She walked them out and stood with her back pressed to the wood. "Why him?" Frustrated, she tore at her hair. "Leave him alone. It's me you want." Her voice dropped to a whisper because of her tears. "Leave him be."

The weight of her sorrow and guilt crushed her, but she didn't have time for self-pity, she had to make this right.

Laughter echoed down the hall. Overcome, Jazz wanted to drop to her knees but headed for the cleaning supplies.

Again.

She picked a corner and started working around the room, starting with picking up the pieces of glass, sweeping up the slivers, and mopping up the food and sauces that covered the walls.

Fresh rage filled her when she spotted a jar of olives that Billy loved under the table. At least it hadn't broken. She put it on an empty shelf that had once been full.

Jazz started on the granite counter, surprised to see fresh blood droplets where she'd just wiped up. She looked down and noticed she'd cut her hand. She closed her fist, and blood trickled down her arm.

"You want me to bleed?" She wrapped it up messily in a towel and kept cleaning while she tried to keep a running total in her head of what she'd have to replace, but there had been so much she'd lost count.

She stopped to rinse out her towel and realized she didn't feel a presence anymore. Bitch had probably lost all her stored-up energy.

Starting with last night.

Last night.

Gypsy.

Oh, God, what was she going to tell her? Though she'd put if off for an uncomfortable amount of time, there wasn't a question anymore. Jazz couldn't— wouldn't—leave another person she loved defenseless against the entity.

Jazz stopped and checked herself. Yeah, she'd been a goner since she'd first laid eyes on Gypsy. She'd only fallen deeper since, and that path had definitely wound into the love category.

She looked around nervously, then quickly shut her mind down. That *thing* could read her mind. She thought it was gone but couldn't be absolutely sure.

The tears she'd been holding back threatened to fall again, but Jazz forced herself not to give in to them. She was afraid if she did, she wouldn't be able to stop.

Jazz finished the kitchen, and anything that was spared, which wasn't much, had been put back in its original place. After she put the supplies away, she headed toward the bedroom to pack her bags.

A nasty leftover of bad energy gave her a chill in the doorway. As soon as she opened the door, she was assaulted with the smell of perfumed products and the sound of running water in the bathroom she shared with Candace.

She didn't possess the level of terror her roommate did, she'd passed that point years ago, but Jazz screamed anyway. Not from a place of fear, but with the pure wrath that flowed like fire through her veins. She continued until her eyes burned, then stopped with a whimper as she sat on her bed and stared at the contents of her drawers and closet strewn across the room.

Already exhausted, she lay down and hugged a pillow to her chest, and because she couldn't hold them anymore, she let the tears come.

❦❦❦❦

Gypsy didn't have any interviews or film shots today and didn't need to go into makeup. But if she had, she thought, she'd be walking in glowing.

She hugged her arms to herself and smiled. The previous night had been perfect just as she'd known it would be. She was full of warm pleasure and the dreamy muscle memory of making love with Jazz.

Though she didn't see a soul, she imagined herself skipping to her dressing room. With a laugh, she sat and spun in her chair. Jesus, she felt like a teenager again, without the fumbling experimentation, of course, but two adults who knew how to pleasure each other with experience behind it.

It had been a delightful dance, she decided. Not even her dark dream could put a damper on the way she felt.

But now that she'd acknowledged it, the nightmare came back to her in full detail. It began much as the last one. The long, dark, and cold hallways that she'd run down while things seemed to follow and reach for her with cold claws.

She shivered with the memory, then realized

what she was feeling must be a draft when her crystal butterfly mobile began to ping and chime. Gypsy didn't feel anything off in the atmosphere in her room but got up to light her white candles anyway.

Small details from the nightmare continued to flow back but out of context and in a jumble of snapshots. Different pictures flashed quickly. A hand reaching, shadows on the stained and peeling walls, bodies in the doorways wobbled like bowling pins that weren't knocked completely down.

Okay, she thought, that was seriously creepy.

Jazz lying on the floor scratched and bloody. She stopped cold and tried to pull that important flash of memory closer, but it eluded her and slipped away.

"Come back, come back," she whispered.

Snap.

"Jesus, I know you get a kick out of this, Tangie, but you scared the shit out of me." Gypsy turned to glare at her, but Tangie wasn't behind her. She rushed to the door and looked out.

The corridor was empty but for what sounded like two men having a conversation in the next hall over.

Wind rushed past her, and Gypsy spun around, heard the outside metal door as the bar was pushed and released.

It wasn't the spiritual activity that upset Gypsy. The inability to discern a presence did. It never happened to her before, and she didn't like that.

Not one bit.

She walked back into the room, and her phone sang in her purse that every breath she took, she'd be watching her.

"Jazz, that is." Gypsy smiled.

It might be a little stalkerish, but Gypsy liked it. She quickly dug in her bag but missed the call. She'd give it a minute to let Jazz finish leaving her message.

After a minute when the notification didn't sound, she called Jazz, and it went straight to voicemail. "Hey, babe. I love saying that, by the way. Anyway, I'd love to see you later." She looked back into the hall nervously. "There's been some weird…"

Heavy static cut her off, and the call disconnected. She tried again, but this time, it didn't ring at all. Puzzled, she put the phone down. She'd have to try later.

Gypsy thought about it and realized the paranormal activity around her had spiked right as she began to work the Edgar case. She made a note to get in touch with her good friend and medium. Shelia would be able to take care of it or at least tell her what was going on.

In the meantime, she should talk with Jazz about it. Tell her to come and talk with her if anything unusual happened.

It was the cost of Gypsy's chosen profession, and she should have warned Jazz before this.

But she hadn't wanted to scare her away.

❧❧❧❧

Jazz pulled herself together. It wasn't as if she'd never experienced this level of paranormal activity before. She'd been living with it for over a decade and had long grown jaded and desensitized. She hadn't realized how much until she'd seen her friends terrified in the face of it.

It didn't mean she didn't get scared. There were

times she feared for her life, and there was no way she'd ever become adjusted to the physical attacks. Jazz needed only to see her scars to relive the horror.

At this point, the best way to describe it was to think of herself as being bankrupt of adrenaline and her flight or fight syndrome was just damn busted.

It was difficult to live with the hopelessness. Never letting herself get serious with someone. Now that she'd allowed Gypsy in, she found a new level of it. She was afraid if she lost her, she'd find the depth had no bottom and she'd fall into the abyss.

Jazz rubbed her hands over her face and pushed herself up. Well, that moment to fall was not on this day, and she had work to do before she packed.

As bad as the food mess in the kitchen was, and it really was, the bathroom surpassed that chaos.

The attack on Billy's house and the destruction of Candace's stuff seemed so freaking childish, but she knew it was to isolate her from those who cared about her. To get her to leave this lovely house and support system.

Abusive bitch.

If Jazz had any conscience at all, she wouldn't return to Gypsy's house. Ever.

But couldn't Jazz have at least a sliver of hope her nightmare could end? Because everything she'd tried in the past failed, it had been a long time since she'd sought any sort of help. Gypsy dealt with these sorts of things for a living and had been doing so for years.

Jazz took towels out of the linen closet, turned, slipped in a puddle of conditioner, landed on her ass, felt a blow to her head as she hit the bathtub, and felt a bright lightning jab of pain before it was lights out.

When she opened her eyes, she was on her side

with her face stuck on the floor. Disorientated, she panicked before she realized she must have landed in a pool of hair glue, the kind Candace used on occasion to spike her hair. If she hadn't been so disgusted about the activity in the house, she might have giggled.

And when she got up to look at the goose egg on the side of her head and saw what she looked like, she did laugh, she laughed until her stomach hurt.

As Jazz leaned against the counter, she couldn't decide if her hilarity was the result of finally jumping over the ledge of madness or if it was really the best medicine. In any case, she felt much better.

The soap and shampoos took longer to clean than the kitchen had and the different makeup harder still.

She'd just finished when she heard the tones of *Lady Marmalade*. Billy had the doorbell specially made. It normally amused her, but the last thing this house needed was more visitors. Corporeal or not.

Jazz looked into the mirror. The stains on her clothes were now unidentifiable, her hair was flat where she'd been stuck to the tiles, and her skin was covered in colorful gobs of god-knows-what.

Jesus.

She thought about not answering the door, but the multiple gitchy gitchy, ya, ya, da, das were getting on her last nerve.

How many freaking times were they going to push it? She yanked open the door to snap at whoever was behind it, then her mouth fell open when she saw Gypsy on the porch.

The smile of greeting froze on her face and mirrored the shock Jazz knew was on her own. Neither said a word for several long seconds until finally Gypsy hit the doorbell again and broke the stalemate.

"Um," she said. "That is so cool." It appeared Gypsy's expression was stuck between biting back laughter and confusion over Jazz's appearance.

Kill me now.

If Jazz could have disappeared through the floor, now would have been a good time.

❧❧❧❧

Gypsy had to blink a few times because she had no idea *what* to make of Jazz's appearance. Her clothes were covered in what looked like fresh stains, and half of her face and hair had dried green goop covering it. She couldn't define only one scent but half a dozen. What on earth had happened here?

The look on Jazz's face, a combination of mortification and anger, had her wanting to back up a step. Humor seemed the best. "New face mask?"

"Ha."

Gypsy tried to step around her, but Jazz blocked her advance. Now she was confused. They'd spent the previous night and half the morning wrapped around each other, and this was a side of Jazz she hadn't seen. "Could I please come in?"

"You shouldn't be here," Jazz said.

"Why?" Gypsy battled her hurt feelings. She thought Jazz would be happy to see her. She herself was more than excited on the way over.

Jazz seemed to hesitate but stepped slightly to the left, and Gypsy ducked under her arm. "I really need to talk to you about something," she said as she walked toward the back of the house. She was avidly curious as to why Jazz looked the way she did. It really didn't seem to be a good time to talk to her about the activity surrounding her from the Edgars.

Come to think about it, they'd never talked about her work. What if the paranormal was something Jazz didn't want to deal with? Gypsy's experience earlier in her dressing room was an occurrence that had repeated itself from time to time in the past, depending on how intense the haunting cases were they were currently investigating, and Gypsy couldn't promise it wouldn't happen again somewhere down the line.

Gypsy put her purse on the counter and sat. The kitchen smelled of disinfecting products.

"Can I get you something?" Jazz asked.

"Water?" Why was Jazz acting as if she were a stranger? Jesus, what if she were one of those bitches who once they'd had you, won their conquest, wanted nothing more to do with you? She hadn't even remotely thought that she was that type. Against her will, Gypsy felt herself draw back a little and placed the first brick in the wall currently being built between them.

Jazz placed a bottle in front of her, and when Gypsy reached for it, Jazz took her hand and kissed the tips of her fingers.

Gypsy smiled and kicked the metaphorical brick. *Whew.* "May I ask why you look like that?"

"I was cleaning."

Jazz's nerves felt palpable, and Gypsy watched her look around the room nervously.

"Is everything okay?" Insecurity was a psychic barrier, and now that she knew it wasn't her causing Jazz's strange behavior, it was easier for Gypsy to read her troubled anxiety.

She had to ask her if she'd experienced something paranormal today, but because she felt it was her fault, she really didn't want to know the answer. She took a deep breath to steady herself, but Jazz spoke up first.

"I can't stand here and have a conversation with you while I look like this. I'm surprised you've been so tactful." The corners of her mouth turned up slightly.

Timid, Gypsy thought, evasive, and embarrassed. She could alleviate some of that. "Is this why you didn't pursue a career as a professional housekeeper?"

Jazz laughed. "Pretty much. I was fired when I attempted it."

The tension between them was gone. "I can help you clean up." She gave Jazz what she knew was her saucy look, her implication clear. She watched Jazz swallow, then answered her with a grin.

One side of her face anyway. The other seemed to be frozen by the green mask.

She wasn't going to wait for an invitation. Gypsy grabbed her purse and headed toward Jazz's bedroom.

Chapter Ten

Jazz didn't know if she'd ever been as confused or torn in her entire life. She wanted Gypsy to stay, and she wanted to run fast and far, far away.

And Jesus, the way she must look to her right now. She grimaced and felt her face stick.

If you keep making that face, it's going to freeze like that, said the long-ago voice of her mother. Guess she was right about one thing. "Now go the fuck away," she said to the memory.

Gypsy was already down the hall before Jazz was done with the thought. Damn it, her room was not a safe place to be right now. She ran to catch up with her.

"It smells like the backstage of a runway show back here," Gypsy said and sat on the bed. "Makes me reminisce."

"Yeah?" Jazz wracked her brain for an excuse while she went through her dresser for clean clothes. "I think maybe Candace dropped some stuff or something." She turned to see a weird expression on Gypsy's face as she looked around the room.

Oh, no. She had told Jazz she was a sensitive. Could she feel it? "I'm just going to…" Jazz gestured toward the bathroom. The very last thing she wanted to do was leave Gypsy alone, but she had to wash this gunk off. Jazz decided she'd just leave the door open.

She started the water and realized there was nothing left in the bathroom to shower with. She couldn't make herself go to Billy's, then she'd have to explain why she was covered in various gels anyway. She'd make do with the single bar of soap available to her.

Jazz began washing off, keeping an ear out for Gypsy in the bedroom, but the problem was solved when she heard her come in and put the seat down.

"Want some company?" Gypsy asked.

Jazz opened the curtain a fraction. "I'll be done in a second."

"Okay, I'll be out here when you're finished." Gypsy's heels clicked out of the room.

Jazz hurried to keep her from getting in, despite her desire. Anxiety nearly crushed her, the threat of the entity was substantial to her, but in retrospect, she was almost certain there would be no more appearances today. The swan song of activity probably drained it completely, and she let out a sigh of relief at the revelation.

She turned off the water and wrapped a towel around herself before walking out to find Gypsy gloriously naked in the middle of her bed. She blinked, and Gypsy was, in reality, dressed and sitting on the edge. Clearly, it had been wishful thinking.

Then she gave Jazz *that* look, and her heart did a slow somersault in her chest. Gypsy got up slowly and backed her into the dresser. Her kiss was tender and excruciatingly slow.

When their lips parted, Gypsy sighed and laid her cheek against Jazz's.

A moment of affection Jazz would treasure. A gesture seemingly so little but treasured nonetheless.

She'd promised herself she'd tell Gypsy of her past, this wasn't fair to her.

But God, Jazz had no defense against the sensation of her body pressed against her. The stress of the afternoon dwindled with each article of clothing Gypsy dropped at her feet until she was down to her lacy underwear and the silver hoops in her ears. "Abracadabra," she purred.

And the tension was gone altogether when the towel joined them.

Jazz ran her hands down Gypsy's back, skimmed her hip, and cupped her ass. Warm breath fluttered along her neck as Gypsy purred, then nipped the tender skin.

Hot flashes of an urgent need for her caused Jazz's thighs to tremble. She wanted her flat and backed her up to the bed. "Take your hair down," Jazz whispered.

"Yes." Gypsy tugged at the band. "Why?"

"So I can do this." Jazz slid her fingers through it and held her still while she returned the long, deep kiss until finally Gypsy pulled her down to cover her. "You feel so good." Jazz propped on her elbows. "I can't keep my hands off you."

Gypsy laughed. "That's a good thing. Because it's mutual." She wrapped her hands around the back of Jazz's neck and tugged her down again. The kiss spun out until she was dizzy with it.

"It's so soon, so soon," Gypsy breathed against Jazz's lips. "My need for you and the desire to have you next to me is overwhelming." She cupped Jazz's face and looked her in the eyes. "It's a craving I can't get ahold of."

Undone, Jazz rested her forehead against Gypsy's. "Nothing feels the same when I'm with you. And I feel the same. I can't get enough of you."

Jazz welcomed Gypsy's legs as they wrapped

around hers, shifting until they were heat to heat, and her body demanded to answer the urge of her hips to move faster, harder. She arched up and cried out and gave Jazz back every thrust with one of her own. She breathed her name while Jazz pet every inch, savoring her, seducing her, so they continued to breathe and move as one.

Gypsy cried out and bit her, holding Jazz's skin between her teeth. Jazz flew higher and higher yet until knots of need unraveled and flowed in liquid warmth through her blood.

The urgency was over, and now they moved gently with each other, the loving and light perspiration making it effortless to fit their bodies together, entangle their limbs, and roll across the bed, every motion in synch with each other, as if this were thousandth time they'd made love.

Gypsy's hands felt familiar as they moved over her, a grip and a caress. Quiet sounds of pleasure filled the room, and Jazz hummed low in her throat before her breath quickened once more and her sighs whispered across Gypsy's neck as she felt the edge of her orgasm right in front of her. Passion became a flash in an instant.

Then Gypsy rose above Jazz, and her sigh was long and deep. Her fingers dug into Jazz's hips as she rocked them both up once more. Flesh to flesh, her breath faster and faster between parted lips.

Jazz felt another orgasm rip through her as she held Gypsy tight while she shuddered and dropped to curl beside her.

Breathless and spent, Jazz's mind and body were still spinning. She tilted Gypsy's face up and kissed her, holding it for several seconds, unwilling to let her go.

When she finally pulled back, the afternoon sun caught strands of Gypsy's hair, and Jazz was overcome with emotion while she waited for her heart to slow down, to swallow the three little words she ached to say.

She looked down, and Gypsy's gaze held hers, dreamy and quiet in the moment "It's almost dinner," she said sleepily. "Are you hungry?"

After, she told herself. She'd say them after she'd told the whole story.

Even guilt couldn't stop the joy that overshadowed the dread. Jazz didn't think anything could.

"I can get dressed, and we'll go out to eat."

"I like you naked." Jazz was about to ask her to stay and she'd fix something, but reality was slowly sinking in. She absolutely couldn't let her stay, not with what had happened earlier hanging over her head.

"I need to freshen up."

"You're gorgeous." Jazz grinned. "All tousled up."

Gypsy stood and stretched. "I feel like a cat."

"Sleek?" A naked Gypsy was a sight to behold, and Jazz would be happy to worship her.

"Sated," she answered.

Jazz decided the sight of her walking away nude was just as awe-inspiring.

"Could you grab my stuff?" Gypsy called from the bathroom.

"Sure." Jazz got up and picked up her girlfriend's clothes. After realizing what she'd thought, she looked down at them and grinned. "Huh."

"And my purse." The shower turned on.

Someone pounded on the bedroom door, and Jazz muffled a scream even as every muscle in her body went on defense.

"Jazz? Are you in there?"

"Billy." Thank God. She threw on the shorts and tank she'd pulled out just in time before he opened the door and peeked around it.

"I see a little red number in the driveway." He pointed at the bathroom where the shower was still running. "Ooh."

She smacked the back of his head affectionately. "Get out."

The water stopped, and she pushed him into the hall. "We'll be out in a minute."

He mimed a zipper shut across his lips, then she shut the door in his face. Jazz felt like a teenager caught by her dad. The image made her laugh.

"Jazz?"

She turned and faced Gypsy.

"Honey, you have no shampoo or conditioner."

Instead of explaining, she grabbed at her towel. Gypsy giggled and stepped out of the way.

Jazz would have happily stayed in her room with her for days, but she knew she wouldn't have that luxury, and the best thing to do was to get her out of the house. How was she going to do that without making it *seem* as if she were trying to get rid of her?

Gypsy dressed, then pulled her damp hair back in a ponytail. "Unfortunately, I have to go. My sister reminded me earlier of plans we'd made with the family. You distract me." She looked up at Jazz from under her lashes. "Unless, of course, you'd like to join us?"

"Let's plan that for another day," Jazz said. *Whew.* "Okay?"

"I didn't mean to scare you with meeting the parents yet."

Jazz hugged her. "Not that at all. Billy reminded me we have plans, as well." She had to pack and leave, but she wasn't going to tell her that.

Gypsy picked up her purse, and they walked out to the driveway. "Oh, I have to ask you something." Jazz opened her door, and Gypsy slid in.

"What's that?" Jazz asked after she'd kissed her.

"Has anything unusual happened here or to you since we met?"

Doused in ice water, Jazz froze and couldn't make herself answer. Was the end to be so soon then? She swallowed the lump in her throat.

Gypsy looked as uncomfortable as Jazz felt when the silence stretched. She waved a hand at her. "It's nothing. I was just wondering." She looked at her watch. "I have to go." She held her face up for another kiss, then sped away, leaving Jazz paralyzed in her wake.

❧ ❧ ❧ ❧

Jazz loathed the fact she'd carry that image of her sweet-natured friend looking devastated and all alone in his pretty living room.

She paused before speaking to make sure her voice wouldn't break. "Billy."

"Don't you say it again. Don't you dare."

"But…"

He got up and went to the small bar. "I need a drink. Do you want one?"

She shook her head.

"I've called everyone, they're coming back to clear the house again." The ice in his drink tinkled against the glass.

Silence grew in the space between them. He didn't want her apologies, and for the life of her, she couldn't think of anything else to say except, "I love you."

"Oh, Jazzy, I've loved you my whole life."

She couldn't bear his tears and crossed to hold him.

They didn't let go for several minutes, and each moment that passed made it harder for her to say goodbye. "I don't want to leave you here alone."

"I don't want you to leave at all." He stepped back. "Jorge will be back here in an hour."

"He's good for you," she said.

Billy nodded. "He is." Then he grinned. "Candace might take a little longer to calm down."

"That's not funny."

"I also told her it was that damn board and kook she brought into the house. For all we know, it could have opened some channel to bring that thing here."

"Billy."

"Well," he said and stuck his chin out. "It could have been. Stop." He held out his hand to halt her reply. "That's my story until I know different."

She wasn't going to argue with him. "I'll bring your truck back."

"You will *not*. What do I need one for anyway? It was a consolation parting gift from an evil film director who left me for an up-and-coming action star. Keep it as long as you need, and I don't want to hear another word about it. In fact..." He waylaid Jazz again. "Just make me small payments. We'll take care of the paperwork later. When you come back."

"Oh, honey," she said. "I can't come back." Her resolve wanted to slip when Billy's eyes filled again, but she couldn't let it. He deserved nothing but the best in her opinion, and if anything ever happened to him, she'd hate herself forever.

Jazz had already packed her bags, and wasn't it pathetic she was in her thirties and her entire life filled only a duffel bag and suitcase?

Billy wrung his hands while walking her to the door. "But where will you go?"

"I'll be okay, I promise. You know I can take care of myself."

"Please stay," he said quietly.

She wanted to, was seriously tempted to give in, but she had a flashback of what the entity was capable of. Jazz never wanted to picture him helpless and at the mercy of some fucked-up demon spirit that gleefully hurt people for the only reason seeming to be because it could.

Jazz hugged Billy again fiercely, slung the green bag over her shoulder, wheeled the suitcase, and tried not to look back while she got in the truck.

"Wait," he yelled. "Don't leave yet." He disappeared into the house.

He scared her to death when two minutes later he threw two huge garbage bags into the extended cab without a word and ran back to the porch. Her heart ached for both of them.

She almost got out to embrace him again when she saw Jorge's car pull up in front. He was early, and this was her exit cue. She waved to him before she turned onto the street.

Jazz missed Billy already.

Jazz paid the clerk for two weeks in an extended-stay room, and she could almost hear her debit card whisper "ouch."

The place had looked bigger and cleaner online, but at this point, she couldn't afford to be picky or have the time or inclination to search further.

Jazz ignored the old man in a bathrobe who stood in his doorway and watched her carry in her things. *Creepy old fucker.*

After a little debate about the neighborhood, she also brought in the bags Billy had shoved at her.

She locked the door and dropped her bags and took a good look at her surroundings.

Jazz took two steps to the tiny kitchenette, which was grossly misrepresented by being called one at all. It included a sink the size of a toilet bowl, a measly foot of counter space, and a tiny refrigerator, which was surprisingly clean. The previous guests, and she used the title loosely, must not have used it much.

The microwave was missing its turntable, and in her opinion, would need a sandblasting before she used it. Thank God, she hadn't seen any cockroaches. Yet, she corrected herself.

She only had to turn around to notice the digital clock was missing its second number, which would make knowing the time ridiculously difficult.

Jazz looked dubiously at the bedspread and tried hard not to think about the last occupants and what might have transpired on the mattress.

She opened her gifts from Billy and was insanely grateful to see a comforter, clean sheets, and pillowcases in one of them.

He would have had one of his famously called "three fits" if he'd seen where she'd landed.

After he threw up, of course.

One thing was certain. No one would ever be invited here.

Especially not Gypsy.

Jazz wanted to call her but realized she'd left her phone at the front desk. If she were a betting girl, and she'd been known to on occasion, she'd put money on it being gone. But she had to check, right?

At least creepy old man's door was closed. Jazz locked the door behind her and returned to registration where slimy attendant guy told her she'd put it back in her pocket.

Asshole.

God, what a night. She was tired to the bone but had to have the phone turned off and change all her information.

Creepy old man became leering creepy man. Jazz thought about flipping him off but didn't want to encourage his attention in any way. It was best to ignore him. She cringed and tried not to think of no-tell motel B movies and the slashers who targeted them.

Then again, her life was scarier than any she'd seen on film.

She could only hope the ancient phone in her room worked so she could handle the details. It did, and after a frustrating hour and a half, she hung up the receiver.

Now she'd have to pick up a new one the next day, and she didn't have Gypsy's phone number memorized. One of the greatest downfalls of the digital age—no one had to memorize a string of digits.

Gypsy, being a celebrity, wouldn't be listed. Jazz tried Billy's, then had to admit defeat when both attempts resulted in wrong numbers. *Shit.*

Well, she thought, there was nothing to do about it that night but be worried that Billy would be stressed. Then be put out that she couldn't talk to Gypsy until she saw her at work. At least she wouldn't be spending much time in this dismal studio.

She washed her face, sat on the newly made bed, glad she'd had her crying jag earlier that afternoon.

Jesus, had that only been hours ago? It felt like an eternity. She prayed the bitch would leave Billy alone now that she'd won. Jazz was effectively cut off from her friends and the woman she loved.

A television blared from another room, and she hoped the entity would freak out creepy leering guy across the hall. It wasn't a very nice thought, but she'd live with it. She wasn't afraid of him, she could take him down, but like cockroaches, Jazz knew worse could come when the lights went out.

A chair went under the doorknob, and every bulb available to her was turned on. Jazz could at least protect herself from the outside. She'd had no choice regarding her personal demon.

As if thinking about it invited it, the air became thick and heavy with malice.

Jazz's shoulders sagged. Apparently, there would be no grace period after this move. She could only be glad to know it was here, and it wouldn't bother Billy anymore.

Has anything unusual happened to you lately?

Gypsy's question echoed in her mind. How could she have forgotten?

The television turned on, and fake moans of bad porn filled the room while the lights flickered and buzzed. She popped off the bed to turn it off only to have it turn back on a second later.

Someone next door pounded on the wall. "Keep it down in there."

Would if I could, Jazz thought sarcastically. The sounds of pseudo sex grew louder until she wanted to throw something through the screen.

The noise cut off suddenly, and the silence that followed was eerie and somehow foreboding.

Jazz heard a squeak in the bathroom, opened the door a few inches, and a black ribbon of smoke oozed through the crack. She wanted to run but knew it wouldn't do her a damn bit of good.

When she felt the cold breath on the back of her neck, she knew it was too late anyway, and the whimper she'd been holding back escaped.

She closed her eyes. *Go away, go away.*

Jazz opened them only to see the mist she was exhaling in the freezing cold space.

She ran to the bed, pulled the comforter around her, and nested in the extra pillows already battling the helplessness and wave of hopelessness she always endured during a physical attack.

Terror marched down her spine like biting fire ants, her stomach cramped, and it felt as if clawed fists were tearing her insides out.

"What the fuck do you want from me?" Jazz had asked the question a thousand times.

But had never received an answer.

And having no choice but to settle in for a night of hell, she began to shake.

Chapter Eleven

an, you look tired." Tangie, sporting a new magenta stripe in her hair, handed Gypsy her coffee. *Snap.*

"That's just a euphemism for 'you look like shit, Gypsy.' And never what a woman wants to hear. Love your hair, by the way."

"Thanks. How come you didn't call me this weekend?" Tangie tapped her pad and peered over the rim of her glasses. "The log shows you worked." *Snap.* "I am your assistant, you know. It's what I get paid to be."

One of Tangie's personal quirks was being needed. As efficient as she was, Tangie was insecure, and she thrived on being indispensable. Gypsy bumped her shoulder. She didn't want to hurt her feelings. "I was only here to finish up some paperwork, the stuff you had already organized for me."

Tangie looked mollified, and Gypsy was relieved. She'd had a rough night, and she didn't need her assistant hovering all day—though she considered *that* her job, as well.

"Okay." *Snap.* "Let's get you to Rhia, you need a miracle this morning."

Gypsy metaphorically dragged her feet on the way to makeup. She may have gotten off with Tangie not noticing there was something beneath the tired, but she wouldn't get it past Rhiannon.

"Wow, you could go to Aruba with those bags under your eyes."

"Flattery will get you nothing," Gypsy said.

"Rough night? Or a long one with Jazz? You looked fine last night at dinner. Glowing, in fact."

"Tangie, could you go get my notes on the Parker case? I left them in my dressing room."

"Really? You're going to send me away for the good stuff?"

When Gypsy only stared at her, Tangie huffed. "Aw, man." *Snap. Snap. Snap.*

"Rough night," she said after Tangie disappeared, and they couldn't hear her gum anymore.

Rhiannon pulled out her brushes and pots. "Tell me."

"After I got home, I tried calling Jazz a couple of times, but she didn't answer." Gypsy leaned back. "I can see you in the mirror, you know, stop raising your eyebrow at me."

"I wasn't hiding it. Hold still."

"Anyway, that's not what's wrong. Hardly. Okay, stop with the face."

"I can't help it," Rhiannon said. "My face is right here—on my face."

"Smart ass. Remember last night I told you about the strange stuff going on at my house?"

"Yes, but you also said you took care of it with one of your little rituals."

"Did I tell you that something might be bothering Jazz? How funny she looked at me when I told her?"

"No," Rhiannon said. "You neglected that tidbit."

Gypsy sighed. "I started thinking that's why I didn't get a hold of her. Maybe she *had* an experience and was scared or something. So when I couldn't get an answer and she didn't call back…"

"Your imagination ran away with you," Rhiannon finished.

Gypsy smiled. "You know me so well."

"Birth to earth, babe."

"Right? So besides that, I was trying to sleep last night, and I kept hearing dogs barking."

Rhiannon started on her hair. "They do that."

"I know that," Gypsy deadpanned. "It was more than one, and it seemed to happen all night long, which is super rare for our neighborhood. Early this morning, it sounded as if someone were crying outside. I got up to look, there was no one there, but when I got back in bed, I could hear it again."

"Odd," Rhia said. "And a little scary."

"Ouch, stop pulling so hard. I could swear it was coming from inside the walls. Even after I did a walk-through with my sage, I still didn't get much sleep."

"We're done. I'm a magician, and no one will ever know." Rhiannon put the hair straightener up. "Do you think it's related to the Edgars? What's your gut say?"

"I don't know anymore. I know that stuff is happening, but I don't *feel* a presence. That's what's so weird."

"Then maybe it was a cat in heat."

Gypsy stared at Rhiannon in the mirror, but before she could make a snappy comeback, Tangie came back with the file.

"Did I miss anything good?"

"No," they said in unison.

"Well, you look a hundred percent better," Tangie said. "And Smiley wants you for another promo."

"Thank you, thank you." Rhiannon kissed her

fingers and waved. "I'll be here all week."

Her sister did indeed perform miracles. "Ha." Gypsy turned to Tangie. "Tell him I'll be right there as soon as I change."

Snap. "Okay."

"Don't ruin your makeup," Rhiannon called after her.

"Yeah, yeah." Gypsy changed into one of her many bohemian outfits, thankful to wardrobe that the dates they were last worn were always tagged.

Tangie was waiting in the hall and walked with her to the haunted stage. Gypsy hit her mark, and while she waited for the clapper, she wondered if Jazz had thought about her at all.

"Take one."

Gypsy faced camera one. "How many believe in the supernatural? Are you one of them?

"What if, as a complete skeptic, you're confronted with undeniable evidence?"

Two steps, left turn, sly smile for the second red light. "When everything you believe changes in an instant, *this* is when your paradigm shifts."

Two steps back to the right, pause, look out fake window, turn, first camera, serious expression.

"Bob and Karen Parker didn't believe." Pause. "Until they moved into a haunted house."

Turn, camera two, slow and sexy smile.

"I'm Gypsy Tanner, and tonight we explore the events that led to the exact moment their paradigm shifted."

"Cut, beautiful, Gyp. Print."

"Thanks, Smiley."

Snap. "Good one. Roger called, the Parker interview has been rescheduled for two hours from now."

"Crap," Gypsy said. On one hand, she was annoyed at the delay, and on the other, she had time to find Jazz. The urgency to do so had increased since she'd talked to Rhiannon.

She realized this feeling had nothing to do with being a needy girlfriend.

Something was coming—and it was bad.

☙ ☙ ☙ ☙

Jazz was way late for work.

The previous night's attack had been horrendous and unrelenting. She didn't know how the entity had amassed its incredible energy, but it lasted until the wee hours. She also didn't know when she'd finally fallen asleep. *Or passed out.*

She wouldn't have to rely on the broken clock had asshole clerk guy not stolen her phone.

It was exhausting living two lives. There was working Jazz and playing Jazz during the day and cowering victim Jazz at night.

In addition to those, there was now love-struck Jazz in the middle.

There had to be some sort of resolution, or she'd end up being stark-ass crazy Jazz.

And it feels as if it's only around the next corner.

Speaking of corners, she thought, she'd just rounded the last and saw Gypsy talking to her supervisor. From the look on his face, he probably wouldn't be too mad at her.

"Sorry I'm late," she said. "Alarm didn't go off."

James looked at his watch. "It's fine. Can you stay late to make up the time? We're on a tight schedule for this contract."

"Sure."

Gypsy touched his arm. "Then you won't mind if I steal her for a few minutes before she starts?"

"Um, no, of course not." He turned to Jazz. "Just clock in when you're done."

After he left, Jazz laughed. "I thought I was going to need sunglasses for that dazzling smile." She pulled Gypsy to her. "Good morning, gorgeous." She kissed the tip of her nose.

"I swore I wasn't going to do this, but I am anyway. How come you didn't return my calls?"

"Because they went to the little prick that stole my phone."

Gypsy looked concerned. "From where?"

"I would have called, but I didn't have your number memorized." Jazz wasn't deflecting, exactly. She was simply changing the subject. "Here." She handed Gypsy the pen in her pocket and held out her hand.

"Ah," Gypsy said. "The original Palm Pilot." She laughed. "I'm glad I didn't send you any racy pictures." She winked, then giggled at Jazz's expression.

"Wait. Is that a possibility? Because I'm getting a new phone right after work."

"Maybe. Look, I really need to talk to you, it's important."

Jazz's skin buzzed. The jig was up, time to pay the piper, and any other stupid analogy she could think of that told her there *was* no more time, not after her experience last night. It was all going to come to a head sooner or later. Later was better, but Jazz knew she wouldn't have the luxury of pretending her life was normal much longer. "Babe," she said. "I have to go to work."

Gypsy smiled and nodded before walking into Jazz's outstretched arms. "Later? Promise?"

"Absolutely."

Gypsy's arms tightened around her, and Jazz couldn't stop her gasp of pain. Before she could protest, Gypsy had lifted the hem of her T-shirt.

"What happened to you?"

Jazz pulled it back down. "It's nothing."

"It's *not*. Those are serious scratches."

"Please, Gypsy. We'll talk after work, and I'll tell you then, okay?"

She stared straight into Jazz's eyes before answering. "Yes, but there's no avoiding this. I'm going to worry all day."

"No, really, don't. I'm fine." Jazz leaned down and kissed her. "Go on, gorgeous, and let me watch you walk away."

She leaned against the wall and did just that, appreciating the view.

Jazz was already dreading it. There wasn't going to be an easy way to explain any of it.

Once upon a time, she thought sarcastically, she'd tried to explain her living nightmare to a girl and was then accused of being emotionally disturbed. Not only crazy but had to be faking her bloody scratches by cutting herself for attention.

Or demon possessed, depending on which ex you talked to. Not exactly budding new relationship material, which was why after that Jazz lived up to her six-date rule. Eight if she pushed it. She was so tired of it, it was exhausting.

She pushed her severe doubts away and prayed Gypsy would see things differently. Working in the paranormal field or not, it was a story that was hard to swallow.

It would be shattering to see Gypsy looking at her fearfully, or worse, disgusted by the details.

❧❧❧❧

Gypsy had just had horrible validation for her premonition earlier of danger approaching. It wasn't a warning for her but toward Jazz, and she couldn't help but feel those gouges were her fault.

Jazz hadn't given an explanation, and Gypsy could only go by her own feelings, which were telling her—no, screaming, she admitted—that something wrong and somehow dangerous was going on.

She'd kicked out the paranormal intruder at her house and somehow into Jazz's. How was she going to explain that?

Then again, there had been something tickling the back of her brain since she met Jazz. Something serious she was hiding, and she'd first felt it at Billy's pool party. With a little time and perspective, Gypsy realized she'd dismissed or allowed Jazz to sidestep everything about her past. She wanted to understand why Jazz sometimes looked sad, even haunted, when she thought no one was watching.

Time was going to crawl while she waited for the end of the day. Maybe if she disengaged her own emotions, handled their talk as an interview, it might be easier and wouldn't hurt too much when Jazz told her she had a wife back East.

Now she was just being ridiculous. Where had that come from? Gypsy had already handed Jazz her heart and knew whatever they talked about that night would change her life. Whether for good or bad was yet to be seen.

Tangie turned the corner, spotted her, and hurried over. *Snap.* "Why do you keep disappearing on me?"

"Not on purpose. I was talking with Jazz."

"Ah." Tangie wiggled her eyebrows. "All fun aside, the Parker couple is waiting."

"Already?" Gypsy picked up her pace to match Tangie's. "Thanks, sweetie. You can take an early lunch."

"Uh-uh, no." *Snap.* "You know I love watching interviews. What's up with you lately?" She poked her in the side. "Oh, that's right. You're distracted by getting a little sumpin-sumpin."

"Jesus, Tang." Gypsy stared at her.

Snap. Snap. "What?" she asked.

Gypsy had to laugh, Tangie had nearly perfected the wide-eyed, innocent look. "Never mind. You go and lurk then."

Gypsy headed for her chair. At least some things remained stationary and normal.

The Parkers looked every inch of the young suburban couple they were. Bob looked a few years older than Karen, but they were both blond, well groomed, and appeared earnest. Gypsy had read their file and reviewed their videos, and she believed them to be genuine.

She tucked her personal issues aside and went to work.

After introducing herself and shaking hands, she sat down and settled in.

"I'm so nervous," Karen leaned forward and whispered. "What if I don't do it right?" She turned to Bob. "What if they don't believe us?"

Gypsy jumped in. "There is no wrong way." And

as much as she'd come to like Alayna Edgar, she didn't want a repeat of her hysteria. "I believe you, and I'll take care of you while we're talking."

She signaled Smiley. "Get ready."

"Parker interview with Gypsy, take one."

Gypsy couldn't help her grin when it was Bob who flinched at the clapper instead of Karen. Here we go, she thought. Smile, camera two.

"I'm Gypsy Tanner here with Bob, a loan officer, and Karen, a working stay-at-home mom of two. The Parkers say they were living a normal suburban life." Pause, camera one. "That is, until they bought and moved into their new house." Pause. "Welcome."

"Thank you," Bob said. "We're glad to be here." He looked sideways at his wife. "I think."

Karen's knuckles turned white as she clenched her hands, and Gypsy wanted to dive in quickly. If she didn't have time to think, perhaps she could shake the nerves off.

Gypsy smiled briefly and glanced down at her file, but it was just for form. She'd already read and memorized them. "We have a lot to talk about, how about we dive right in? Is that all right with you?"

They nodded together.

"Karen, you were the first to notice odd things happening in your new house, is that correct?"

"Yes. We have two children. Lisa, two, and Lance, who is four." She smiled nervously. "That's why I work at home."

Gypsy knew the editors would cut in a family photo into the conversation. "That's lovely. You have a beautiful family."

Without further prodding, she began. "Thank you." Karen's pride was evident. "I started to pick up on it the day we moved in. Looking back, what I thought was moving day nerves must have been more like an inkling, you know?"

Gypsy nodded. "Instinct." She appreciated Karen continuing in a strong clear voice. They might just get through this in one take.

"I imagine you hear a lot of the same stories that begin in exactly the same way. You could probably recite it for me."

She's right, Gypsy thought, most all the interviews she'd conducted started the same way. The astute statement surprised her, but she didn't want the Parkers to think their story wasn't important. "Every case is always different because each family, such as your own, has a unique perspective of their experiences. We're more than interested in hearing yours." She smiled to reassure them.

In spite of the turmoil of her own emotions, Gypsy managed to be fully present for the Parkers, and that mattered to her.

"Go ahead, honey." Bob put a hand on his wife's knee.

At his physical contact, Karen appeared to relax. "Okay. Again, in hindsight, it started with the dogs."

It brought to mind the previous night's occurrence of the neighborhood dogs going nuts, and the hair on Gypsy's arm stood up, but she kept her interview face on for the camera.

"I remember that," Bob said. "Charlie, our dog, didn't want to come in the house, I had to drag him. He'd bark at things we couldn't see, and if he did come in, he'd run around as if chasing something and snarl at everyone. He wouldn't come into the bedroom. Ever. Not even after bribing him with treats."

Karen's eyes filled. "We had to give him to my mother because he *changed*, you know? We were scared for the children."

Bob nodded. "Since we brought him over there, he's reverted back to his sweet self."

"That's important," Gypsy said. "And it ties back to what's been going on in your house to the location rather than behavioral."

His sad expression told her it wasn't any consolation at all. "Before a week was out, we started hearing knocking or scratching noises."

"And you thought they were easily explainable and dismissed as normal when you move into a new house." Gypsy tapped her pad with her pen.

"Right," Bob said. "That's what we did, made excuses and debunked them."

Gypsy raised a brow, and Bob chuckled. "We watch your show and others, we know the lingo." He looked over to Karen, who sighed, then picked up the narrative smoothly.

"Then we started hearing the cries of an infant, you know, the ones that break your heart and you want to run and pick them up."

Again, the hair rose on her arms. These were classic symptoms of a new haunting, and she should have seen the hints in her house sooner, *before* the hangers did a jig in her closet.

She'd been in denial. She'd read somewhere that coincidence was simply your mind's way of making sense of what it can't believe is real. How ironic that in her profession, she'd missed the clues. Gypsy made a mental note to have a professional cleansing of her house and soon.

The interview was long, but from that point on,

most of it resembled similar narratives of escalation she'd heard several times before.

It didn't mean Gypsy didn't pay attention or project her genuine compassion, but because it felt routine, it allowed her mind to cloud and worry about her own problem.

The Parkers were an engaging couple, and she would make sure they got all the help they needed. Her investigative team had already informed Gypsy they didn't find any indication of a dark energy. She was relieved none of their story seemed to hold any implication of evil, and the Parkers seemed to be more baffled than scared.

Good, she thought on her way to her dressing room, Roger would *not* send Jane Boren to scare them or their kids into believing something that wasn't true.

She heard Tangie's gum snapping behind her before she caught up with her in the hall. "I liked them."

"Me too." Gypsy turned toward her. "Did everything look okay?" Gypsy hoped her distraction hadn't been noticeable.

Tangie tilted her head and stared at Gypsy. "As always, yeah. Why?"

Slightly reassured, Gypsy continued down the corridor. As much as she loved Tangie, she also wanted some alone time to further process what was happening at her house. The best way to do that was to give her something to do. "Would you get a hold of Shelia for me? Ask her to review the team's tapes. I'm sure she'll be able to tell us what the problem is, then I can appropriately know who to send to clear the house. I have a feeling it's not going to be problematic." She paused. "And if in the rare case it turns out to be, we'll try the next solution."

"Sure." *Snap.* "We haven't had a failure yet. Close your door, get some rest, or better yet, leave early. The only thing I need from you is to sign off on the Edgar interview, and I can send it to your email. You can easily do that comfortably at home instead of having Roger breathe down your neck."

Gypsy was tired after comparing the Parkers escalation to her own made her sick to her stomach.

❧❧❧❧

Jazz had worked late and stopped to pick up takeout. By the time she got to Gypsy's, the sun had already set. She parked and took the path around to the back deck, knowing she would be breaking her self-imposed taboo to keep silent on the subject and with each word said she could be jeopardizing any chance of a future relationship with Gypsy.

The waves crashed, taunting her with their power, making her feel small and insignificant once more. Close by, a dog barked viciously, and she nearly dropped the big paper bag.

She was well used to swallowing her PTSD during the day, but the previous night's attack had left her more than a little jumpy.

On top of that, Jazz felt like she was walking a tightrope of tension, trying to keep her balance without falling off the top of the fence. It felt incredibly self-centered of her, the desire to be with Gypsy, love her, and continuing to try to contain a horror belonging only to her without letting it invade any part of Gypsy's life.

Jazz stood on the deck and looked in the folding door to where Gypsy was standing at the counter. She smiled and looked up. Jazz fell off the fence, and the part of Jazz's heart she'd kept locked to keep Gypsy safe fell selfishly at her feet.

Gypsy rose and hugged her. "Thank you for coming. God, I'm starving."

Jazz forced a grin. "Just a delivery person?"

"Absolutely not. I'm happy to see you." She looked over Jazz's shoulder. "That's way more than I ordered."

"You were missing several have-to-have items on their menu. In my mind, you should never have Chinese food without pot stickers and honey walnut shrimp. There should be a law against it."

"I stand chastised then." Gypsy leaned back and kissed her long and slow. "Mmm," she said. "This is what I wanted most of all. Let me get the silverware."

Gypsy picked up a random carton and carried it back to the table.

Jazz grabbed two more containers and sat in the chair next to her, making a concentrated effort to appear nonchalant. "What's up?"

Gypsy flipped a switch, and a cleverly hidden television slid from behind a large painting. "Some things have been occurring lately, peculiar things."

Jazz held her breath and felt her nerves kick up another notch. She wanted to ask for details, but at the same time, she never wanted to hear them. Instead, she exhaled slowly and decided she'd wait until Gypsy elaborated a little more.

"What are we watching?"

"The final cut of the Edgar investigation. I'm going through the evidence, some of them being visual, but most are EVPs. The guys are excited about this one."

Though she knew already, she asked, "EVP, electronic voice phenomena?" Gypsy's team would have had a freaking party if they'd ever been to her father's house. They wouldn't have needed to amplify or clean up the sound at all to hear the entity's threats.

"Yes, exactly."

"Why do you have to sign off?"

"It's my show. I don't mean that to sound arrogant, but I want to verify what's been found. It's important to me to know everything about the investigation because for me, I want integrity versus ratings. I don't ever want to stand behind something that's fabricated or false."

Jazz understood that perfectly and realized she was stalling. Then she ordered herself to quit being a baby. These people had nothing to do with her or her personal story. "Okay, let's get started." To cover her nervousness, she stabbed her fork into her food and began to eat.

Gypsy hit buttons on the remote and waited while it loaded.

Jazz saw three people in a dark room staring at the camera, the night vision turning their eyes eerily white. Immediately, she was struck by how much they resembled the thing haunting her in the dark. She concentrated instead on the group. "How come they all look blond?"

Gypsy paused the show and stared at her. "Have you not watched any yof the episodes yet?"

Jazz swallowed. "No, not yet."

"The woman who Googled me?"

"It's not for the reason you may think." *It's time.* Jazz pointed at the screen with her fork. "I need to tell you a story, and if unexplained things are happening to you, I promise, it has nothing to do with that case."

"But that's when it started, and I think it's tied. How did you get those scratches? Jazz, you have to believe me. I'm sorry that my work has overflowed onto you."

Sweet mother of Jesus, Gypsy thought it was her fault? That did it. Jazz reached and cupped her cheek. "Honey, turn that thing off. I can guarantee you that what you've seen on that investigation, or any other, is child's play compared to my life."

"So it's paranormal then? Is it bad?"

Jazz nodded. "It's really bad. Listen to my story, and if when I'm done, you want me to leave, I'll understand." She could already feel her heart fracture.

"I knew there was something you weren't telling me, I could feel it," Gypsy said. "As far as wanting you to leave, that won't happen."

God, she hoped not. "Make up your mind when I'm finished."

Jazz set aside her food, then crossed her arms on the table. "Thirteen years ago—"

"Wait," Gypsy said and left the room. She returned with several white candles and what looked like a miniature cast iron pot.

"What is that?" Jazz asked.

"Sage, to cleanse and clear energy, sweet grass draws the new and positive, and keeps dark forces away."

"Babe, look at me. We'd have to fill a burn barrel to avoid that."

"You know what I do, Jazz. Do you think I'm going to tear at my hair and run screaming out of the house?"

She couldn't help it, Jazz grinned at her tone.

"You might. But, god, I hope you don't."

"Pu-lease," she said, then lit the candles and herbs. "Okay, I'm ready."

Gypsy might just make all the difference. Jazz was handing faith and her fate to her in both hands.

Jazz took a deep breath. "Thirteen years ago—"

"No once upon a time?"

"Gypsy."

"Sorry. You look so serious, just trying for some levity. Okay, interview mode. Go."

"Thirteen years ago—"

"Wait. I want some wine, do you want some?" Gypsy got the bottle and two glasses, then walked back to the table. "I'm nervous, I'm never nervous."

"Maybe I should—"

"No, you can't stop there." Gypsy sat down again. "I'm ready."

Jazz sighed. "I was working at—"

"Aren't you going to say—"

"Gypsy."

"Jazz."

"Oh, my God." Jazz laughed. "Enough." As silly as the conversation was, it relieved some of her apprehension. Maybe that had been Gypsy's intention.

When she smiled and looked knowingly at her, Jazz knew she was correct. "Sneaky minx."

"Thirteen years ago." Gypsy tapped her nails on the table repeatedly. "See? I'm being helpful."

Jazz studied her. "I've never seen you like this."

"Like what?"

"Scattered, a little ADD. You've always been so steady, confident, and sure of yourself."

Gypsy looked appalled. "I'm all of those things."

"I know. So what's going on?"

"I'm in love with you."

The words hit Jazz with a rush and square in the chest. "I thought it was because you were scared." She got up and cupped Gypsy's face with her hands before kissing her. "I want to drop this right now and let you know how much I love you back, but what I'm going to tell you might change your mind or at least give you pause."

"It couldn't possibly," Gypsy said and reached for her. "And if you think I would, you don't think very much about either of us."

"Please, it's not that. Let me just get this out, okay?" Jazz backed away and sat on the other side of the table. "Right after graduation, I got a job working the graveyard shift at an old asylum, and one night after a miscommunication, I got left there."

"That's horrible," Gypsy said. "What happened? Were you a tour guide?"

"No, I was in charge of special effects." When she saw her quizzical look, Jazz expanded. "There was a special cordoned-off section in the basement where management had a room with a console and several humongous computer screens showing live feeds of the groups. When the tour reached certain places, I had the means to cause the activity they experienced."

Gypsy appeared disgusted and shook her head. "I've gone to several similar places in the past. I don't know why they felt they had to cheat, places like that are hotbeds for activity."

"Right?" Jazz was grateful Gypsy knew so much, she wouldn't have to paint her a picture. She might just survive this yet. Or at least until she told her the part about the entity. "I agree. There's enough going on to begin with without their tricks. Of course, they tried to justify it. The bosses told us, the employees, it was because they wanted the paying visitors to get their money's worth, but I think it was more about lining their pockets. The fees they charged were outrageous."

"Of course," Gypsy agreed. "It's business practices like that that give the profession a bad reputation. With the vast amount of grief and suffering inside those walls, the truly insane, psychotic, and sociopaths living alongside innocent lambs, convenient prey, really, how could there *not* be leftover energy? I've learned violence and sexual and psychological abuse leave psychic scars. Scientists have proved that trauma lives on and stays in one place long after it's gone. It creates a kind of synergy, emotional tornadoes that create a paranormal Disneyland." Gypsy took a sip of her wine. "I'm sorry, I get carried away sometimes, hazard of the job."

Jazz was at the point of no return. Her life, the one she wanted desperately, was hanging in the balance. Still, she felt as if she couldn't draw enough breath to start.

After a minute, Gypsy sat back in her chair, her expression open and positive. "I almost feel as if we should have a drumroll." She grinned at her. "What happened to you there, baby?"

"I got locked in."

"Oh, my god, that's horrible, and I'm sorry. I wasn't expecting that." Her smile went from amused to serious in an instant.

"That's okay." Jazz closed her eyes. "After shift, I dozed off waiting for my ride, who had canceled unbeknownst to me. After I couldn't get a hold of anyone else, I freaked. I never wanted to spend any more time in that place than I had to. And with no other choice, I would have to make a run for the entrance.

The electricity had been turned off at the main office, as it always was, so it was dark."

"That just gave me chills," Gypsy said. "How terrified you must have felt."

"There isn't a word to describe how much," Jazz said. "Even so, I do remember thinking when I heard voices and footsteps that there was a rogue ghost-hunting group playing around with me. Though I was scared out of my mind, I wanted to justify the noises around me, who wouldn't? I ran to the entrance and found even security was gone. That's when I panicked and beat on the doors until my fists bled, I was hysterical to get out."

"Oh, honey, I don't know a person alive who wouldn't feel the same way trapped in a place like that. I think every skeptic out there needs to have a field trip to a similar place."

"I'd love to see their faces," Jazz said.

Gypsy moved to take Jazz's hand, her voice was smooth and quiet. "Then what happened? How long were you there?"

"My phone died. Here's where things get a little blurry. I know I wasn't in my right mind but crazy with fear." Jazz paused and swallowed. "You know how every sound amplifies in the dark?"

Gypsy nodded but stayed silent.

"Yeah, that. I heard what I thought was laughter, but it just sounded evil. Could I have been misleading myself? I don't think so. That place was never quiet, it's as if the energy there never sleeps, never relaxes, it's a buzz across your nerves that doesn't end until you're far away from it."

"As I've said, I've been to a few," Gypsy said. "I know exactly what you're talking about. I've always felt oily and nauseated after leaving."

Jazz nodded. "So I heard that laughter, and I was panic-stricken, the kind where you're frozen solid, can't move, your eyes feel as if they're going to pop out of your head, and you can feel the chill right down to your bones, and you just know something is going to happen in a very bad way. I felt claws scratch me from my neck down my spine."

"Physically attacked?" Gypsy gasped audibly. "I hate that you had to go through that."

Jazz shrugged it off; she didn't want sympathy, she just wanted to get through it. This part was easy, there was much worse to follow. "I don't remember much after that. They told me later it was hours until I was rescued. Billy and Stacy, my girlfriend at the time, told me they found me blubbering on the floor. My memory is a bit hazy on that part, but I do know I crawled out of that place."

Gypsy nodded and continued to pat Jazz's hand.

"At the hospital, they bandaged me up and concluded I must have cut myself on a piece of broken metal lying around or something. That my…" she used finger quotes, "imagination had been in overdrive and created the scenario."

"Then they'd never had personal experiences or were too embarrassed to admit it around their colleagues," Gypsy said. "They didn't want to open themselves to ridicule."

"And they didn't want to listen to a hysterical teenager screaming about evil entities. They wanted to assume I was on drugs."

Gypsy sneered. "It's always their fallback. You were victimized twice that night."

If Jazz was grateful before, her cup was running

over now. That Gypsy would see that, understand that, brought a lump to her throat.

She wanted to stay detached, but in the face of the love she saw, it was becoming impossible. She thought about not continuing with the rest.

But that was not what Gypsy deserved.

Jazz was facing the sliding door and saw a shadow move. Her ears started to ring right before the hag's face, three times as big as Jazz had ever seen, pressed against the glass, and Jazz jumped in her seat.

"Have you heard what I've said? What's wrong?"

Thank god, Jazz was the only one who saw it. "Nothing," she said quickly. She couldn't tear her gaze away from the fat black lips mouthing words at her. Fear cramped her stomach when she realized she'd brought it straight here. She had to get away from here, far away.

"Nuh, uh, uh." It waved a hideous clawed finger in the air in a no, no gesture while she mouthed a kiss toward Gypsy before licking the glass. Jazz wanted to throw up and curl into a ball. This was exactly what she was terrified of happening.

"Come out, come out, or I'll come in and play-yay."

"Gypsy, please go upstairs. Now."

"What?" She spun her chair around. "Why?"

"Don't argue. Just do it," Jazz yelled at her. "I said right now." Jazz grabbed her arm and pushed her firmly toward the steps.

"You're hurting me."

"I am so sorry." Jazz turned to look her in the eye. "Please, please trust me." She would beg if she had to. "You have to go upstairs now."

Gypsy stared at her, and whatever she saw on

Jazz's face must have gotten through to her because she walked backward toward them, then up the same way.

A black fingernail tapped at the window, but Gypsy didn't appear to hear it as she reached the landing and stopped. "Please tell me what's going on."

"I can't right now. Go to your room and lock the door." Jazz didn't know why she said it; locking a doorknob was only an illusion of safety, but it was all she had.

"I can help you," Gypsy pleaded.

She shook her head. "No one can," Jazz said and crossed to the doors. The entity was no longer visible, but the immediate and imminent threat remained. Jazz looked back once as her heart cracked in pieces.

Then she ran out the door.

Jazz was shaking so hard, she dropped her keys twice, then fumbled to fit them in the ignition and look behind her at the same time.

She had to get out of here before Gypsy came out. She didn't have a meek bone in her body.

I'm in love with you.

Love with you.

With you.

You.

The words echoed over and over, then slowed to match each beat of her thundering heart. What had she done? The words she knew should fill her with joy now invoked fear.

Not for herself but for Gypsy.

Jazz drove like a bat out of hell, barely noticing the stretch of highway she normally thought so beautiful, the smell and sound of the ocean through her open window.

The radio turned on full volume and assaulted her ears. Jazz reached down to turn it off, and something freezing brushed her arm before curling around her wrist like a vise.

The truck accelerated at an alarming rate as Jazz fought with the unseen force while trying to watch the road in front of her.

Shock was ice cold as she attempted to hold on to the steering wheel. She hit the brakes repeatedly but only gained more speed.

Headlights came toward her, and additional terror squeezed her chest. She didn't know how much more her heart could take before it stopped entirely.

Jazz was aware of the entity's breath as time slowed and her reality shrank down to focus on the other vehicle approaching her head-on. She couldn't go that way, her only option was to go over.

She viciously yanked the steering wheel to the side where the silver guardrail loomed, and the sound of screeching metal and shattering glass were the last things she heard before impact.

Chapter Twelve

After a speedy and harrowing drive to the hospital, Gypsy hit the doors at full speed and barreled toward the counter.

The nurse sitting at it held up a finger to silence her while she continued to talk on the phone.

Unfazed, Gypsy raised her voice and asked her questions rapid fire. "Where is Jazz, Jasmine Miller? What room? How is she?" She was a little surprised she was able to articulate them at all through the panic.

The nurse turned her back, and Gypsy had a violent vision of grabbing the receiver and rapping it against her bleached blond head.

Fortunately for her, her co-worker looked over, and from the way her eyes lit up, Gypsy knew she'd been recognized.

"Hey, aren't you—"

Flies, honey. "Yes." Gypsy read her nametag. "Ellie, could you please tell me which room Jasmine Miller is in and her status?"

Someone tugged her arm, and she pulled it back viciously before she saw Billy. "Oh, honey, I'm sorry." She turned and faced him. His eyes were red-rimmed from crying, and his breath hitched.

"I tried to remember all her information. How can they expect it when you're scared out of your mind?" He shook his head. "Here," he said. "We're over here." He led her to a crowded waiting room where worry and despair floated like fog through the mass of people.

She clutched him, though he seemed to be as unsteady as she.

They stood against the wall along with Jorge, and before Gypsy could pepper him with questions, she saw a tiny woman with bright blue hair rushing over to her.

Tangie.

When she reached them, she shook her head. "No," she said. "This won't do at all. Come with me."

"Where?" Billy asked. "We were told…"

Snap. "I've already been on the phone with the admins, and they have a private waiting room for you."

Gypsy's shoulders sagged, and she let Tangie take her hand and the lead.

After she shut the door behind Jorge, she pointed at the chairs. "Sit."

"How did you—?" Billy whispered.

"Tangie can do most anything," Gypsy said. "Anything. First, Billy, who called you?"

"State patrol. He only said there'd been a bad accident, and they were bringing her here."

Gypsy took a breath. In her frantic rush, she'd missed it. The unmistakable scent of antiseptic and depression, even in the pretty waiting room Tangie procured.

And whose bright idea was it to put that giant clock in here? The seconds loudly ticked and reverberated in the room, building more into the minutes of anxiety while waiting for word on Jazz's condition.

Any news at all would help contain the scream of frustration building in her lungs.

Billy sat and held hands with Jorge, and now, Tangie seemed lost. It must be killing her, Gypsy thought, as she was someone who *always* had answers.

It was in her nature.

The door opened, and all four of them surged to their feet, but no one spoke. Gypsy's throat was coated with terror, anticipating horrible news.

It took a few seconds before she recognized the nurse, Ellie, from registration who stood with her hands clasped at her hips.

"Do you have some news?"

Ellie looked carefully behind her before shutting the door. "Privacy laws," she said. "But I knew you were all waiting. Please don't tell anyone I was here."

As she'd discerned earlier, Ellie was a fan, and Gypsy rushed to reassure her. "We won't." She pointed to Billy, who wiped his eyes as he approached. "He's her brother."

"You don't have to convince me," Ellie said. "Your friend is still in the operating room."

The words felt like a slap. Gypsy's arm came up around Billy's shoulder automatically when he slumped against her and began sobbing.

She wanted to cry herself. "Surgery?"

Jorge came up to Billy's other side. "How serious is it?"

Ellie smiled but looked grim. "I'm sorry, but it's too soon to know, and it'll be a while before she moves up to the ICU."

"Thank you." Gypsy took one of her hands and held it. "We appreciate it."

Ellie smiled warmly. "I have to get back before I get in trouble. It was nice to meet you, though I'm terribly sorry it was under these circumstances." She cracked the door open to peek into the hall before opening it, then turned. "The doctor will come as soon as he can and let you know the details."

"I'll be back." Tangie followed her out, shutting the door behind her.

She moved off in her purple Converse high tops, and how silly was it, Gypsy thought, that she even noticed them?

I must be in shock.

Billy dropped into a chair and covered his face. "She's in the operating room? It has to be bad, right?" His shoulders shook. "I couldn't bear it if she…she…"

Gypsy felt the same way but needed to be strong for him. "Stop it right now, and don't talk like that, I mean it." She crouched in front of him. "We'll find out what's going on. It's a good hospital, and I'm sure they're doing everything they can to help her, okay?"

He sniffed, nodded miserably, and leaned against Jorge's shoulder.

"Can you tell me what happened?"

"I've already told you, the state patrol called me. They said her truck had been in an accident, and they were bringing her here."

"I drove him," Jorge said. "The officers wouldn't tell us more than that. They said pending an investigation."

"Jazz would never drive if she were impaired in any way," Billy said. "I don't know how this happened."

Despite the calm front she was projecting, Gypsy felt herself tremble, and she rubbed her hand over her heart. She didn't know how long she'd be able to keep herself together. She wanted to wail and weep herself but knew it wouldn't do any good.

An hour went by, then another before Tangie walked back in. Gypsy shot to her feet. "What did you find out?"

Billy rushed to her. "Are they still working on her?"

Tangie pulled a notebook out of her monster bag, and Gypsy noticed she wasn't chewing any gum. "I've been assured Dr. Lee is the best in his field, and he's the surgeon in charge. They say Jazz is very lucky."

"Who are they?" Jorge asked.

Gypsy shook her head in his direction. "Please, let her finish."

"I was told he would be in here to talk to you as soon as he can. They're still working on her, then transferring her up to the intensive care unit."

"What are her injuries?"

Tangie nodded. "I'm sorry," she said to Gypsy. "I've lost my perfect track record. I couldn't wrangle any more than that." She was close to tears.

Gypsy knew how much that admission cost her, would fracture her sense of confidence, and she pulled her in. "It's okay, Tangie. Nobody here will blame you." She also knew that she would do better with a task to perform. "Could you go see about getting us something to eat while we wait?"

"If I can't do anything better," she muttered. "I might as well, but that doesn't mean I'll stop trying."

"Thank you, I know you will," Gypsy said and steered Billy back toward his seat. She went over to the window and listlessly watched the parking lot.

"It's been hours," Jorge said. "You think they would know how much better we would all feel if they just let us know what's going on."

Billy nodded. "I know, right?"

"I would rather it take longer than have someone come in with horrible news," Gypsy said. "I'm trying to think of it as a positive thing."

Jorge put a hand on Billy's knee. "Then we will, too."

Gypsy picked up the remote and turned the television on. Not that she or anyone else would really watch anything, but it was something to look at.

After another hour, Tangie picked up the barely touched food containers and tossed them in the trash. "I'm going crazy, I'll be back."

Gypsy kept running the evening through her head and tried to explain to herself why Jazz would run off. They had just told each other they were in love, but she also gave cryptic clues Gypsy might not want her after she explained.

Explained what? Logic told her that night she'd been trapped wasn't the end of the story.

"I was wondering," Billy said and interrupted her thoughts. "Was Jazz coming from or going to your house?"

"Leaving, and I don't know why. I had asked her over to help me with a case I'm working on, and instead, she started telling me how she'd been locked into that hospital a long time ago. All of a sudden, she ordered me upstairs, then ran off.

"I couldn't even call her because she'd lost her phone and hadn't given me the new number yet. I waited for a while to see if she would come back, and I was on my way to your house when you called me about the accident."

"What happened right before that? Did she say anything else?" Billy asked.

"I told her I was in love with her."

"Anyone can see that," Jorge interjected. "That couldn't be it."

The look that passed between Billy and Jorge spoke volumes to her.

"What are you not telling me? My instinct tells

me she was scared *for* me. I could feel it."

"You should tell her," Jorge said.

Gypsy was going to ask, but two sharp knocks preceded a man in scrubs. He paused in the doorway and looked at Billy.

"Are you her brother?" He looked down at his chart and raised a brow. "William…Sweet, is it?"

"Yes." He stood and grabbed Gypsy's hand in a vise grip, but the doctor gestured them to sit back down, then chose a chair for himself.

He's trying to make us comfortable before he gives us bad news.

The doctor's face was unreadable. Gypsy imagined it must be a long-ingrained skill after what must be thousands of meetings with families.

"First let me say, she came through surgery."

Relieved, Gypsy felt herself exhale. Dr. Lee looked at her briefly, then back to Billy. "A broken leg along with two fractured ribs. Her chest was severely bruised, we're assuming by the steering wheel, and we were concerned with internal bleeding. Though we'll be running more tests, everything looks okay there. There's trauma to her face, probably from hitting the airbag. When that swelling goes down, we'll be able to determine more."

"Dear God," Jorge said.

Dr. Lee went on. "We were most concerned with her skull."

Gypsy heard Billy's squeal, and his fingers tightened around hers painfully.

"It's a small linear fracture." He pointed to the top of his forehead. "We're going to need to keep an eye on her for swelling and monitor any pressure on her brain."

"Is there a chance of any lasting damage?" Gypsy

asked, surprised her voice seemed so calm.

"Not at this time, I don't think so." Dr. Lee's expression finally softened. "She's holding her own. It doesn't hurt that she's young, in good physical shape, and appears very healthy. All we can do is wait and see."

❧❧❧❧

After her trip to the restroom, Gypsy saw Billy was sitting in Jazz's assigned room. "You should go on home. I'll sit with her when they move her up."

"What if she comes out of the anesthesia and I'm not here? She's the sister of my heart, Gypsy. What if she never wakes up?"

"Of course she will. The doctor said it was only a medically induced sleep."

"Isn't that like a coma?"

Gypsy shuddered inwardly. She didn't want to use that word at all. "They're in control of it, Billy."

"The night nurse was just by and told me visiting hours were over," he said. "But I don't want to leave her alone."

"Is Jorge still here?"

"In the restroom fixing his face, as he says, he's not a pretty crier." He waved that off. "The nurses said they would get in touch with me immediately if there were any changes and that I could call anytime with questions or to ask how she's doing.

"Okay," Billy said and stood. "I'm going to go pick up some of her things. Maybe she'll feel better if she has some of her own stuff."

A new nurse came in and introduced herself as McKenna. "It's going to be a couple more hours before they move her up from recovery, so you may as well leave." Gypsy couldn't help but notice her tone was as sour as her features were sharp. As long as she took excellent care of Jazz, they wouldn't have a problem.

Gypsy ignored her and turned to Billy. "I can help you," she said. "And bring it here."

"Are you sure? It's kind of far." He rattled off the address Jazz had given him.

Gypsy waited until McKenna left the room before she questioned Billy. "When did she get her own place? She didn't tell me she'd moved." Now she had more to comprehend, additional questions, and her nerves were already on overload.

"I can't tell you and please don't pressure me about it. It wasn't my idea. I'll tell Jorge to take the car home if you'll drop me back off before coming here."

Her head felt like it was spinning. "Yes, of course." She needed answers, and hopefully, she'd get him to spill some during the trip. That, or she just might scream her throat raw.

When they got to the parking lot, Billy punched the address into Gypsy's GPS, and the map came up. "Oh, I didn't know she'd moved that way. That is such a seedy neighborhood. I feel horrible." He covered his face with his hands. "Poor Jazzy."

"You never did tell me why she moved. I thought you were all happy with the arrangement."

Billy closed his eyes and leaned back. "Gypsy, I'm tired, and I'm just going to rest for a few minutes."

He was strikingly pale, and Gypsy didn't want to push. The level of secrecy was frustrating. To fill the quiet and settle herself, she turned on the radio but kept the volume low as he began to snore lightly.

He was right, it was far away, but the relief she felt when she heard the smooth voice telling her she'd reached her destination was short-lived. She was devastated to see the old broken-down motel, and it hurt because Jazz had felt the need to stay there. Why?

She could and would fix that. Jazz needed someone to take care of her for several weeks at least when released. Gypsy would hire someone to bring Jazz's things to the Malibu house.

Billy looked up after she parked the car. "Fuck me." He looked horrified.

"I know. I feel the same way. She can't stay here," Gypsy said. "I'll have her move in with me."

He looked at her as if he were struggling to keep from saying something but nodded instead. "Good idea," he said. "But you might want to ask her first."

"If you think I'll leave her to live here, reconsider."

"It's not that." He sighed heavily. "I'd take her out forcefully myself if I had to." He shook his head. "I agree with you."

They walked past a large, potbellied man wearing a shirt at least four sizes too small who didn't appear to have showered in a month. She shuddered. Scruffy didn't cover it.

"Here it is." Billy took out a key. "Jesus, what the hell happened in here? It looks like the place has been trashed."

"Should we call the manager?" Gypsy asked.

"No. Her electronics are right here. Help me pack up some clothes."

Watching him, he was clearly nervous, and she knew he was being evasive, but the place was giving her the creeps, and she wanted to get back to the hospital as soon as possible.

Billy and Gypsy threw some things into a suitcase, and she was devastated at the thought of Jazz living like this.

"I have to get out of here," Billy said.

"Let's go then. I can have someone over here tomorrow to pick up the rest. It won't be much, but I want to leave right now."

As soon as they left the room, they heard shouting from the parking lot, and when they got there, a barrage of questions rang out.

"Gypsy, look this way."

"Why are you here?"

"Are you having a secret affair?"

"What's in the suitcase?"

They pressed around her, but she circled around and managed to ignore them while she hurried Billy to the car. "How did they know I was here? Crap, this is going to end up on TMZ and the supermarket rags."

Billy flipped the visor down and peeked into the tiny mirror. "I look terrible."

Gypsy couldn't help but laugh, even if it was tinged with hysteria. "Let's not talk about this. Ever," she said. "I'm going to get you home."

After they left the paparazzi behind, she looked sideways at him. "I don't understand all the cloak and dagger here. Can you at least tell me why you won't talk to me?"

He looked out the window. "If—no, I mean when—Jazzy wakes up, you'll have to ask her. It's a promise I made a long time ago, please don't make me break it."

Gypsy was disappointed and burning with a need to know. "I respect your loyalty, but I'm dying here," she said. "Oh, god, sorry. Bad choice of words."

Billy continued to stare at the glass, and Gypsy let the silence hang. When they were close to Billy's exit, she tried again. "Billy? Are her nightmares connected to that night?"

He turned to look at her. "She told you about those?"

"No," she said and thought about the morning she woke her up, how frantic and jumpy she'd been. "I've witnessed the aftermath. I have to get her to talk with me, I can help her."

"I hope you do," he said. "And yes, it haunts her to this day." He said it with a finality she wasn't going to argue with.

"She's going to be fine," she said. "I know, I can feel that." Just as she knew she'd been distracting herself from Jazz's accident. At this point, did it matter whether or not Jazz had been hiding something? No, she thought, all that mattered was she was lying in that hospital bed and she needed to get through it to the other side. Whatever it was wouldn't change how she felt, how much she loved her, nothing would.

When she turned into Billy's driveway, she was relieved to see Jorge's car. He didn't need to be alone. "Good night, sweetie. I promise to call you the moment I know something."

"You better." He smiled, but it didn't reach his eyes. "Tell her I love her."

"I will. You get some rest."

He nodded, got out of the car, and walked up to the porch with his shoulders hunched as if he carried the weight of the world. Gypsy waited until the door opened and Jorge hugged him before he brought him into the house.

≈≈≈

On the way back to the hospital, Gypsy called

Tangie from her car. Twenty minutes later, she called her back.

"Okay," she said. "Handled. That particular nurse, McKenna, is on report for leaking the address she overheard." *Snap.* "Meanwhile, she's off Jazz's floor. She did, however, let them watch while she deleted pictures she'd taken of you on her phone. I hate rude people."

"Me too, Tang. I'm back at the hospital now."

"Everything's going to be okay. I've already rearranged everything on your schedule for a few days. Come to think of it, Roger was uncharacteristically accommodating about it."

"I'm going to text you an address. Could you please arrange for someone to box up all the personal items and bring them to my house?"

Snap. "Sure."

"What, no questions, my curious cat?"

"I figured you'd tell me later."

"I will. Also, I need to hire a private nurse. I don't know for how long until I see how she is and how long she's going to need to recover. I want you to find a reputable service for that."

"You got it. Make sure and tell Jazz how much we care, and we're all pulling for her."

"Absolutely. Thank you so much for everything. I don't know what I'd do without you."

"Good thing you don't have to." *Snap.* "Love you, boss, bye."

That girl deserved a raise, she thought. Now that she could let go of the details, Gypsy felt the weight fall off her shoulders and could concentrate solely on Jazz, her recovery, and care.

When she reached Jazz's room, Gypsy tightened her lips against the gasp that wanted to burst out of her throat. Jazz's left leg was in a full cast and in traction. Bruises looked violently red and purple against her pale, pale skin. Tubes and wires seemed to sprout from every direction. Gypsy couldn't compare the sight to anything other than what it was—Jazz being in a horrible car wreck. She looked small and defenseless under all the bandages, and Gypsy's instinct to protect and nurture went into full gear.

After she'd unpacked and put away the things she'd brought back, she made mental notes of what was still needed, then made her way to the side of the bed. Tangie and her ever-blessed efficiency had made sure the private room was stocked and comfortable. Though she was certain it hadn't hurt when Gypsy told her to spare no expense.

She slid her shoes off and after folding Jazz's hand in her own, leaned forward to rest her head near her shoulder, being careful not to jar her IV. "What happened to you, baby?"

Gypsy took a huge breath and finally let the tears she'd been holding out of their prison. She managed to cry softly despite the fact she wanted to sob her heart out. "I just found you."

She slipped into the place between wakefulness and sleep while staying aware for any changes from the monitors or any movement Jazz might make. Gypsy synced her breathing with Jazz's until she imagined their pulse beating in tandem.

"You don't get to leave me," she whispered.

She knew she was in a dream state when time became irrelevant, heartbeats her only reality. She floated in the warm darkness until she felt a beckoning toward a tiny light in the distance.

The light became an ember, the ember a flame,

and the flame a burning fire where Jazz stood in the center.

Gypsy jumped into the heat and finally let sleep take her.

❧ ❧ ❧ ❧

Jazz was disoriented, and every inch of her body hurt.

What the fuck?

Where was she and how did she get here? She felt as if she had a migraine, and her thoughts were sluggish. There were sounds around her that led her to believe she was in the hospital, and she searched for the reason.

The guardrail.

Her lids were heavy, but she managed to open them to find Gypsy inches from her face, staring at her. "Hey, gorgeous," she said. Her tongue felt like cardboard.

"Hello." Gypsy smiled. "You're probably thirsty."

"Read my mind." Jazz felt a stabbing pain in her ribs as she tried to sit up. "Fuck." She fell back.

"You're pretty banged up. Here, let me help you." Gypsy offered her a spoon of chipped ice.

"Thanks."

"Stupid question," Gypsy said. "But how do you feel?"

"Worse than I look."

"Oh, and Tangie wished so hard against that."

"Ha." Jazz drank her water through a straw. "I don't want to look into a mirror any time soon. How long have I been in and out?"

"Four days," Gypsy said. "But doc says you're definitely out of the woods now, and you're going to completely heal. We were so worried."

Four days? She struggled with the information. "Was I lucid at any time?"

Gypsy smiled. "You were asleep for two of them. After that, you said a few things here and there, though you were very cryptic and very insistent someone was in the truck with you."

Jazz searched for answers, but everything was so foggy. She was too high to remember and do any damage control. *Deflect.* "Did we have sex?"

"Are you kidding? We sold tickets, set the hospital on fire, then you pinched the phlebotomist's ass."

"Don't make me laugh, please, it hurts." Jazz held on to her side.

"I'm so happy you came back to me," Gypsy said. "We were all worried to death. After you ran off, I was sure it was something I did and the accident was my fault."

"Oh, honey," Jazz said. "That had nothing to do with you." She was still trying to find the details in her muggy memory bank.

"Then tell me what happened. Why did you order me upstairs and run off?"

Her stomach sank, and she really wanted another shot of morphine to escape into the haze she'd been in for days, or at least to put off the inevitable. She looked down at her lap. She picked up the cup to keep her hands still.

"I would never forgive myself if something happened to you." The lump in her throat came back.

Gypsy crossed her arms. "How about you let me worry about that? I'm not taking no for an answer." She looked meaningfully at Jazz in the hospital bed. "You can't exactly run off."

Jazz hadn't yet seen this mile-wide stubborn fierce streak, either.

"In case you haven't noticed," Gypsy went on, "I'm not a wuss. I can kick ass and take care of myself."

Jazz choked on her water. "I never said—"

"You didn't have to. Either you trust me or you don't, but that excuse you keep telling yourself you're protecting me is dead, and I'm not letting you get away with it anymore."

"Wow," Jazz said. "That told me."

"Hi, Lydia," Gypsy said to the nurse who walked in. "Look who's awake and interacting."

"Wonderful," Lydia said. "The doctor will be happy to hear it."

"How was your blind date last night?" Gypsy asked Lydia.

"Fine, it was fine." She paused and grimaced. "No, no, it wasn't. He bored me to death. All he talked about was his ex-wife."

"Kick him to the curb," Jazz said to Lydia, then turned to Gypsy. "How come you know so much about her?"

"Oh, I'm on a first-name basis with all your nurses," Gypsy said. "Billy said he'd be by tonight after he picks up Jorge."

"Can't wait," Jazz said. "We'll have a party."

"Sarcasm, ha," Gypsy said. "At least you can't leave, wild woman."

Lydia laughed. "You sound like a couple. I miss that. Anyway," she said to Jazz. "The whole staff is really surprised at how fast and well you heal. You're lucky. Are you excited to be able to go home with your girl the day after tomorrow?"

Jazz looked over at Gypsy. "Going home?" She

hadn't been able to think about it yet. Where was she going to go and be safe? "To your house?" Her stomach sank. It would put Gypsy right in the line of danger. "Who decided that?"

Lydia seemed to catch on to the energy building. "I think I hear my boss calling. I'll be back later." She rushed out.

"What's she talking about?" Jazz asked Gypsy, who was tapping her fingernails, red today, on the wooden armrest of the chair looking a bit sheepish. "I'd thought I had to be here at least a week, or I think that's what he said."

"If you think I'm going to let you go back to—"

Jazz interrupted. "You've been there?" She felt herself pale. She'd never intended for Gypsy to see that place. "Please tell me you weren't alone."

She shook her head. "Um, I went with Billy." She handed Jazz the tabloid paper sitting on the empty chair beside her. "What's this?"

"Page twelve," Gypsy said.

"Gypsy Tanner, queen of the paranormal and an unabashed out lesbian, was seen leaving this seedy motel on the arm of an unidentified male. What we want to know, Gypsy, is when exactly your *paradigm* changed."

"Oh, my god," Jazz said. "Really?" She laughed but then realized Gypsy might not think it funny. "Sorry."

Gypsy's eyes lit up. "It's hysterical. I've gotten quite a few calls that Tangie took care of. But nobody that matters believes the crap that's published in those papers. Price of being a celebrity, at least that's what they tell me." She winked. "Anyway, it's a good picture, right?"

"It is. Has Billy seen it yet?"

"Are you kidding? He had it framed."

"I want a copy, too."

Gypsy chuckled. "I'll make that happen."

"Now," Jazz said. "About going to your house."

"What about it? You're coming, and I'm not going to argue about it. I'm having a nurse checking on you when I'm not there."

"Honey." Jazz was aghast. "I can't afford that." She motioned around the room. "Or this place."

"But you don't need to worry," Gypsy said. "I've taken care of everything."

"That's just it. I don't want my girlfriend to mollycoddle me. I don't want you to pay for anything." Closer than it had ever been, hiding beneath her pride, her sadness welled up. She turned her head toward the wall because she didn't want Gypsy to see any of it.

"Jazz," she said. "Haven't you ever had anyone take care of you?"

Though it was somewhat disconcerting, as usual, Gypsy got right to the heart of the matter. She was amazingly astute. "Look," Jazz began to gear up for her argument. "I love you, and—"

"No, you listen, okay? It's going to happen just that way."

"When did you get so bossy?" Now what? Frustration was making her head ache. Jazz wouldn't go back to Billy's, and she shouldn't go back to the hotel because logically she knew she couldn't manage her injuries on her own. Jazz had never asked anyone for help. It felt humiliating to her. "I'll pay you back."

"I have money, Jazz. This isn't going to break me."

"It's your money, you worked hard for it."

"Yes." Gypsy got up and stroked her shoulder. "But I also have lucky DNA." She tapped, then walked her fingers up Jazz's chest. "You have some pretty lucky genes yourself."

Jazz would concede, for now. "Are you trying to distract me with sex?"

"Maybe." Gypsy looked relieved. "Is it working?"

"I'll make you a deal," Jazz said. "If after I finish telling you what's happening and you want to rescind your forced-upon-me invitation, I'll understand, and there won't be any hard feelings, okay?" She paused when she saw Gypsy's expression. "You haven't won yet, so stop looking like the cat that stole the cream."

Gypsy grinned. "But I do it so well. As far as your deal goes, I'll agree to it, but I want you to know I'm sick to death of the evasions. It can't be bad enough to change my mind about anything. It makes me feel disposable."

"That's not what I intended."

"I know that. Have you ever considered that not talking about it is what makes it so big? Bring the secrets out into the light and diminish their power so we can move on to better and bigger things."

"That told me," Jazz said again. "You're kind, beautiful, funny, smart, and super stubborn. I don't know why I'm with you at all."

Gypsy laughed. "Save it."

"And so charming, too." Jazz exhaled. Gypsy sat next to her and held her hand out.

Jazz took it.

Chapter Thirteen

Finally. Gypsy wanted to tie the ends together and be grateful she would finally know what was going on. She continued to hold Jazz's hand, making sure to keep her energy open and positive to help facilitate Jazz through what felt at this point to be a confession of epic proportions. "You want your drumroll?"

"There's that funny side again," Jazz said.

Though the comment had been sarcastic, Gypsy could see it had the desired effect because some of the tension lines around Jazz's mouth and she remained silent, Gypsy kicked into her interview mode to facilitate the beginning. "We left off where you had been trapped in the asylum, after being physically attacked."

Gypsy knew from her interviews, paranormal assaults could and usually did have very real, very traumatic aftereffects. The solution would have to be an approach at a deeper level.

"That's where it began," Jazz said.

"Okay," she said. "A horrible experience for anyone. I can understand why you don't want to talk about it. So far, I've heard nothing that's making me take a step back."

Jazz sipped water through a straw and stared for a moment. "The only person who knows the whole truth is Billy."

"I'm honored that you trust me, Jazz."

"Thank you. Okay, Stacy had been my girlfriend for more than a year at this point. We were in love and stupid with it at that age. She was my first love."

"I know that feeling," Gypsy said. "I like that you have a fond expression when you mention her, it says I'm right about your character. Tell me about it."

"After the hospital, I quit that place. Well, I walked off and never went back for my last check. I ended up getting a job at a fast food place where Stacy worked, but we had different shifts. It wasn't unusual for her to come over and slip into bed with me. One night, I felt her come in and I didn't turn around, but I felt the mattress dip. I knew she was there. I'm positive we had made love, but I couldn't tell you the details. I was in that wonderful floaty feeling before you fall asleep, you know? Where everything is magical?"

Gypsy nodded. "I do."

"The sun woke me up and I felt wonderful, relaxed, and in that state you're in when you've had great sex." Jazz covered her face with her free hand. "God, why am I telling you this? It feels incredibly inappropriate."

"You're trusting me," Gypsy said. "I asked you to tell me, it's okay."

"All right, but still. I turned to say good morning to Stacy, but she wasn't there. I thought, okay, no problem, she's up making coffee or something. Sometimes, she'd get up early and visit with my dad. Despite his drinking, he could be somewhat lucid in the mornings."

Gypsy let that go. There was a story there, as well, but she wanted Jazz to finish, and she hoped that telling her would be somehow cathartic for her.

"So I took my time in the bathroom, I didn't have to work that day. I was anticipating hanging out, maybe returning the favor. I finally go out to the kitchen, and my dad is sitting alone at the table in a bathrobe. I don't know why those specific details stand out, really, but they do."

"Important ones usually are." Gypsy smiled to reassure her.

"I asked him where Stacy was, and he'd said he didn't know she stayed the night. I didn't think too much about it, maybe he'd drank too much the night before, or something. Then I thought she must have left before Dad got up, which would have been unusual because she always left a note.

"I'm still feeling all warm and loose, and she's nowhere to be found, so I called her and woke her up. Very funny, I said to her. What time did you leave? And she asked me what I was talking about, she didn't come over. I thought she was joking. Of course you did, I say, I didn't have sex with myself. Stacy got really quiet and asked me who I *did* have in my bed last night. I told her to quit kidding around, and she insists she's not. I finally drop it because she's so pissed at me. Like it's my fault and I actually did sleep with someone else. I would have never cheated on her.

"I wasn't going to talk to my dad about it because, hey, it was about sex. I didn't talk to anyone about it. I relegated the whole experience to a very real, very vivid dream. But I've often wondered if that's how the door opened for this thing."

Ah, Gypsy thought. Here we are getting to how her story was currently relevant. The fact she was so upset warned her there was worse to come. "That would freak anyone out, Jazz, you're not alone."

Jazz nodded slightly, and she took another deep breath. "The next time, I *knew* it wasn't Stacy. She'd called me earlier and said her mother had asked her to come home after her shift because her father was having a bad night. He had cancer and was going through chemo at the time, and there would be no way Stacy would have ignored the request." She paused again as if looking into the past, then her expression faltered.

It was obvious to Gypsy she was struggling to find her next words. She leaned over and rubbed her good leg over the blankets. A gesture of understanding and love. She continued to look her in the eye to convey how she felt without interrupting the story.

"The second I came to the feeling of someone behind me, the tone changed. I heard whispers in my ear but couldn't make out the words. I was frozen for a second and tried to fly out of the bed. All pretense of being gentle disappeared. The whispers became a snarl, and I became paralyzed while it held me down."

Gypsy broke her silence. "Oh, my god," she said. "That's petrifying."

"You know," Jazz said and shook her head. "I know how ludicrous this sounds."

"I believe you," Gypsy said. "And I want to hear the rest. Just pull it off quick like a Band-Aid, I'm here for you."

Jazz tilted her head for a second before continuing. "I must have blacked out because I don't remember the details that time, either, but I remember waking up in a lot of pain. I thought being trapped was the worst night of my life, but this one topped it." Jazz took another drink of water. "After that, she, it, whatever started to terrorize me and come maybe once a week. It's hard to recall, it's been happening for so long. I'll never forget it, and I still shudder when I think of it."

"Who wouldn't?" Gypsy asked. "I'm heartbroken you went through this alone. You couldn't talk to Stacy?" She'd heard the underlying fear in Jazz's voice and the unspoken reality of continuing assaults, and it told her where they were going in the conversation.

"I tried telling her, but she didn't believe any of it. Long story short on that is she witnessed one of the attacks on me, then left and never came back. It's not her fault, I understand she was scared."

Gypsy wasn't going to say anything but decided she would, she had to get it out. "Don't you dare give her that excuse. She should have believed you in the first place, helped you, and not walked away. I'm sorry, it's none of my business, but that pisses me off."

Jazz raised her eyebrows but didn't address it. "I knew they had to be connected to the asylum, and who the hell wants to face that shit? I wouldn't have wished these experiences on my worst enemy."

"I have a few," Gypsy said.

Jazz laughed. "I can't believe you said that. Don't make me laugh, please, it hurts, it hurts."

To watch Jazz's amusement made Gypsy feel a little better for the comment she made. Though she wouldn't have abandoned Jazz, or anyone she loved for that matter, in her need. She hated to do it, but she needed to move her through it. "What happened that night, I mean the one she witnessed?"

"I was pinned to the bed, I couldn't move, couldn't scream, and I knew there was something, someone else in the room. She happened to turn over and see me, she thought I was having a seizure or something, and when it was over and I told her about it, she basically ran for the door telling me I needed a priest because I was probably possessed."

"We've had a guest dealing with sleep paralysis. The symptoms sound remarkably similar."

Jazz made a sound of derision. "I tried rolling with that. I went to talk with a so-called professional Billy made me go to after I told him of the night terrors I was going through. We wanted so desperately to believe it was something other than an entity had followed me home from that cursed forsaken place."

"Good for Billy. What happened?"

"God," Jazz said. "It was such a waste of time. They tried to give a scientific explanation. You know the one, the part of your brain that keeps your body in bed when you're asleep to keep you from acting out your dreams?"

Gypsy nodded. "I'm aware. It has something to do with chemicals. Your brain wakes up, but your body stays asleep. Did they have you participate in a sleep study?"

"Couldn't afford it. You don't really believe it's sleep paralysis?" Jazz's eyes snapped with anger.

That surprised Gypsy. "I'm just going through a mental checklist, honey. I can't get to solutions without eliminating the obvious, there's no need to be snarly. I didn't say that I agreed with them."

"I'm sorry, you're right."

"I don't want to be right, Jazz, I want to be helpful."

"I'm remembering how they treated me, and they all came to the same conclusion: I was crazy. Their bullshit explanation, their so-called scientific proof didn't pertain to what was happening to me. Their nice and tidy explanations didn't apply."

"I agree," Gypsy said. "I've always contested the theory. Why do others describe and have such detailed descriptions of who they call the hag? If it's a waking dream while you're immobile, why do thousands and thousands of people all over the world only suffer from horrific nightmares? Why don't they have pleasant ordeals also? Like say, walking on the beach at sunset? It should go both ways."

"Huh." Jazz nodded. "Good point, I hadn't thought of that. Anyway, that's kind of moot because they never took into account the shadows. Well, other than trying to convince you they're hallucinations. And it doesn't explain over a decade of attacks along with the poltergeist activity several people have witnessed over the years."

"We've *so* eliminated sleep paralysis," Gypsy said and mimed checking off a list.

"Could I have more water, please?"

"Of course." Gypsy poured another glass and handed it to Jazz before sitting on the bed. "You must be thirsty."

"I feel drained."

Gypsy smiled. "I can't imagine why."

"Again, it's the first time I've shared that side of it."

"Thank you for trusting me with it. We'll get into the entity activity you've mentioned and gather all the information we need to defeat it. So far, Jazz, none of this even has my psychic antenna quivering, let alone enough power to scare me away."

"My father didn't have a choice. To run, that is."

That took her by surprise. Jazz never talked about her family. Gypsy let the silence hang for fear if she made any comments, Jazz would stop talking about this sensitive subject. She was right, after a few seconds, Jazz continued.

"My poor dad. He fell apart after my mother left, and that's when he started drinking. Over the years, it progressively got worse until he was a full-blown alcoholic. It started picking on him."

"That makes perfect sense," Gypsy pointed out. "His alcoholism and his altered state could be a trigger, too."

"Yes, but at the time, I attributed it to the drinking. At this point, I was having the nightmares, slash attacks, maybe two or three nights a week but didn't put two and two together. I was too busy working and trying to keep the household going."

So much responsibility, Gypsy thought, for such a young woman. Jazz's energy was dimming and becoming darker, and she didn't want her to fall down the rabbit hole if she could help it. "You were very young. You're looking at events with hindsight, that wonderful tool we only pick up when we're older and wiser."

"Wonderful?" Jazz asked. "Was that sarcastic?"

Gypsy smiled. "Just a little. But it's true when you think about it. It's more of a reason to beat ourselves up when we look at past events. If you had known then what you know now, I promise you, you would have handled it differently."

"Huh," Jazz said. "I'll have to look at that later. I can only tell it from my frame of reference I have right now."

"Okay," Gypsy said. "You're right. Go on, please, I'm sorry to have interrupted."

"Anyway, he would hear banging and had eventually been scratched in his sleep, but at the time,

I believed he'd done it to himself. I would say to him, 'there, there, it's okay.'"

"I'm thinking that he'd probably done it before all this," Gypsy pointed out.

"Yes, but I'll still probably never forgive myself for that. For thinking he had the DTs and hallucinations. I should have known better. The only thing close to forgiveness I have for myself was that I'd been in denial. I tried so hard to put that night behind me. I didn't even pick up my last check. If it had been a million dollars, I wasn't going back. I insisted they mail it because I'd have rather eaten stale Top Ramen than get the money for groceries that week. I would give anything to block that memory forever."

"As would I," Gypsy agreed. "You're still being too hard on yourself."

"Not really." Jazz shook her head. "I *discounted* him. How hard that must have been on him."

Jazz turned away again. "This thing follows me everywhere and anywhere I've gone, it's found me. I'll skip the times I've tried explaining this to others and wasn't believed or told I was batshit crazy, and we'll fast forward thirteen years later when I moved here. It took a couple of months, then it…she…whatever, began to terrorize Billy. I had to leave to protect him."

"What happened?" Gypsy asked.

"A rerun of my life," Jazz said. "It starts with the attacks, then spreads out to include whoever is close to me. Candace was having nightmares, then the entity had a poltergeist party destroying Billy's kitchen and my bathroom."

Gypsy thought back. "The day I came over?" It made sense. She knew she'd felt something there that day, but she was easily distracted by her want and need to be with Jazz.

Jazz nodded. "For some reason, it has more strength here. I didn't have any grace period at all after I got to the hotel. The assaults were immediate."

"I may have an explanation for that," Gypsy said. "It's believed that Los Angeles has a ley line through it. Meaning the entire area is kind of a vortex for energy. Good or bad."

"Hmm," Jazz said. "Giving that theory credibility, if you think about it, people flock here by the thousands, and the city is either really, really good to you or really, really bad."

Gypsy smiled. "In a nutshell. I have several books that give detailed explanations and examples."

Jazz waved that off. "Not on my reading list right now. I just want to get through this. Maybe then you'll realize why I can't go home with you."

Gypsy didn't blame her. She couldn't imagine having to carry that self-imposed responsibility to keep everyone around her safe. What a tremendous weight it must be to carry it around for so many years. "Still not going anywhere."

Jazz didn't acknowledge her comment. "I had a particular violent night the day before I went to your house."

"The morning you were late and I saw your scratches?" Gypsy asked.

She nodded. "I knew I was going to tell you everything, but when I saw it outside the window threatening you, I had to leave. I couldn't live with myself if anything happened, if that *thing* hurt you in any way."

"You could have told me," Gypsy said. "It's not the first time something has shown up at my house. I might have been able to help."

Jazz looked down. "I couldn't take that chance. I've never let her out, so to speak. I protect the people I love and keep it close to me instead."

"Have you ever considered this thing wants you isolated? Not to talk about it? It could be the only thing providing it with power?"

She shook her head, and Gypsy filed the questions away for future reference to bring up again when Jazz was willing to look at the solutions.

"I was driving, worried about seeing it outside your window, then she popped in my truck and grabbed my hand, and we fought for the wheel." Jazz closed her eyes. "And that's pretty much all I remember before I went over."

"There are no words for how frantic and worried we all were. The thought of losing you kills me." And, she thought, the first chance she got, she hoped to annihilate the entity for it. Though it went against her sense of honesty, Gypsy held back the activity and nightmares in her own house. Jazz would only feel guilty. They could talk about that later, when Jazz wasn't so raw. "I'm so sorry this has been happening to you. All I can say is thank god you're going to get better. It's finally time to kick the hag's ass."

The corner of Jazz's lip twitched. "And you're the one to do it?"

"You're damn right," Gypsy said. "I'll fight for you. She won't win, I promise you."

Nurse Lydia appeared with her tray. "It's time for your meds, Ms. Miller."

"Jazz, please."

"Okay," she said. "I'm sure you're probably wanting this right about now." She held up the syringe.

Gypsy stood to the side while Lydia added the painkiller to Jazz's IV port.

Ten seconds later, Jazz's eyes drooped. "Sleepy, sorry."

"You rest. I'll be back later." Gypsy walked to the door, then turned back. "Oh, hey, is it okay if I share some of this, not the private stuff, I promise, with Tangie? She's trustworthy and knows everyone…"

"Who knows everyone," Jazz finished.

"She'd be a tremendous amount of help."

"I trust you," Jazz said, slurring her words a little. "Love you, Gypsy."

"Love you, too."

"Hey, babe?" Jazz opened her eyes.

"Yes?"

"Bad things happen in the dark."

Her chest ached. Jazz's voice was full of pain, and Gypsy said the only thing she could think of at the moment. "Then we'll leave the lights on."

Gypsy waited until she was in the elevator before she called Tangie to get this ball rolling. That bitch's reign of terror was going to end, and she didn't care what she had to do to accomplish it.

She had a lot to do before she brought Jazz home.

Chapter Fourteen

Jazz sat in Gypsy's dressing room and recalled the set of events that led her here, trying to bolster herself for what was coming.

From the moment she'd been wheeled into Gypsy's house, her nerves had been shot. Jazz seemed to always be holding her breath and waiting for an attack that had yet to happen, ready to leave on a moment's notice if anything threatened her, despite Gypsy's vehement denial.

So far, nothing out of the ordinary had occurred, but there had been lulls before. Jazz ordered herself to quit thinking about the possibilities. She would give anything to keep this peace. If all she got was this brief time, she'd still be grateful for it.

Boredom and anxiety aside, daily life had been awesome. Was there anything better than watching Gypsy walk in after work? The sight of her sitting on the deck and watching the sun set with her? She felt her face grow warm thinking about the times Gypsy had undressed, then proceeded to show Jazz that having a leg cast and cracked ribs could make sex tricky but not impossible. Was it any wonder Jazz was stupid in love with her?

It didn't stop her from feeling like a burden. Not only because she needed help, but because she didn't feel as if she contributed anything. Jazz had always paid her own way, had always taken care of herself for as long as she could remember.

It was the reason she was here preparing for her interview on *Paradigm*. Roger had come over one morning while Gypsy was at work and made her an offer she didn't feel like she could refuse. Once she got past her resentment he'd been snooping on Tangie's desk and had found her vague notes, she'd agreed to do it, with conditions.

She tried not to think about how pissed Gypsy had been that he had, in her opinion, bribed her to put her situation out there for entertainment.

After matching her own stubborn streak against Gypsy's, it was Jazz who'd insisted on going through with it.

She'd felt so much better after sharing what happened to her, Jazz hoped by doing it publicly, it might help someone else being terrorized who was afraid to talk. That it could open doors for them to seek help. And deep under that, there might be a sliver of hope that it might really be over.

Jazz had felt helpless for so long, it was hard to believe she *could* have hope. She wanted nothing more than to have a future with Gypsy and be free of her baggage.

She heard Tangie snapping her gum all the way down the hall.

"Hey, Jazz, doing wheelies in that thing yet?"

Jazz popped one and held the front wheels up while she spun around. "Pretty impressive, huh? I can't wait until the cast comes off."

"When?" *Snap.*

Jazz grimaced. "Ugh. Weeks."

"Well, they're ready for you. Are you ready for them?"

"As much as I'll ever be."

When Tangie reached for the handles, Jazz turned in a circle. "Just lead the way, please."

They set her up in front of the haunted stage's fireplace where deep shadows were created with studio magic to keep her shaded.

It was the main condition of her agreement with Roger. If any of her features did make it through the lighting, editing would make sure to blur them. She wore a hoodie, and they would film her below the shoulders. Because of the nature of her condition of anonymity, most of the show would be done in B-roll re-enactments behind Gypsy's and Jazz's narrative and inserted at a later time.

Gypsy kissed her on the cheek. "I want it on the record. You can back out if you want."

"Nope, I'm ready." Jazz's other condition was that everyone connected to the story was to also remain anonymous—the city, the asylum, Stacy, and Jazz's first encounter. Gypsy simply wouldn't bring any of it up. They'd decided together to protect the innocent, and because they legally had to, and by association, shield the guilty, as well. "Love you, let's get this over with."

"Your wish, my command, and all that. Love you, too," Gypsy said and smiled at her before crossing to her chair.

Jazz was relieved she didn't have to worry which camera was filming her and barely flinched when the clapper rang out.

"Welcome. Tonight on *Paradigm*, we have a special episode with Rose—"

Jazz couldn't help it, she broke into laughter.

"Cut," Smiley called out.

"Rose?" Jazz asked. "Where did you come up

with that name?"

Snap. "That was me," Tangie called from the other side of the set. "Joke, you know? Jasmine, flower?" *Snap.*

"Find another." Jazz laughed again and pointed at her. "Gawd."

Tangie tapped her chin. "Lily? Ha, just kidding. How about Carla? Can you live with that?"

"I don't care which one you use," Roger called out. "Time is money."

"Fine," Jazz said. "Let's go with that."

"Miller interview, take two."

"Welcome to *Paradigm*," Gypsy said. "I'm here with Carla, who prefers to stay anonymous…crap, I lost where I was going with that."

Now it was Smiley who laughed. "Cut. You never do that, Ms. I-can-do-every-scene-in-one-take Tanner."

The atmosphere was lighthearted, but Jazz felt her nerves slam down like bricks, her laughter faded.

"Um, Carla interview, take three."

"Welcome, and thank you for joining us on *Paradigm…*"

Jazz's ears began ringing, and she missed most of Gypsy's opening monologue, only really hearing the last line. "Thank you, Carla, for joining us to tell your story."

"You're…uh…welcome." She'd only just started, and she was anxious. Thankfully, she knew Gypsy would take care of her. They'd gone over the questions beforehand. Jazz didn't know if anyone else could tell how tightly controlled Gypsy's expression was.

There were so many people behind the lights, listening, watching, and she tried to ignore them and focus solely in front of her.

"Take us back," Gypsy said. "To the night *your*

paradigm changed."

Jazz cleared her throat. "Actually, I already believed in the paranormal. When I began working at the hospital, I'd seen, heard, and experienced many things that made me a believer." Jazz left it at that and skipped the asylum and its fakery, protecting the guilty, she thought again. And perhaps skipping possible lawsuits.

"I can imagine," Gypsy said. "If at one time I'd ever been a skeptic, I've witnessed more than enough in those places to become convinced." She paused. "Carla, can you tell us what happened that night, thirteen years ago?"

Jazz winked at her and watched Gypsy's mouth twitch while she tried to keep a straight face at the inside joke the line had become.

"I was working a graveyard shift at the hospital. The guy I usually rode home with went home early, and I missed the call. I ended up falling asleep."

"Graveyard shifts are hard."

"Right?" Jazz said. "Anyway, when I woke up and saw the texts, I tried calling other people I worked with, but no one answered, and I realized I was alone."

"You must have been scared," Gypsy said.

"Terrified is a better word actually." This was going easier than Jazz expected. She could only assume it was Gypsy's presence that made it so she'd almost forgot the cameras.

Almost.

"Go on, please." Gypsy prompted her.

"The only place with electricity was in the small part of the basement I worked, and when I left, I used my phone as a flashlight to find my way up to the front door exit."

"There wasn't any security?" Gypsy asked.

Jazz shook her head, then realized the camera wouldn't see it. "Yes, I mean no. At that time of night, security locked them to keep out kids and vagrants but mostly those amateur ghost hunters looking for chills and thrills."

Gypsy smiled. "I bet they got some along the way."

"A lot more than they bargained for, I'm sure. The building is notorious for its activity."

"Which only added to your horrible predicament."

"You're not kidding." Jazz still shivered with the memory of her flight through the hallway. She knew at this point production would insert the B-roll re-enactment. The slamming doors, the footsteps, and since she'd already viewed it, a clip of her beating her hands against the glass, the freaky fingers scraping her neck, and how she lost consciousness. She only had to pause briefly for a moment to give the editors a clean splice point.

When she'd watched the daily on it, in her opinion, the actress in the segment was excellent. She'd built up an illusion of heart-clenching fear, and the whimpers in the clip were so realistic, Jazz could have made them herself.

"Uh, yes," she said. "Horrible." She realized she'd lost her place and looked over to Gypsy for a cue where she was. Gypsy had told her of guests who were hard to interview, and she didn't want to be that way, the one who had multiple takes because she couldn't get it together.

"So what happened when you got to the main exit?"

Relieved at the save, Jazz continued the narrative that would run along with the actress's flight. She only had to remember and keep her story concurrent with it. "It was locked, security had already left, and it seems like I banged on that door forever. I tried to call for help, but my phone died, and I was left in the dark."

"I would have been petrified." Gypsy's expression was sympathetic.

"When I felt something scratch me from my neck down my spine, I screamed until I passed out. There isn't a word strong enough to describe how I felt."

She happened to glance to the side of the set and saw Billy and Jorge, and her gratitude erased some of the hard edges she was feeling.

Gypsy put her hair behind her ear. "I'd be hard pressed to hear of another experience so terrifying."

"I wouldn't wish it on anyone," Jazz said.

"So what happened next?"

"I'm not sure. I know I must have been out cold because I was told when I was rescued it had been more than four hours since my shift ended."

The re-enactment reel would play out being found by Billy and Stacy, her frantic crawl outside to the garden path, and the worried night guard holding his keys with a scared paternal look on his face. Then it would cut to the ambulance and the bandages on her hands.

"And that was the experience you believe to be the cause for your long ordeal?"

"It's what I know started my living nightmare," Jazz said and paused for ten full seconds as Gypsy had advised her earlier.

"Cut," Smiley yelled. "Short and sweet, love it. Take five, stretch, whatever."

Short and sweet? Jazz thought. It seemed like hours.

"Thanks, Smiley." Gypsy got up and came over

to her. "You're doing great."

"The actress is doing all the hard work," Jazz said. "She made it look real."

"You wrote it." Gypsy rubbed her shoulder, and Jazz was tempted to pull her down on her lap but decided not to because of the crowd. Instead, she waved at Billy and Jorge.

"We can still cancel this if you're uncomfortable."

"Do you say that to all your guests? Come on, Gypsy, all these people are here. I can do this."

"Since you've insisted," Gypsy said and sighed.

"Babe," Jazz said. "You're going to have to get used to someone else having their way."

Gypsy laughed. "I'll remember that. I love that about you."

"Thanks," Jazz said.

"For what? The backrub?"

"That too. I didn't think it would be as cathartic the second time around, but it is."

"That's good, though, right?" Gypsy asked.

Smiley ordered them to their marks.

Knowing where the conversation was going, Jazz's palms began to sweat. She was already hot and didn't know how Gypsy managed to look so cool under the hot lights directly above her.

Gypsy gave her another smile, the one usually reserved for their most intimate moments, and Jazz relaxed, still wondering how she'd ever got so lucky.

It was at that second, her perception of her long nightmare changed. Feelings came up, and she overflowed with adoration and gratitude. If all the events over the years had led her here, she'd suffer it all over again. The realization was so big, Jazz wasn't sure she could hold it in.

Aha, she thought, she could honestly say, her paradigm shifted. She was amused and couldn't wait to share it with Gypsy later. She sat across from her, knowing the lump in her throat wasn't at all from anxiety. It was love.

Jazz snapped back when Smiley called out.

"Carla, can you take us back again and tell us what happened after your ordeal?"

Jazz squelched the need to clear her throat again. They had already agreed not to talk about how explicit the first experience was and would instead discuss a much watered-down version of the events. "How many people start this part of the interview in hindsight?"

"Most all of them," she said. "Recently, in fact. I think in the beginning, people are too busy denying and justifying what's going on around them and that it's only with time, distance, and personal experiences we find where it really begins."

"Good point," Jazz said. "So, in hindsight," she chuckled, "activity began immediately. I didn't realize it as such because I didn't even want to remember what happened let alone analyze it."

"Perfectly understandable," Gypsy agreed, "for you to want to bury the trauma of it."

"Looking back, on the same night after I came home from the hospital, I can remember it started with my dog." Jazz had forgotten that until right that moment. "She usually jumped all over me, but that night, she shook and whimpered and was acting cautious because she kept backing away. I didn't really think too much about it. I assumed it was that my hands were bandaged up like boxing gloves."

"I've heard animals always know. That they're torn between wanting to be near and being frightened by a negative energy."

"Exactly," Jazz said. "From that night on, she slept in my father's room. The way I recall the next chain of events is this, and I'll try to leave out most of the denial and excuses or we'll be here until next Wednesday."

Gypsy smiled at that. "We're interested in hearing what you have to tell us."

They'd practiced this. "I started having dreams. At first they were kind of sexy. I was young, and my hormones were all over the place. I didn't think anything about having them." She paused, happy to have been able to cut down the nightmare within the nightmare down to one sentence. It was still hard, but she knew sharing the actual experience with Gypsy beforehand had gone a long way to erasing her guilt and shame. It was easier to act nonchalant as she continued.

Jazz took a deep breath and dove in. "Then they turned to where I was constantly being chased, but I attributed that to being trapped at the asylum."

"That wouldn't be a bad assumption," Gypsy said. "I would think that would be normal, given the circumstance."

"If I saw a shadow out of the corner of my eye, I was desperate to assume it was my imagination. I took all the hours I could get at my new job. I hated it, but I didn't want to be at home. I guess on a subconscious level, I knew there was something wrong. Something not normal was creeping paround.

"More hindsight, it picked on my father first." By agreement, they were also going to leave out her father's drinking.

She swallowed the lump the memory brought and kept going. "When he told me that the television was turning off and on, things were flying out of the cupboards, I didn't believe him. I would just say, 'there, there, it's okay.' He was being terrorized, and I was in denial. I came home from work one day, and the kitchen was destroyed. I blamed him." She recalled but didn't share the crawling; rustling sounds she'd heard outside her door late at night were in fact her father trying to get to his room after a binge.

"From what I've heard, it sounds like a poltergeist," Gypsy said.

"I know that—now. I finally had to take my head out of my…uh…the sand and truly open my eyes to what was obvious. That thing terrorized him."

Gypsy looked down at the notes. "You said your dad was handicapped. Some experts in the paranormal believe entities choose the most vulnerable for a way in."

"Yes, my father was…" Jazz hesitated and stopped when she realized she'd about said he was impaired. *And his altered state by default was drunk. It had been a perfect invitation for the hag I brought home.* "My dad was scared, and I was scared for him. I stopped working so many hours, and now that I was paying attention, I began hearing things. First tapping on the wall coming from rooms no one was in, and when I would get up to look, it would stop. Over time, it became louder and more insistent. The taps became knocking, which became banging so hard the pictures on the wall would shake."

"I know exactly what you mean," Gypsy said. "It's almost as if it's calling for attention, saying notice me, notice me. I think that behavior is designed to keep you off balance and fearful."

"Yes, you're right. That's a good way to look at it.

Anyway, the activity escalated from there. The house, especially the hallway, would be chilly, then cold, then to the point it was downright freezing. We'd hear footsteps all hours of the night, the electronics in the house would fritz for no reason, and the lights were freaking out all the time. The air was always so thick, you know?"

"Dark and heavy?" Gypsy asked.

"Exactly," Jazz said. "I felt I could cut it with a knife. At this point, it started leaving my dad alone and concentrated on me. It centralized into my room, and it felt different. As if someone was always there and yelling at me an inch away from my ear. I always felt as if there was something under the bed. You know, where you're afraid to hang your feet or hands over the mattress? I knew it all had to be connected, and while I was scared out of my mind, I was pissed, too. Why me? It wasn't my fault I got locked in that damned place. In the end, my emotions probably gave it just what it wanted or needed to get stronger."

"Another point," Gypsy said. "They feed off negative emotions."

"At the time, I had no clue, but I would wake up and know something was in the room with me. I was paralyzed and couldn't move, but I knew it was there. And I knew it was going to happen again. There isn't a word I can use that's bad enough for the terror and helplessness I felt when it would approach me. At times, the hag would stand at the end of my bed and stretch until she nearly hit the ceiling. Other times, she hovered inches above me, making me look at her, and since I couldn't close my eyes, I had no choice. She can shift between the hag and a demonic-looking figure with red eyes. She looks horrid, her long hair hangs in ropey strands, she has empty black eyes, and her ugly hands have ragged nails." Jazz shivered. "She *is* your worst nightmare come to life. Worse than any movies I've seen with possessed people."

Gypsy tapped her nails against her notebook. It was, Jazz knew now, her thinking mode.

"It sounds absolutely repulsive. I still can't imagine how you've coped all these years."

Jazz didn't answer her comment but continued. "I would be overcome with a nauseating dread, and I swear it would wait until I was scared enough to scream, but of course, I never could. The hag would crawl up my legs, slither up my body, and pin me to the mattress. Where her skin touched me, it burned like dry ice. It would laugh in my face, call me names, and say horrible things I can't repeat here. Every time it happened, I thought I was going to die."

"You're talking in past tense," Gypsy said. "Do the attacks still occur?"

"Yes," Jazz said. "The entity hates me with a passion I can nearly taste."

"Some would argue this could be sleep paralysis because of the classic symptoms of the hag, so to speak."

She and Gypsy decided it was best to have a short answer to address the sleep paralysis and not get into a drawn-out conversation about it. "I might have believed it was—if not for the poltergeist behavior and the fact there'd been no paranormal anything in our house before I was trapped in that haunted place. I might have even been talked into believing a little of the theory if that thing, the entity, hadn't begun to leave marks. Deep red scratches and bruises most everywhere on my body. The only thing I can agree with and is a fitting description is that people all over the world describe it as a hag. And it fits."

Jazz blew out a breath to simmer down her anger before she continued. "Anyway," she said. "The attacks continued, and the banging and dish-throwing went on. No matter what conclusion those doctors came to, the attacks went on. And on."

"Did they suggest medication?"

Jazz almost wished the camera would pick up her snarl. "They talked me into sleeping pills, which didn't work. When they started making noises I might be schizophrenic, I never went back."

"I hate that," Gypsy said. "The paranormal is outside their paradigm, so they blame the victim and suggest it's a mental health issue. You had physical proof."

"Which they dismissed as self-inflicted."

Gypsy wasn't even trying to hide her anger, she let it show. "I hate bullies, skeptics, especially doctors, when they refuse to shift aside their egos and try, even a little, to open themselves up to anything other than their pompous beliefs."

Surprised, Jazz didn't know what to say. She let the pause hang for a second, in case they wanted to edit out Gypsy's little tirade. She really hoped they didn't. As corny as it sounded, Gypsy really was beautiful when she was mad and protective.

Gypsy pulled it together. "Is this when you decided to get help from the paranormal community?"

"No, that was decided when I saw something crawling on my bedroom ceiling." It was the most, freaky fucked-up thing Jazz had ever seen. She hated when that happened with a passion. And the hag *knew* it.

"Good lord," Gypsy said. "I would have run out

of the house screaming."

"I pretty much did, but who was I going to call? Ghostbusters? I had no idea, and my father wasn't much help. We hadn't been to church in years, but a friend of mine finally found someone who would come out to the house. Their explanation was I must be possessed, and I'd have to find a clergyman to perform an exorcism."

"What did you think about that?"

"I pretty much told them God had never helped me before, why would he start now?" It brought up the memory of her as a young girl who prayed every day for her mother to come home, and each night for her father to stop trying to kill himself one drink at a time.

"So," Gypsy said. "What happened?"

"They brought over a minister anyway. They prayed, threw holy water on me, and waved a cross in my face."

"Then what happened?"

"I got wet," Jazz said and laughed. "No, really, they did their rituals throughout the house and over me. They said they chased it to the basement, and couldn't I see how much colder it was down there? I told them it was winter, it was supposed to be cold. They told me they'd gotten rid of it, and didn't I see how bright the house was?"

"And was it?" Gypsy asked.

"No, but if it would get rid of them, I'd agree."

"Did any of it work?"

"No, it only seemed to piss the entity off. Things actually got worse after that."

"I'm sorry to hear that."

"I've tried other things, as well. Psychics, other denominational priests, something called a deliverance."

"Is that a ritual that involves several religious beliefs?"

"Something like that, but none of it worked. It still continued to come every night and throw stuff around, usually just in my space. It became all terrible, all the time. A virtual Evil R Us."

Gypsy's expression was pure compassion. "It must have been trying to have any kind of relationships."

Jazz paused. "Impossible. When I became close to anyone, it would chase them away. No one wants to be with someone who comes with that kind of extreme baggage." Not one, Jazz thought and recalled one woman in the past she truly cared about who left screaming and never returned her calls after that.

"So, this hag, entity, it wanted to keep you isolated to terrorize you."

"It worked. My life got to the point where I didn't let myself get attached to anyone. They didn't understand, and I stopped trying to explain the situation over a decade ago."

"You must have been very lonely," Gypsy said.

Jazz shrugged, forgetting again the camera might not pick it up. "I got used to it. I still had my father and my best friend, Ricky." She made Billy a pseudonym on the spot. It was the first name to pop into her head, and he'd have to live with it. "They'd witnessed the activity and always loved me without judgment. Well, up until the time Ricky moved across the country."

"Carla, you said this has gone on for thirteen years. I can't imagine the fortitude it takes to go through this. Most people would go stark raving mad."

"Who says I'm not?" Sarcasm was still her first reaction, but she knew Gypsy wouldn't take it personally. It was her defense against the hurt she was feeling walking through these memories.

"You sound lucid to me," Gypsy said. "I think you're strong. What did you do then?"

"I moved. And when the entity found me, and it always did, I had to move again. I couldn't put the people around me through it."

"You lived with it all this time?"

Jazz nodded, then remembered to answer. "Yes."

"Thank you, Carla, for sharing your experience with us. I think here at *Paradigm* we can do better than that. Will you accept our help and come back at a later date to update us?"

"Sure, and thank you for having me."

After the scene was cut, Tangie said Jazz could leave the set while Gypsy tied up a few ends with Smiley and Roger.

Jazz hung out in the hall for a few minutes, then decided to wait in the dressing room. It paid to know the host, she thought with humor. She didn't have to wait in the green room, and in any case, it wasn't green at all but stark white.

"You did great." Gypsy caught up, then kept pace with Jazz's wheelchair.

"It wasn't as bad as I thought it would be actually."

Tangie came up behind them. *Snap.* "Good show and good news. I've seen how the B roll looks that show your experiences. They look awesome. Super scary. This will be a viewer favorite."

"I'm glad to entertain," Jazz said. She knew her retort sounded snarky, but Tangie didn't pick up on it.

"Well, it has everything. You know, I'm sorry it happened to you and all, but the paranormal community is going to love it. Oh, and Billy and Jorge told me to tell you they'd see you later." *Snap.* "More good news, I just heard from Alayna Edgar."

"You did?" Gypsy looked wary. "And did the team of psychics and clerics we sent work to help her get rid of the damn mother-in-law?"

Tangie smiled. "Yes. One of the psychics, our favorite by the way, Shelia, managed to find the source. Evil MIL had bound her blood into one of the large stones of the fireplace with the help of a voodoo priestess."

"Sounds like a movie," Jazz said. "Blood and bones, curses and spells."

"Actually," Gypsy said, "from my experience, it's much like that."

"Once they learned what had been done, they called another priestess in, and she helped them remove the stone, reverse the curse, cleanse, and bless the rest of the house, and voilà." Tangie waved her arm dramatically. "Then they sent the entire entourage to Junior's house. Anyway, Alayna said she'd call you later and fill you in on all the details."

"I'm so happy and relieved to hear that," Gypsy said. "After how easy it was to remove the poltergeist for the Parkers, I felt guilty that the Edgars were still suffering."

"Well." *Snap.* "All's well that ends well."

Jazz yawned. "I'm exhausted."

"Don't you feel a bit lighter, as well?" Gypsy asked. "Bringing light to the shadows you buried for so long?"

"Yes, of course, but draining. Can we go home now?"

"I'll take you," Tangie said. "Gypsy has meetings for the rest of the day."

"Oh, okay, I forgot about that. Guess I'm more

than a little squirrelly."

Gypsy kissed Jazz goodbye and assured her she'd be home as soon as possible.

On the way to Malibu, Jazz fell asleep but woke when she heard Tangie struggling to get her chair out. "Sorry for nodding out. The interview drained me but Gypsy was right. I do feel better."

"Might be the drugs, too, Kimosabe, but yes, she's always right."

Jazz laughed. "Good to know."

Tangie squinted against the sun. "It's going to be all right, you know. There hasn't been a case yet we haven't been able to help on."

They made it into the door, and Tangie reached to help her down the two stairs into the living room. "No," Jazz said. "Watch this." She pulled up the front wheels and bounced down them.

"Cool beans." *Snap.*

"Lots of time on my hands, ha ha, to practice." She rolled over to the glass doors and looked out at the ocean. "Jesus, there couldn't be a more peaceful place to be an invalid."

"You make her happy."

Jazz turned to look at her. "Abrupt subject change."

"I work for her, and I believe us to be good friends. I've never seen her like this." *Snap.* She looked Jazz dead in the eye. "You're almost good enough for her."

"I'm working on it, Tang. I'm working on it."

"Look, I have to get back. Don't worry, okay? I have interviews set up for different paranormal professionals. If one fails, I have several more on tap."

Jazz sighed. "I've tried several rituals over the years. A few worked for a while. It always finds me."

Tangie kissed her on top of her head. "Have a

little faith. They weren't my contacts, and you didn't have me and Gypsy on your side."

Surprised at the affection, Jazz only nodded and turned back to the view. "Faith? I'm a little short on that."

"That's okay. We have enough for all of us." *Snap.* "See ya."

After Tangie left, and though she was rusty at it, Jazz Prayed to a God that she still wasn't quite sure was there.

It was a start.

Chapter Fifteen

Jazz was exhausted, drained further than she ever thought possible.

The last couple of weeks had been hell.

Witches, warlocks, priests, ministers, and psychics.

Oh, fucking my.

All claimed they could help.

Each one failed, and with each session with said denominations, hope skittered and slipped farther away.

And with another nightmare the previous week, last night, and the night before, Jazz had none left. She was back to feeling she'd have to leave at any minute. It was only a matter of time before the entity was strong enough to manifest again. Only a matter of time, she thought sadly.

Gypsy had ordered her out of the house that morning to spend the day with Billy.

They spent it on one of his famous shopping marathons, which she actually enjoyed this time because Billy was forced to slow down, and she didn't mind having to hold his bags while she was sitting in the wheelchair. She let herself be entertained during lunch as he gave his running commentary on the people who passed by. It was almost like old times.

At least she stayed awake during the drive home. She was grateful that with each day that passed, she had a little more vitality. This forced into being an invalid thing was worse than she could have imagined. And in the back of her mind, as she gained energy, so did her nemesis. The knowledge haunted her most of her waking moments. She was learning to be adept at hiding it from Gypsy.

They sat in Billy's car in her driveway.

"I really wish you would let me help you," he said as Jazz hopped out on her good leg, opened the back door, and reached around for her wheelchair.

"I need to do it myself. Besides, I've been practicing on the crutches. Though I wouldn't have been able to use them today being dragged around the mall."

Billy sighed dramatically. "The things we do for friends, right?" He laughed. "So what's going to happen in there?" He pointed toward the house.

"Does it matter? Whatever Tangie and Gypsy cooked up is going to fail like all the rest."

"If you think it's going to, it will."

Jazz cut him off. "Here we go." Jazz managed to pull out her chair. She was getting good at it. "I'm going to hear another one of your positive thinking lectures."

"Hey, don't judge. It works."

"Don't get defensive," Jazz said. "None of it has worked. Zero, nada, zilch. I repeat, nil, buddy."

He sighed. "What was the excuse for the last one?"

"That I'm not possessed, therefore, it's not their fault it didn't work. They're not returning calls at this point."

He nodded to the black truck by the curb. "What's that one going to do?"

She knew she was acting nonchalant and keeping a brave face for Billy, but deep down, she was worried. She didn't know if she could take any more of these disappointments. "Something super-secret that no one is supposed to know about. Some kind of out-of-body experience thing. I think Gypsy said she's a Sky Soldier. And yes, I'm going to say it. If I tell you the rest, I have to kill you." She laughed. "Can you imagine? A Sky Soldier?"

"Don't be like that. Have you ever tried one?"

"No. I doubt I would find one in the yellow pages."

"Ha," Billy said. "Wait, no one ever uses those anymore, do they?"

"Hardly, but I betcha I could get a thousand or more hits on Google if I wanted to look it up."

"You're so funny today. Not. How can you make fun of it if you've never heard of the ritual?"

"Sorry, Billy. I really am. It's not that I mean to scoff or belittle this woman. You're right, I don't know her, but I've gone through prospects at an alarming rate, and my expectations were low to begin with." Jazz settled into her chair. "I've got it from here."

"Are you sure you don't want me in there?"

"Please, let me at least try to keep you safe. Gypsy gives me no choice when it comes to her."

"She loves you."

"I know." As wonderful as that felt, she couldn't help but feel bad about what had become a circus to her. God, she just wanted this to be over, so they could lead a normal life. Maybe get married, if Gypsy would have her. But not, Jazz ordered fate, until this was over.

Billy kissed her cheek. "See ya. Call me when it's over, please?"

"Absolutely. Love you and drive careful."

He waited until she wheeled up to the door, then took off.

God, she hoped this wasn't a farce. Gypsy held this

dream soldier Una in such high regard, Jazz wanted to keep her doubts close and her sarcasm to a minimum. She had serious reservations this experience would go the way it was promised to. Who'd ever heard of dream travel? She hadn't. Not to mention Gypsy said they might be able to interact with the dead.

Worse, even worse than that, they were supposedly going back to the beginning of Jazz's ordeal. Her shoulders slumped. There had been absolutely no arguing with Gypsy. She insisted she was going to complete the ritual with Jazz. God, she was the most stubborn person Jazz had ever met. The best thing at this point to do was humor them both.

Gypsy led her to the living room where she introduced the other woman. Una's hair was long and red, contrasting with her dark complexion. Her eyes were shockingly light blue, nearly white, her entire appearance seemed otherworldly.

Fitting, Jazz thought. "It's nice to meet you."

Una laughed. "You're thinking I'm a crackpot and hoping this isn't another waste of your time."

Jazz stuttered. "That's not…"

Gypsy put a hand on her arm. "It's no use protesting, Una can hear your thoughts."

"Ah." Jazz looked away. Now this was awkward. "Sorry."

"It's fine, I get that a lot," Una said. "I've learned to turn it off and on." She grinned. "Right now, it's on."

In the middle of the room, three blanket pallets were in a circle around a low table in the center where herbs were already smoking and several candles in assorted colors burned around the perimeter.

Una was taking several various-sized packages wrapped in cloth out of her huge bag. "We're going to lie down with our heads in the center and our feet facing the outer circle." She carried the parcels to the table. "If you have an item, something that reminds you of a family member who's passed, bring them to me."

"I don't have anything." Jazz folded her arms. "Guess this isn't going to work."

"Wait," Gypsy said. "You said 'remind.' So it doesn't need to actually have belonged to them?"

Una looked over her shoulder at them, and Jazz wondered how she could be so calm thinking she was going to have to battle a demon. Unless, of course, she knew it couldn't be done. It would just be another monumental failure. Well, there goes the no sarcasm promise to herself. Jazz looked at the floor when Una smiled at her.

Crap. She was going to have to be even more careful.

"It doesn't have to be something they owned. Any possession that holds a memory of a certain individual is infused with energy through yours." She paused. "Powerful magic."

Jazz racked her brain. "I have an old picture of my mother and her sister."

"That'll work."

"I don't know," Jazz said. "That whole side of the family is crazy."

"Even better," Una said and continued to put items on the table.

Gypsy laughed. "Sorry, I was just thinking of my Uncle Jimi, he loved a good fight. And um, cigars, yeah."

Una smiled back. "Bring him on in then. We could use him."

"I'll be right back." Gypsy darted out of the room.

Jazz opened her wallet and dug in the back of it

to pull out a small picture of two teenage girls, one of them her Aunt Mary.

"Who's the other one?"

Jazz swallowed. "My mother, Sally, her twin."

Una closed her eyes and held the photo between her palms. "Your mother is not on the other side, but there is separation, yes?"

"I wouldn't know if she was dead," Jazz said. "She left us a long time ago."

Una looked at her, then tilted her head slightly. "Do you want to find her?"

"You can do that?" Jazz was surprised but only gave it two seconds of thought. "Nope. Not interested, but thank you."

Gypsy returned with some jewelry, photos, and a cigar clipper, and handed them over. She pulled at Jazz's arm. "You look nothing like her."

"I'm the spitting image of my father and happy for it. Can we not talk about her anymore?" She studied what looked like branches, moss, and twigs tied together, other pictures, and by their appearance, probably of Una's family, a wallet, a church hat, and peculiarly, an unopened can of Coke. *What?*

"My grandmother loved them. It's an offering." She pointed at other items still in their wrappings. "Some of them are very private, and we'll leave those covered." She then took out a large knife and placed it in the middle. She looked over at Jazz. "It's a ritual symbol of our intention to fight. You can't actually use it."

"What are all these other things?"

"Stuff," Una said. "I can't go into the details, I took a sacred oath. I *can* tell you the ability has been passed down to the daughters from generation to generation until me, and when it's time, I will pass it on to mine, as well."

"But it boils down to having the ability to separate from our conscious bodies and astral travel?" Gypsy nodded. "So, in other words, kids, don't try this at home?"

Una laughed. "Funny, har har."

"Seriously, I can't tell you how much we appreciate the fact you came."

"You don't have to. I can feel it, just as I know Jazz doesn't have an ounce of faith this will work."

"I didn't say…never mind. What happens if the entity doesn't show up?"

"The demon, entity, hag, it, or whatever you choose to call it will come. If it doesn't, we'll take the fight to her." Una tapped her temple. "Because of the other things you tried, the entity is licking its wounds right now and is pissed. Literally, it's as if you've been poking a bear with a stick." Una lit more herbs and sage in the black bowl, then white candles on her altar table.

She handed them each a teacup and a large crystal. "Drink this, and make sure you hold on to that."

"Alice in Wonderland?" Jazz laughed nervously. "Anyone?"

Una took her own drink and downed it. "Lay down."

Jazz drank it and did as she ordered. "God, this is nasty."

"But necessary," Una said and lay back herself.

"Ick," Gypsy agreed, then turned to Jazz. "Whatever happens, I love you."

Jazz reached for her hand. "Love you, too. Be careful."

"Will do, and back at the both of you."

"Okay, kids," Una interrupted. "There are places in the world where evil really does dwell, and this hospital is one of them. The amount of pain and suffering experienced in its walls only brings more to it. It's more than a building, more than the souls trapped there. It was and is a playground of sorts for sadists, rapists, and the like on both sides of the bars. Not one of those souls belongs there, and they need to move on one way or another. Now close your eyes."

Not a ringing endorsement for her trip, Jazz thought. "What do we do now?"

Una chuckled. "Now we go kick her ass."

❧ ❧ ❧ ❧

Gypsy felt as if she were falling in a rabbit hole.

Weightless, she fell down, down, down.

Her body felt light and tingled, her stomach lurched, and she briefly wondered if what they drank might have hallucinogenic properties. She dismissed that notion. Una would have warned her. She could have, however, cautioned her about how hard she would land.

Her eyes took a few seconds to adjust before she looked around. "Jazz?"

She was alone.

Gypsy registered the cold concrete she was lying on, and when she got up, the sign on the wall opposite read *First Floor*.

First floor of what? Yet another sweep of her surroundings revealed she was in the hallway from her nightmares. She shuddered with the realization that they did indeed get where they needed to confront the entity.

"Jazz? Where are you?" The air felt heavy, and Gypsy strained to hear any noise, but her ears felt stuffed with cotton.

All of it was weird and disconcerting, but being alone was worse.

She startled at the giggle behind her, and knowing it wasn't Jazz or Una, she hurried forward.

The hall itself stretched to an impossible length until she couldn't see the end.

Her hand hurt, and Gypsy looked down and saw she was holding the crystal Una handed her before they left the circle. Her fingers were bleeding. She loosened her grip, then stuck it in her pocket. She could see about any injury later.

She ran on.

Disbelief shocked her when she turned and found she hadn't moved twenty feet beyond the reception desk.

Shouting from the distance drew her attention toward the other end.

Gypsy began running again.

❧ ❧ ❧ ❧

Jazz fell the last four feet, igniting sharp pains in her hip and shoulder. Her first thought was for Gypsy as she leapt to her feet, barely registering her cast was gone, and she *could* stand.

Jazz spotted Una, who was already standing, and crossed to her on shaky legs. "Where's Gypsy?"

"I don't know, but I feel she's safe."

"We have to find her."

"Yes, and we will."

They turned to the double doors, and Jazz recognized the area they were in.

Holy fuck, it worked.

The hospital.

She'd just taken three steps when the doors opened with a crash, bouncing off the walls and back again.

"Wait," Una said and grabbed her arm. "It's not safe."

"Gypsy's out there."

"I said she's fine," Una snapped at her. "Stay close."

Jazz whispered, "We have to get to her, she must be so scared."

"We have more important things to worry about right now."

"Yeah, like what? What could possibly mean more than the woman I love?" Her patience snapped, and anger replaced her fear.

Una's grip tightened on her arm. "Them."

"What are you talking…?"

The harsh fluorescent lighting zapped on, and the space looked nothing as she remembered. Mold and mildew disappeared as the walls stitched themselves back together, and graffiti erased itself. Trees and vines disappeared as wire-meshed glass filled in the broken frames. Tables and worn sofas and chairs manifested, decades of neglect were erased. The day room filled with people.

It was as it must have looked when the place was still in operation, and Jazz knew she'd never witnessed such a heartbreakingly horrific sight in her life, the sad attempt to have a bright spot in this cursed place. Watercolor paintings reminiscent of kindergarten attempts hung on the walls, checkerboards, decks of cards, and other harmless distractions were around the room.

Jazz stood as still as a statue as patients seemed to go about their day. Una's fingers twitched on her arm. "What?" she asked, keeping her voice low as possible.

Una's eyes were wide as she scanned the room. "I didn't expect so many."

Jesus. If Una was worried, Jazz was beyond that. And what was Gypsy going through out there all on her own?

✥ ✥ ✥ ✥

Though she went nowhere, Gypsy continued to run. She ran until she collapsed. Her need to get to Jazz overcame her fear and exhaustion, and she struggled to get to her feet again. The sweat that dripped from her hair and body pooled around her, and she slipped onto her knees. She gasped against the pain but finally gained her feet, and as she leaned against the wall for support, the lights went on.

She didn't know why, but she was more afraid of it and the way the hospital renewed itself than stumbling in the darkness. She blinked several times against it, and as her eyes adjusted, she spotted a figure down the hall. When she took a step, she gasped and drew his attention.

An elderly man appearing to be a janitor mopped the floor in a sweeping motion from left to right. "Now what are you doing out here?" he asked. "You know you're supposed to be in your room."

Gypsy was terrified but then registered what he'd said. "Oh, I'm not…"

"Hurry," he hissed, then looked down another hall she couldn't see from her position. "She's coming, now go." He pointed with his mop behind her. "Now," he repeated.

Gypsy turned and went that direction back toward reception. Nurses sat at the desks and behind the counter, but they didn't seem to notice or register her presence.

What the hell was going on?

A voice whispered in her ear. *Hide.*

Gypsy looked frantically one way, then the other. Nothing but closed doors. Her only option was the desk at the station. She prayed she'd stay unnoticed and crawled swiftly sideways and around the nurse's legs to hide under the desk. She bit her lip at the pain in her knees and curled up.

Where is Jazz? As she hid, the sentence became a mantra she used to keep herself from going stark raving mad.

❧❧❧

An old man walked by, shuffling in his slippers along linoleum scarred by what looked to have been a thousand trips back and forth.

A meticulously groomed woman played cards with another who looked as if she hadn't brushed her ratty hair in months.

A skinny young man stood in the corner yelling for everyone to repent their sins because they were all going to hell, over and over. The sound rattled Jazz's already overstimulated nerves.

The rest of the patients scattered around the room. Another young man in a wheelchair turned circle after circle in place, going faster than what seemed humanly possible.

Then the screaming started.

The wave of sound came from every direction, and Jazz backed up along with Una into the center of the room.

Several burly orderlies ran in, and Jazz watched in horror as they began beating the patients, and a cacophony of screeching intensified, piercing her eardrums, and the pain of it nearly bent her in half.

"Shut up, you fucking freaks. Shut the fuck up." One of the men slapped the well-dressed woman who crumpled to the floor.

The old man took off his slipper and batted at them, having no more effect than a fly swatter. The orderly backhanded him into the wheelchair-spinning teenager.

"Repent, repent, repent," the patient in the corner screamed, then began laughing maniacally as he struck his head against the wall, paying no apparent heed to the bleeding it caused.

Jazz's stomach was turning flips as panic set in during the bedlam.

"Try to calm yourself," Una said and locked elbows with her. "It's all just a distraction."

"Calm?" Jazz's eyes felt as if they would pop, but as her mind attempted to take it all in, she had no idea how to process it or react.

Fight or flight?

Una's body tensed next to hers. There was no way in hell Jazz would run, she had to go through them to find Gypsy.

The noise stopped instantly, and in the absence of sound, Jazz could hear her pulse pounding and

Una's heavy breathing.

As if they were puppets, every person in the room swung around, and terror choked Jazz as the crowd stepped, hobbled, or wheeled toward them.

Una shifted until she and Jazz stood back to back. "Get ready," she said.

"Ready?" Jazz asked. "For what?"

❧❧❧❧

The phone rang incessantly, and the old-fashioned bell tone was driving Gypsy crazy, as if being here weren't bad enough.

The nurses either didn't hear it or ignored it until Gypsy wanted to scream.

Answer it, answer it.

The second it stopped, an alarm went off, and Gypsy felt her entire body jump.

The nurse above her said, "We have to move."

"You know it's my first night, what's the alarm for?"

"It means lockdown. Patients are loose in the ward."

"Whadowedo?" the younger one screeched, her words tumbled together.

"Shut up and follow me."

Gypsy couldn't hear any more over the sounding alarm, and she didn't know what to do. Then she remembered Una's warning echo through her mind. "They can hurt you."

Well, she wasn't going to sit here and wait for it. Gypsy unfolded herself and cautiously came out of her hiding spot.

Which way to go? The same direction the nurses

had run or the opposite where the danger seemed to be coming from? Unsure, Gypsy was caught in the middle and only wanted the choice that would bring her to Jazz.

Maybe, the entity *wanted* her to run with the nurses and away from where she wanted, no needed, to be.

Just as she took a step and decided to run, the elevator doors across from her slid open.

The janitor peeked around the hall and whispered. "Take it," he said. "Up to the third floor."

She still hadn't seen his face, his hat was low and his features were blurred. "Who are you?" she asked.

He shook his head. "Go."

Gypsy had no way of knowing if he was steering her wrong, and she didn't know if she had a better option.

The elevator dinged, and before she could justify it, she dove into it before the doors closed.

It could be the stupidest thing she'd ever done. She would have never done it in the actual hospital where it was an ancient death trap. Or, she thought, it could lead her to Jazz.

The car lurched and squeaked on its climb, reminding her stomach to clench again.

Gypsy swallowed bile and got ready to jump when it came time.

The seconds ticked by, and she grew more agitated, frightened it wouldn't open again, and she'd be trapped.

But it did, and she saw the third-floor nurse's station. She moved fast toward it and hoped it would give her cover until she decided or was shown what her next step might be.

When she looked around, she saw a sign across from her announcing she was in the surgical wing and wondered why she was directed here by the old man.

The halls were as empty as the desks in front of her.

Gypsy couldn't hear the alarms anymore, but the phone lights were blinking as if they were all on hold.

Right, left, or forward? Think, Gypsy.

When she heard a door open to the left, she started that way. It could be Jazz.

She heard crying, and as she drew closer, it turned into inconsolable sobs that grew louder and more desperate as she approached. Gypsy felt her heart ache for the woman's obvious grief and distress.

She was four feet from the door when the lights flickered and went out.

Gypsy pressed herself against the wall and froze in an attempt to hear what was happening, but the crying was too loud. The smell of antiseptic and copper seemed to emanate from the spot and only grew stronger until she gagged on the stench, but it didn't stop her progress.

When she reached the door, it slammed in her face and nearly stopped her heart. Over the crying woman, she was able to make out two other voices that sounded as if they were having a heated argument.

Another voice caused her to stumble. It was the sound of a newborn baby in distress.

It might be horrible bait and a lie, but regardless of her anxiety, it wasn't anything she could ignore or run from.

Gypsy turned the knob, stepped in, and nothing. The silence was much worse than the screaming and crying.

"Get out," a growling voice ordered her, but she held her ground even as she trembled.

A gale force wind knocked her back against the wall, and she slid down it after hitting her head.

No, no, no. Stay awake. Even as she said it, Gypsy felt herself slipping out of consciousness.

❧ ❧ ❧ ❧

The patients in the room drew closer, surrounding Jazz and Una, then more poured through the doors until the circle was three people deep. They stopped and swayed side to side, their eyes looked like black holes.

Jazz had seen a lot over the last thirteen years, but she decided this had to be the creepiest.

She turned slightly to whisper in Una's ear. "What's going on?"

"They're waiting."

Jazz was glad Una seemed calmer because she was freaking the fuck out. "For what?"

"Her."

The answer hit her like a blow to the head, and every hair on her body stood at attention. Jazz could cut the tension with a knife, and dread built to an almost impossible level until she thought she might pass out.

"Oh, no, you don't," Una said.

"Are you reading my mind?"

Una shrugged. "Yes."

"Please tell me where Gypsy is."

She closed her eyes and hummed.

Jesus, this was well beyond the realm of insanity. "What the hell are you doing?"

"Looking for Gypsy's energy." Una opened her

eyes again. "She's gone."

Heedless of the demented crowd, Jazz spun around. "What do you mean gone?"

For the first time since they'd come here, Una appeared more than distressed. "I can't locate her."

"I mean, that's good, right? She's at home safe?"

"Let's hope so."

"What else could it be?" Anxiety poured through her like molasses, and she shook Una by the shoulders. She didn't answer, but the small amount of moisture in her eyes told Jazz she knew what else it could be. "No," Jazz said.

"We'll pray she never left. We don't know anything yet."

Jazz didn't know whether or not to believe her, but Una had known everything up to that point. She was the most gifted person Jazz had ever met. As far as she was concerned, she had to trust her. She had no choice if she wanted to get out of here.

Jazz found her rage under the panic and began to feed it with more.

"Good," Una said. "Focus on that."

The comment didn't at all surprise her this time. She'd assume from now on her emotions and thoughts were an open book. "I'm done waiting. What's taking this bitch so long?"

"She's drawing us out, prolonging the fear so she can feed off it."

With a clap of thunder, the room was instantly empty and derelict once again. As another sounded, the people were back and surrounding them.

Time slipped back and forth, completely disorienting Jazz and making her dizzy. The floor shook under their feet, and she and Una locked elbows again to hold each other up and keep from falling.

It was like being in a demented pictograph with someone turning the handle to make the slides go faster and faster.

Past. Present. Past.

Dark. Light. Dark.

"Enough," Una shouted.

Jazz was shocked it worked. Patients stayed solid and resumed their freaky swaying.

Metal doors slammed up and down the hallway faster and harder than any human could manage. Could she consider dead patients human?

"Yes. They're human spirits and have thoughts and feelings, but this is something unknown to me."

Una had read her mind again. "What's that?"

"They're still mentally ill. They should have passed on to the light and been free of it."

"Why haven't they?"

"They've been trapped here for so long." Una's voice was sad.

"By what?" Jazz looked around. Against her will, compassion filled over some of her animosity.

"Not what," Una said. "Who."

The front line took a step forward, then another. God, she hoped Gypsy was home and safe. The patients were now less than six feet from them. She wished desperately for a weapon.

Una's smile was feral. "Remember they can hurt you. They may be victims, but we have the ability, as well."

Jesus, Jazz didn't want to hurt them. She had to stop this and go back.

"Jazz?" Una asked.

"What?"

"Gypsy just came back online."

❧ ❧ ❧ ❧

The first thing Gypsy was aware of when she came to was the smell, and there was no mistaking it for anything other than blood.

Using the wall, she got to her feet, and at first glance, she was in a small dirty surgical room. She looked to the bed where a young girl was in stirrups and strapped to a bed. She took a couple of tentative steps toward her and was relieved to find she remained unnoticed.

A man and woman were arguing in low but spitting harsh tones, and Gypsy ignored them to finish crossing the room.

When she stood at the young woman's bedside, she covered her mouth to muffle her distress.

She was younger than she first thought, maybe sixteen or seventeen. Long dark hair clung to her sweating face and neck, half of it shading a large bruise on her cheekbone, and her lips looked painfully dry and cracked.

There was blood, a lot of it, and it covered the girl's thin hospital gown and thighs and pooled under her to drip on the floor.

Gypsy had never seen so much gore outside a horror film, and she involuntarily stepped back and slipped, landing in a warm puddle. It took several tries to get up while she attempted not to throw up.

Disgusted and nauseated, she wiped her hands on her jeans before she reached to unfasten the buckles of the straps holding the girl down.

Her fingers passed through them, and she was

devastated that she couldn't help. The girl's cries were getting weaker, but Gypsy clearly heard her begging for her baby.

The nurse in the corner spun around. "Shut up, Bridget. Your bastard is dead and better off for it, I say, than to have a whore for a mother."

Gypsy shivered. Where her face should be was a black hole.

Bridget shook her head slowly from side to side. "No," she said. "I heard him crying. You're lying. Give me my baby."

"But," the orderly stuttered.

"You shut up, too." She hissed, then slapped him. "And if you don't do as I say, I will absolutely ruin you and tell your wife about this harlot."

"Yes, Miss Dorinda." He hesitated. "Ma'am."

Gypsy heard a mewling sound from behind them, and from Bridget's reaction, she'd heard it, too. She struggled harder. "You give her to me, you fucking bitch. Bring me my baby."

The nurse laughed. "She won't make it through the night, and neither will you."

"Save our child, Brian. Don't let her do this. Please," she begged, "you said you loved me."

He glanced at Bridget, turned back to Dorinda, turned red, and shook his head. "I don't know what you're talking about. Everyone knows you fuck all the patients in here. That's why you've been in solitary for the last seven months. I never touched you."

"I'm going to kill you," Bridget said. "If it takes me until the end of time, I'm going to haunt you for the rest of your miserable life."

Her voice grew weaker and trailed off, and Gypsy watched her eyes dim. She couldn't change what was happening and only wanted to comfort.

Dorinda picked up the bundle and stalked toward the door with Brian following weakly behind her. She stopped and looked back at the bed. "I'll be back after I take care of this little problem. So I'll see you later." She laughed. "Oh, that's right. You won't be here, and I'll have killed two birds with one stone."

Gypsy felt the nurse's dark energy crawl into her and knew without reservation the head nurse was stark raving crazy herself.

A sociopath in charge of helpless patients.

"Who are you?"

The small voice from the bed startled her, and Gypsy's scalp tingled. Bridget could see her. Working quickly, she reached for the buckles again, but Bridget shook her head.

"I'm already dead," she said. "Are you an angel?"

Gypsy reached for her hand. She wouldn't leave this victimized girl to die alone. With her other hand, she gently smoothed her hair from her face and cried when Bridget drew her last breath. "I am so sorry this happened to you."

She felt lost and didn't know what to do. How long had she been in this place? It felt like days.

Wind rushed by her seconds before Gypsy found herself standing in an empty room once again.

Though she'd watched them leave, the feeling of evil intensified. Maybe the reason she couldn't see Dorinda's face was because she was the entity who'd attached herself to Jazz.

Gypsy needed to get to Jazz before Dorinda did.

She was in danger.

The tension of standing still had Jazz's entire body cramping, and she made a conscious effort to relax.

The crowd still circled them, still swayed, and just stared with dead, empty eyes.

Una had told her they couldn't strike first. Whatever was coming, Jazz was impatient to get it over with.

It felt as if they'd been standing for hours, and every time she tried to talk to Una, she'd shushed her, told her not to disrupt the energy.

Jazz felt a scream of frustration building, and she didn't know if she'd be able to hold it in much longer.

Just as she opened her mouth, people in the back row began to drop one by one around the circle, then the second row fell until they were only surrounded by the original group who took a step back and fell onto the bodies behind them.

The rec room furniture disappeared, and they were again alone in the dim light.

Jazz let out a slow breath, then another. She looked at Una. "I'm out of here," she said and sprinted for the doors. "I have to find her."

Una caught up with her, and they went through together. She looked left then right, but the lack of light in the hall made it hard to see. When a rat ran over her foot, she yelped, and the sound echoed back to her.

She saw a shadow at the farthest intersection. "This way."

The sound of her shoes hitting the floor gave her a horrible sense of déjà vu, but she shoved it down in the face of her need to find Gypsy.

Jazz stopped when she reached the point where

she'd seen the shadow and was faced with two more separate directions. She turned and looked helplessly at Una. "We have to split up."

"Not a good idea," she said. "But I agree with you. Our time is running out, I can feel the drawback to our bodies."

"Not until we find her," Jazz snapped. She turned and ran again and around the next corner, found a broken-down reception area.

A crash followed by a growl sounded behind her, and Jazz jumped under a desk. When she was in the small confined area, she could smell Gypsy. On an exposed nail, she found several long hairs wrapped around it. "Where are you, baby?" she whispered and rubbed the strands along her cheek.

Even the nightmares she'd suffered couldn't hold a candle to the fear she felt for her.

She heard footsteps approach, and Jazz popped up, hoping it was Gypsy, but it was Una who came around and sat with her.

"Nothing that way but more rooms."

"That leaves our third option." Jazz pointed.

"You told me you worked here," Una said. "Do you know where we are?"

"The rec room is on the first floor." She reached over and shook Una's shoulder. "Do your woo-woo thing and find her, damn it."

Una nodded, looked around the edge, and stood.

The hands with black jagged fingernails Jazz had seen a thousand times grabbed Una around the waist and pulled her backward through the hall faster than Jazz could move to help her.

Jazz heard her screams fade until it was silent once more.

What if it had been Gypsy? Jazz nearly lost it. Which way was up, what was real, she didn't know anymore, all she felt was fucked and desperate.

"You're next. I've been waiting for you."

The sinister raspy voice came from behind her. Crossing through acid rain wouldn't have been as scary as the terror washing over her.

Tears formed. She didn't want to be here. She was so tired of being afraid and pretending not to be. Nightmares had recurred too many times over the years, pulling her into dark places she never thought to recover from.

Until Gypsy.

Grief crippled her as hopelessness took over. She should have never agreed to her help and kept Gypsy as far away as possible.

Now Jazz was going to die here, alone. Maybe as she should have done on that night so long ago. She curled under the desk and waited for the inevitable.

She jerked when something poked her. It was the nail Gypsy's hair had been caught on.

She was livid. These were not her thoughts. They had seeped in slowly until she hadn't been able to tell the difference.

Jazz jumped up. She was *not* going to lie here and feel sorry for herself.

Or die.

She was going to find Gypsy and Una and get the fuck out.

Jazz stood up straight and squared her shoulders, turned around, and came face to face—with herself.

The stranger wore a blue uniform and one of those weird hats that reminded her of a nun and a nametag that read *Dorinda*.

The shocked and surprised expression on the nurse's face mirrored Jazz's feelings, and they stared at each other until her eyes burned and stung.

She was wrong, of course. Dorinda's hair was longer, her face fuller with hard frown lines etched around thinner lips. She was definitely older, and Jazz shivered.

But the resemblance was there, far more than was comfortable. "Don't tell me," Jazz sneered. "You're some long lost relative or some shit like that." She was done being afraid. She was through with cowering, and she knew this freaky fucked-up ghost in front of her was the key.

There was something wrong with her. Jazz knew that right off the bat—other than the fact she was dead. Dorinda had crazy eyes, and bad energy pricked at her skin and the nerves beneath.

Then Dorinda began to laugh, "Oh, this is rich." She slapped her thighs. "You're the reason."

"I literally can't see the humor in this, *Dorinda*." Jazz poured out her bitter sarcasm.

Dorinda stood back up, and the laughter stopped on a dime.

Despite her resolve to show no fear, the look she gave Jazz raised the hair on her neck.

Heavy footsteps came down the hall, and an orderly appeared behind Dorinda. "Brian," she said. "Meet our salvation."

"Huh?" He looked puzzled.

Oh great, Jazz thought, keeping her derisiveness. Not only was he huge and hulking, he was smart, too. "What are you talking about?" she asked.

Before she received an answer, Dorinda and the dumbass Brian faded as Jazz jerked against a vicious pull in her chest. She briefly wondered if she were having a heart attack, but when she sensed a presence behind her, she swung around with her fist raised, ready for battle.

"Easy, easy." Una raised her hands and soothed. "It's just me."

Jazz felt her chest jerk again.

"That pull you feel? It's our bodies calling us back."

"I'm not leaving without Gypsy," Jazz hissed when Una stared at her.

"You may not have a choice," Una said. "But I can stay longer. I've trained for it, and I promise I'll find her."

Jazz realized she must be in shock to not have asked what happened to her. "Jesus, are you okay?"

"Not now, talk later." Una held a hand up as Dorinda and Brian reappeared. "You bitches."

The venom in Una's voice had Jazz backing up a step.

"You keep these souls trapped here."

Dorinda smiled wickedly. "I had power when they were alive." She laughed. "I have more now."

Jazz pointed at her. "She's the hag that haunts me?"

Una didn't answer. She locked gazes with Dorinda until, to Jazz's surprise, she saw her smile falter.

Brian trembled, and he stepped behind Dorinda. "You coward," she spat at him. "You're useless to me."

"Let me go," he whined. "I don't want to be here."

She shook her head. "You loved it when you could torment the patients. What made you think you had a choice *but* to stay when you should have gone to hell?"

He looked down at his feet. And if ghosts could look ashamed, Jazz thought, he pulled it off.

Dorinda turned back to Una. "You will not fix this. We've been free since the night," she pointed at Jazz, "she was stupid and got locked in here alone. It's not my fault she looks like me." She paused. "Though I am prettier." She shot Jazz a smarmy look. "You look like a boy to me."

"What kind of junior high bullshit is this?" Jazz took a step toward her. "You've been my paranormal terrorist for more than a decade? Fuck you." She turned to Una. "Can I hurt her?"

"You won't have to. She'll get what's coming to her." She tilted her head to the right. "Right about now."

Dorinda grabbed Brian's arm and tried to pull a fade but without effect, and this time, it was Una who grinned wickedly. "Gotcha."

They turned to leave around the short corner and were met by a wall of people.

※ ※ ※ ※

The lights never came back on, and even if they had, Gypsy didn't want to chance the elevator again. She searched the third floor but felt she was only going in circles.

At this point, she'd be happy to think this was only a nightmare, but her jeans were stiff and crusted with dried blood, and her hip, knees, and tailbone still hurt.

As unreal as this all seemed, she thought, the pain was certainly genuine.

The place was a damn maze, but she finally came

around to a stairwell, carefully moved around the sharp metal of the broken hinges, and started down.

It must be the worst part of the building, she thought. She could see daylight through the holes in the roof where the leaks over the years caused a green sludge to cover everything and threaten her balance.

The rain was gone, and the last thing she wanted to do was fall again.

Banging from the third floor followed her down the next flight. Gypsy didn't care what it was, she made herself move forward.

The growling stopped her in her tracks. It grew in volume until she felt the cement wall vibrate next to her.

She shook off the fear. She had to keep moving. Gypsy felt trapped and scared to death but wasn't going to stay a sitting duck for whatever was stalking her. She certainly wasn't going to make it easy.

When the noise stopped abruptly, she quickened her pace and made it down to the first floor.

The idea of having to search another floor made her want to cry. Only the thought of Jazz kept her going.

Her muscles ached with the longing to go home. She'd felt as if she'd been here for years and briefly wondered if they'd traveled into the bowels of hell itself. Better not to think too hard about it.

"Psst."

Gypsy nearly jumped out of her skin but looked behind her.

The janitor peeked out of a maintenance closet. "She's back, she's pissed, and time's nearly up."

"Where do I go?" Gypsy strained to see his features, but his face remained a blur.

"That way."

"I don't know who you are, but thank you for helping me."

She ran a few steps, then turned back. The storage closet door was still open, and he was smiling at her. She looked closer and realized it was her Uncle Jimi. "How?"

He cut her off. "No time now. That way."

She took off in the direction he'd indicated, and up ahead, she spotted the cursed reception counter.

Right back where she started.

❧❧❧❧

As she looked at each person in turn, Jazz could see the resemblance they bore to Una. The ancestors, she presumed. "Took them long enough," she muttered under her breath.

But there was also a man who she assumed to be a maintenance man by his clothes, a blond woman she thought looked like Rhiannon, and the last caused her heart to twist, an excruciating pain that nearly knocked her to her knees.

"Mom?" she asked.

Una tapped her shoulder. "No, sweetie, your mother's twin, remember?"

She shook her head. "I never saw my aunt Mary as an adult." And this was not the time for some weird-ass dysfunctional reunion.

Jazz's attention drew back to the others who remained in their hospital gowns.

She and Una were in the center while on one side was the family, the other the patients, and the only hall remaining was on the left, and they all turned to look down it as the doors began to open and slam close again. Jazz counted twenty of them, and each blow made her increasingly nauseated.

Fluorescent lights flickered as a dark mass formed in front of the window at the very end of the hall. Then each one popped as the shadow of smoke passed under them.

Wind and a foul odor preceded the entity. The patients' mouths opened to scream, but only whispers escaped as they seemed to be paralyzed in place. Dorinda and Brian violently attempted to escape the area but couldn't get past the group.

The floor buckled underneath them. "Get ready," Una said as the wind picked up and a swarm of bats came with it.

Out of the mass, an entity appeared, its hair twisting like snakes around a hideous blue gray face. It stared at them with dead, empty eyes, and a horrible demonic smile showing black craggy teeth.

"You fucking idiot," Dorinda yelled at Jazz. "You brought her back here. Bitch, you have no idea how hard it's been to hide from that little whore."

"Bullshit," Jazz hissed. "I most certainly do."

The entity grew in height until her head nearly hit the ceiling.

Speechless and terrified, Jazz could only stare in horror.

"Here is where her power originates," Una said. "She's the strongest here."

Dorinda shoved Jazz toward the entity's clawed hands, and the patients vanished in an instant.

"No," Una shouted over the gusts, which became a spinning vortex around them.

Jazz managed to put her back to the wall to avoid

the entity's reach but had to duck from the bats dive bombing and their high-pitched squeals.

Rain poured down on their heads.

Over the horrendous sound, Jazz heard running and screams approaching.

Gypsy.

"Stay back," Jazz yelled, but in three seconds, she saw her shadow behind the entity, and her heart threatened to stop when the hag turned toward Gypsy. "No. Leave her alone and take me. Here, look at me, take me."

Gypsy approached, and the janitor moved to her side as she stood at the edge of darkness. "Bridget," she said. "Stop!"

The entity turned and tilted her head. The howling wind died down, and the rain slowed as the bats disappeared down the hall.

The apparition wavered, and her image flashed between the huge demon and a young girl in a bloody hospital gown.

Water dripped from her hair, causing the blood to run in rivers, spreading across the floor until all of them were standing in it.

"Gypsy?" Jazz called out.

Instead of answering, Gypsy waved Jazz and Una back. The ancestors stayed where they were but showed no signs of retreat.

"Bridget," Gypsy repeated and pointed at Jazz. "She's not your enemy."

"You're lying." The voice roared as her visage grew large again. "I've been trying to get her back here. She needs to pay for what she's done."

Panic hit Jazz like a freight train when she saw Gypsy move closer to it. "Hey," she said to distract.

"I'm over here, leave her alone."

The entity growled and reached for her again.

"No. She's mine, Bridget. Look at me."

Jazz had to get to Gypsy.

"Watch," Una said, then pulled her arm as if she read Jazz's mind. "And don't move."

Jazz would rather die by the entity's hand than let Gypsy be hurt. She bunched her muscles and rolled up on the balls of her feet to prepare herself to jump anyway, but Una tightened her grip. Stronger than she looked, Jazz thought bitterly, and began to struggle in earnest.

"Bridget, listen to me."

"Why does she keep calling it Bridget?" Jazz gave up fighting Una.

"She's repeating her name to call to the part of it that was once human before she turned into…" Una pointed. "That."

"Mine, mine, mine," the raspy voice insisted.

Gypsy took another step, her hands out by her sides, and the entity's image flickered again. "No. I love her, and her name is Jazz Miller, and she's mine, Bridget."

"Yours?" The girl appeared and looked confused. "Trick," she growled.

"No, no, no," Gypsy said.

Jazz felt the pull to go back as the hospital itself faded in and out.

"We're out of time," Una said, then gasped.

Did that mean they were going home?

"Hurry." Una yelled, and Jazz screamed when she saw Gypsy lunge straight at it. The entity's arms went around her, and the rain came back.

Over the deluge, Jazz heard Gypsy call out

Bridget's name several times.

An instant later, an ear-shattering scream pierced her eardrums, but before she could panic, she realized it wasn't Gypsy's.

She had her arms around the girl and rocked with her on the dirty floor.

"I remember you. I remember you." Her voice broke as though unused to human syntax. "The angel who came." Bridget pulled back and grabbed Gypsy's shoulders. "Angel, Angel, Angel."

The moment seemed to hang in time until finally Bridget pointed at Jazz. "Yours?"

"Yes," Gypsy said. "And innocent."

Out of the corner of her eye, Jazz caught movement, and the fog was much like the smoke from the entity's first appearance. Jesus Christ, she thought, there are *two* of them?

"No," Una said. "It's our help."

The ancestors turned the smoke to a ball of light, and dropped Dorinda and Brian in front of Bridget.

A roll of thunder crashed through the hospital, the walls shook, the doors rattled in their frames.

There was several seconds of silence before the patients looked around in wonder, none of them appearing mentally ill. The young man in the wheelchair got up, smiled beatifically, and stood tall.

"Jazz, come here," Gypsy said. "Slowly."

She walked around the ghosts who surrounded them, dropped to her knees, and pulled Gypsy into a death grip. "I'm never going to let you go."

Bridget made a sound like a bark and reached for her, but Gypsy put herself between them, shook her head, and pointed to Dorinda and Brian. "Yours," she said.

She turned back to Gypsy. "Mine?"

Jazz saw the tears that ran down Gypsy's face and neck. "Yours," she repeated.

Bridget went scary again, grew, and turned into the demon Jazz had associated her with for years. She towered over Dorinda and Brian, then roared while she reached for them.

Faster than Jazz could comprehend, the entity that long ago used to be the young girl Bridget disappeared back into the black fog with her prize, the sources of her trauma.

As the screams faded, Una came over to them. "We have to go."

Jazz nodded and drew Gypsy up. They held hands in a circle. "Please, let's just get the hell out of this place."

"It's over," Gypsy said.

Una shook her head. "No."

Jazz jerked. "What do you mean, no? We went through this for nothing?"

Una bowed to her ancestors, Gypsy smiled at the janitor through a cloud of cigar smoke. As confused as Jazz was, she managed to wave slightly to her aunt, who smiled radiantly at her. Wow, she was going to have to process that later.

"Thank you," the groomed woman said. "For all of us."

Sunlight flooded the halls, and the previously captive patients began to rise in a sight so beautiful Jazz felt her own tears. The spirits that chose to remain, for whatever reason, scattered in all directions.

"Thank you," Una said to the ancestors. "Until we meet again." Then, one by one, they also disappeared.

The floor tilted, and Jazz, Gypsy, and Una

traveled back.

※ ※ ※ ※

Jazz was alone when she woke on the couch. The circle was gone, and everything looked as if Una had never been there or performed the ceremony.

Was any of it real or another one of her screwed-up nightmares? "Gypsy," she yelled, then heard bare feet running across the hardwood.

"You're back," Gypsy said and kissed her. "Una said you'd be out for a few hours detoxing from the energy and psychic hooks Bridget had in you."

"So it *was* real?" She tugged Gypsy, pulled her down onto the couch, and noticed her leg was back in her cast. Damn it, she thought.

Gypsy smiled at her. "It was."

"How can you be so calm?" Jazz asked. "We were stuck there forever."

"Time is fluid in that reality. We were there for twenty minutes from this side, and you've been recovering for about three hours now."

It was impossible to get her mind around it, but she had only one question. "It's really over?"

"Yes, finally." She looked up and smiled at her. "You're free."

※ ※ ※ ※

Later that night, they spoke in whispers, then didn't talk at all.

Gypsy surrounded Jazz in scent and wrapped her in pleasure.

Their hands glided, lips slid over heated skin,

ache and pleasure rolled together in a swirling storm.

The trauma Jazz lived with for so many years fell away and under Gypsy's sighs in the dark, surrendering to her, fusing them as one.

Gypsy's eyes glowed in the twilight as they fell together. Jazz pulled her close and knew if she were ever lost, Gypsy's would be the light that drew her back.

She could, at last, be home.

About the Author

Multiple award-winning author, Yvonne Heidt, lives with her wife of 17 years in East Texas, where she battles mosquitos the size of Chihuahuas, is chief nanny to their 4 dogs, and has long conversations with visiting ghosts. Sometimes they even talk back.

Check out Yvonne's other book

Meet Me in the Middle - ISBN - 978-1-943353-63-7

Veterinarian Aislin O'Shea runs a busy clinic. She wasn't looking for a relationship. She'd already had the perfect one. She certainly wasn't attracted to fancy pants executive, Ms. Zane Whitman - she wasn't her type.

Zane Whitman had it all. Stellar career, wealth, exclusive social circle, and models vying for her attention. Impulsive, emotionally charged Aislin was not her type.

Two women from the opposite side of the tracks.

Neither one expects meddling from an unexpected source on the Other side.

Neither one knows the train is coming.

Other books by Sapphire Authors

The Travels of Charlie - ISBN - 978-1-948232-24-1

In 1884, Charlene Dieter needs a new life, away from unwanted male suitors and from Jo, her best friend who has rebuffed her romantic overtures. Charlene finds her new self in "Charlie," the man she always thought she should have been. Charlie decides to start a new life in Illinois, motivated by letters from a cousin of Charlie's deceased dad.

Kitty McIntire, a young woman managing her prairie farm after her father's death, also fends off a suitor, John Cameron. John, however, presses on, despite a rival for Kitty's attentions in cousin Charlie, newly arrived in their small town. Charlie does his best to be a farmer, but sustains injuries that lay him up. Kitty attends him while he recuperates, and they begin to fall in love, when circumstances force Charlie to let Kitty in on his secret.

Charlie and Kitty together face the escalating verbal and physical attacks from John, as he tries to get Kitty and her farm for his own purposes.

Will John come between the love that Charlie has found with Kitty? How can they, two women in a time that men rule, bring John to justice?

The Four Seasons - ISBN - 978-1-948232-26-5

Music begins the story, and music weaves itself around each changing time period and evolution, Vivaldi's transcendent notes encapsulating the various moods of the Four Seasons.

Irene has taught their intricacies for years, as the music of her life gently coils around her and her longings. As the result of a radio contest, she ends up in Tasmania, crossing over hemispheres and seasons, leaving behind winter for the warm sands of summer.

Helena, mountain woman, humanitarian, and yogurt baron, takes her yearly trek to Tasmania to assess her culture providers, unaware that she will meet her match and love in life.

Individually and together, these two women blend a musically rich tapestry of passion, eroticism, humor, intrigue, and the simple and complex layers of the human existence.

Twisted Deception - ISBN - 978-1-939062-47-5

There are two types of people who can't look you in the eyes: someone trying to hide a lie and someone trying to hide their love.

Addie Blake's life isn't black and white--more like a series of short bursts of color that sustain her until the next eruption. She isn't a ladder-climber in the corporate world. Instead, she works long hours at the office and even at home, something her mechanic girlfriend, Drake Hogan, can't stand. If Addie can't focus on Drake, then Drake finds arm candy that will. After a long week of late nights and a series of text-messaged demands, each one a bigger bomb than the last, Addie has had enough of her Motor Girl.

Greyson Hollister inhabits a world where everything is either black and white, or money green. She's a polished, certified workaholic. As head of Integrated Financial, she has built the ladder others want to climb. Now she intends to attend a business mixer to confront a rumormonger and kill merger rumors involving her company.

Detective Nancy Hill, the lead detective on the Elevator Rapist task force, has just been called in to investigate an attack at Integrated Financial. She can't quite put her finger on it, but something doesn't add up with this latest assault, and Greyson Hollister isn't exactly lending a helping hand.

A storm's brewing on the horizon. Can Addie and Greyson weather it, or will it blow them over?

The Treehouse – ISBN – 978-1-948232-00-5

Camilla Thompson, a Humanities college professor who never did write that Great American Novel, hasn't seen her son Nico for two years.
One morning she drives to the house where her ex, Allison, is still raising Nico. Knowing that they are away for a week's vacation, Camilla begins to build a treehouse as a surprise for the son she's not allowed to see.

But Camilla's regrets, grief, and lack of construction skills aren't the only challenges she'll face. Old friends and unexpected visitors show up to help—and complicate matters. Free-spirited Taylor, Camilla's best friend, arrives with her lover, Audrey, whom Camilla finds herself falling for. Then Wallace, Camilla's Department Chair, disrupts everything with startling news that threatens to end Camilla's career.

At first an impulsive idea, the treehouse soon promises to be an oasis for Camilla's redemption that could free her for another chance at love and family. Then again, it might simply be just a bad decision.